MEAN SEASON

MEAN SEASON

SALVATORE DIFALCO

Mansfield Press

Library and Archives Canada Cataloguing in Publication

Difalco, Salvatore, 1958-, author
    Mean season / Savatore Difalco.

ISBN 978-1-77126-085-5 (paperback)

    I. Title.

PS8557.I397M43 2015   C813'.6   C2015-906197-0

Copy Editing: Stuart Ross
Cover Design and typesetting: Denis De Klerck
Cover Image: Shutterstock

The publication of *Mean Season* has been generously supported by the Canada Council
for the Arts and the Ontario Arts Council.

 Canada Council **Conseil des Arts**
for the Arts **du Canada**    **ONTARIO ARTS COUNCIL**
CONSEIL DES ARTS DE L'ONTARIO

Mansfield Press Inc.
25 Mansfield Avenue, Toronto, Ontario, Canada M6J 2A9
Publisher: Denis De Klerck
www.mansfieldpress.net

"I believe the game is designed to reward the ones who hit the hardest. If you can't take it, you shouldn't play."

— Jack Lambert

ONE

One question I would have asked my father, were he alive today: why Hamilton? Why, of all the blessed places on earth, all the gleaming cities of the world, all its sunny, green-shagged corners—why did he ever decide to emigrate from Sicily, the jewel of the Mediterranean, to Hamilton, that sooty eyesore on the shores of Lake Ontario? What was he thinking? What did he think of the place when he first stepped onto its grimy one-way streets? Or when he took in its belching smokestacks? Or caught a whiff of its fetid air? My mother, also Sicilian, who married my father by proxy a few years after he arrived, and had little choice in her relocation, said the city depressed her on first impression, its filth, its stink, its ugliness. Adjusting was difficult, there were sacrifices, setbacks, even tragedy, but they had made a life here. It was home now.

Still, she never could explain exactly why my father chose Hamilton. He was here, so I came here, she'd say, and leave it at that. I suspect he would have credited his uncle Ignazio, who owned a north-end boarding house, or work promised at the steel mills, for drawing him to Hamilton, some such story. But he also had an uncle in Buenos Aires, another in Melbourne, Australia, and his aunt Rosalia lived in Brooklyn. Not to mention family in the north of Italy, namely Genoa and Milan. I understood the reasons why he left Sicily: postwar *miseria*, lack of work, the rapacious *mafia* and so on, if not the reasons why he never returned—and maybe he would have, had he lived longer. But Hamilton? The Hammer?

Back in the spring of 1980, as I crammed for my third-year finals at the University of Toronto—about an hour away on the QEW—another summer in Hamilton seemed inconceivable. I'd had my fill of it: the steel mills and sulfurous air, crumbling sidewalks and buildings, the misnomered "mountain," and that overblown blue-collar gusto and grit.

No, the Hammer wasn't in my plans. I'd grown fond of the big city. University life appealed to me; I was playing varsity football, excelling at my English studies, and expanding my horizons, as they say, intellectually and socially. I'd made scores of new friends, including artists, thinkers, poets, and we talked about things like aesthetics, existentialism, and politics. Existentialism! I loved it. And I had my choice of cool summer jobs—waiting tables at a hip café in Little Italy, or working doors at the chi-chi Hippopotamus Club on Yonge Street with some Varsity Blues teammates. But despite the tipped scales, family matters forced my hand.

My widowed mother had been struggling with my sixteen-year-old brother Joey, whom I'd lost touch with on sporadic eat-and-run visits. My mother respected my ambitions. She knew I wanted to stay in Toronto, and agreed that I should, but despaired for Joey, who no longer abided by her rules, coming and going as he pleased. He had threatened her, stolen money from her purse, and had smashed things around the house. And she'd heard he was mixing with a bad crowd. She feared for him, and for herself. Hoping to lessen her suffering, and to intercede before Joey wrecked his life, I decided to return for the summer; I'd be the good brother and son, and help my mother find peace of mind. Then I could get on with my own life.

But I'd be less than honest if I held that was the only reason why I returned. For all of its grime and grit, the Hammer had lots of *action*. Sex, drugs, gangs, and violence: the full buffet. Toronto was still Toronto the Good, tight-assed, circumspect, held in check. Nobody calls it Toronto the Good anymore, but back in 1980, despite its evolving cosmopolitanism and cultural diversity, it had yet to loosen its girdle. If you wanted to get down and dirty, Toronto wasn't the ticket. Hamilton had the goods.

On a dull Tuesday morning in late May, 1980, I left the U of T campus, duffel bag and books in tow, and with misgivings hopped a bus to Hamilton. Little did I grasp the acuity and prescience of those misgivings. If working doors at Banisters—a Wild West saloon masquerading as a discotheque—last summer had been any indication, another roller-coaster ride awaited me. My old boss had sold Banisters that winter, but had offered me a job at his new club near the cop shop—not that being near the cops meant any less action. I knew what to expect. There were risks. But risks also meant kicks, adult excitement, and maybe, after months of lectures and overdue essays, I needed these. But then it's always a question of biting off more than you can chew. Or getting in too deep. Or thinking that, somehow, you're immune to the downside of risk, and to those dark, untidy forces raging beyond your control.

Though only weeks had passed since my last visit, my mother welcomed me with tearful hugs and kisses. She promptly marched me to the kitchen, fired up the stove, and started cooking. Years of stuffing hot dogs in the vaults of Essex Packers had led to chronic neuralgia, for which she collected a modest disability pension. In pain, or exhausted, her blue eyes sparkled youthfully that morning, and her movements were light and quick. In minutes she had a mess of steaming cutlets plated.

"Ma, it isn't even noon yet."

She circled me with her hands on her hips, studying my thick arms and neck, then touching my chin with a tender gesture.

"You look thin, Bobby."

"Ma! I've gained twenty pounds this year."

"Your face is thin."

"Where's Joey?" I asked, stuffing an end of Italian bread in my mouth.

She glanced up: he was sleeping.

"I'll go wake him," I said.

"No, let him sleep." She placed a hand on my shoulder. "You can talk later, Bobby. Let him sleep. Eat now. It's so nice to have you home."

I demolished the veal with a loaf of bread and some black olives. My mother watched me eat with a smile. My buddy Tony Demarco rang me up in the middle of espresso and lemon cake. Our mothers often mingled in the neighbourhood; mine must have mentioned my return.

"What, no call, you prick?" he said.

"Why would I call a loser like you?"

"No one else will talk to you."

"You're hurting my feelings."

"Feelings? Does a prick have feelings?"

"Even a prick feels pain."

"Tell it to the marines, prick."

Demarco's raspy, high-pitched voice warmed my heart. We'd been friends since nursery school. He had just finished his last exam of the year—toward a science degree at Hamilton's McMaster University—and was keen to catch up; we hadn't talked much since last summer. It was as though I'd moved to another country, not a far cry from the truth. No mistaking Toronto, Canada's burgeoning financial and media hub, with Hamilton, the country's major steel producer.

Demarco wanted to hit the gym that afternoon but I had to get my Camaro on the road and run a few errands. I suggested we go for drinks that evening and he cited lively Tuesday-night crowds at the Street Scene, a pub in the basement of the Royal Connaught Hotel. I had dated a bartender there last summer, Nancy Ormond, but had lost touch with her that winter. Demarco told me not to worry about it, she'd be happy to see me—something I doubted.

I spent the afternoon prepping my silver ragtop Camaro, which I kept on blocks during the school year in my cousin Rocco's garage. It was a classic, better for cruising the one-way streets of

Hamilton than hauling around a stop-and-go city like Toronto. Rocco had tuned up the engine but it needed new rubber, so I hit a Firestone outlet and grabbed four fat radials that set me back a chunk. A high school graduation gift, Uncle Giuseppe had scored me the Camaro, a '68 327 two-speed powerglide, from an old widower in Fort Hope whose wife had only driven it on Sundays.

Anyway, inevitable mechanical decline had begun. Even with Rocco tuning it up for next to nothing, it was costing me money I didn't have. Government loans and grants and summer earnings went only so far. Selling it had crossed my mind. But when I took it out that afternoon for a boot along Burlington Street with the roof down and the radio cranked up—*Jim Dandy to the rescue/Jim Dandy to the re-es-cue*—the wind rushing through my hair and sunlight dazzling the silver hood, I felt lucky to have it. I gunned the shimmering beauty past the old navy barracks and the abandoned brewery, then crossed the railroad tracks that led to the pungent soybean factory on the bay front. Just ahead, the steel mills loomed like fire-breathing colossi, obnoxious, foreboding. I turned the car around and headed home.

When I got there, Joey had already split. My mother didn't know his whereabouts or when he'd return. I pulled out the hose from the back and washed and polished the Camaro. The neighbours, Mr. and Mrs. Warden, stared on from their porch, both in beige safari jackets and bucket hats. I wondered what ailment had sent Mrs. Warden to Chedoke Hospital—and its esteemed psychiatric ward—for a month, according to my mother. Pale and tremulous that afternoon, she had never looked otherwise.

Sunny but on the cool side—a stiff fishy breeze gusted up from the bay. Not a pleasant view, either: across the street, buckled snow fences still girded the perimeter of Eastwood Park, a rutted and muddy mess. Many of the leafless trees had been blackened by fungus, and I saw no flowers, an oddity in late May. As a kid, I'd played football and soccer on the usually well-tended back field, but now it looked carpet-bombed. I buffed the Camaro's metallic silver paint to a twinkly gleam under the bland, avian scrutiny of the Wardens.

Joey didn't resurface that afternoon. My mother made ricotta-and-spinach lasagna for dinner and watched me eat in silence. She looked tired, drawn. When I finished, she put a foil-covered plate of food on the stove for Joey and without comment went to the living room; she stretched out on the chesterfield, covered her legs with a light blue blanket, and shut her eyes.

At seven that evening, with rain clouds threatening, I drove to Demarco's house. He lived around the block with his parents in a stuccoed bungalow. On the front lawn, a pale marble fountain imported from Italy featured a pissing cherub, the only one in the north end, evidencing his old man's taste for the rococo. I pumped my horn and jumped out of the car. Demarco charged out the door with his head down and we collided on his lawn near the fountain, locking up like two grapplers, until I hip-tossed him to the ground and pinned his arms.

"Get off me, you prick!"

"Say uncle, dumdum."

Demarco bucked his hips, but I held his forearms fast and dug my knee into his liver.

"Quit struggling."

His mother appeared on the porch, wiping her hands with her apron, and shouting so loudly that flanking neighbours' heads popped out of doors and windows.

"Stop it! Stop it, you two!"

"It's okay, Ma!"

"It's okay, Mrs. Demarco," I said, jumping up. "It's me, Bobby Sferazza."

"Roberto?" She clapped her heart. "Dio—you scared me."

Demarco hopped to his feet rubbing his ribs. "He's lucky I didn't kill him."

"He's lucky he's your son," I said.

"You're huge," he said. "Look at you! Look at him, Ma."

He hugged me fiercely around the shoulders and gave me a rasping kiss on the temple. He reeked of Royal Copenhagen Musk.

"Show some control! Mrs. D, I'm ashamed for your son."

"You should both be ashamed. Two big salamis behaving like children." She shook her head. "How's your mother, Roberto?"

"She's doing okay."

"She must be happy you're back for the summer. Say hello to her for me."

"I will, Mrs. D."

"We're going out, Ma."

"Be careful. And don't drink alcohol, Tonino. Make sure he doesn't drink alcohol, Roberto, you know how he gets."

"I know, Mrs. D. I'll give him a beating if he drinks. Promise."

Mrs. Demarco smiled at me and accepted a Judas kiss from her son.

"Look at you," he said, slapping my neck as we walked to the Camaro. "You're a frigging side of beef."

"Yeah, and if those lats of yours get any wider, you'll attain the frigging power of flight."

My observation put him off.

"Seriously, you're starting to look weird, man."

A belted beige wool cardigan compounded the weirdness; he'd taken to wearing thick sweaters the previous summer, even in heat waves, maybe to give the illusion of body depth.

"And lighten up with the musk. You smell like a dead civet."

"Tell me what you really think, Bobby."

We drove to the Royal Connaught, trading more jibes and picking up pretty much where we left off last summer. As we turned into the parking lot, it started pouring rain. We sprinted round the front of the hotel to the Street Scene side entrance but still got doused. Demarco's cardigan must have soaked up a gallon of water and he was bitter about it.

We descended a flight of concrete stairs and entered through a red steel door with iron grillwork. I paused, wondering what complications lay beyond the door, if any. A few years older than me, Nancy was as sharp as she was sexy. I'd thought about her often that winter, and though I'd felt tempted to call her periodically, prolonging the relationship seemed pointless: we had very different aims and ambitions. I was skeptical if any spark remained.

As I shook raindrops from my hair and let my eyes adjust to the gloom, a hot waft of cigarette smoke, beer, and ammonia pinched my nostrils. I held my breath and took in the scenery. Not much had changed since last summer: the same amber street lamps lit the place; pressboard urban landscapes passing for décor remained uncorrupted; vintage graffiti zigzagged the cinder-block walls. The Zodiac jukebox gleamed in its traditional corner, heavy-metal roster intact. Everything had survived the winter.

Nancy Ormond had survived. She was tending bar in a dark red shirt, her long hair blonder than I remembered, her features sharper. Pouring a pitcher of draft with great concentration, she didn't notice me, or if she did played it cool.

As promised, the place was buzzing for a Tuesday evening. "Black Dog" boomed from the jukebox—*Hey hey mama said the way you move/Gonna make you sweat, gonna make you groove*—and liquored chatter filled any silences. I recognized some faces by the bar and at the tables, nodding acknowledgments, then spotted Oscar Flores, a teammate from high school football, sitting with Ricky Tartaglia and John the Greek of the Barton-Sherman gang. That made me pause, take a better look around.

Other gang members sat nearby in their trademark flannel work shirts and steel-toed boots, clutching bottles of Blue and glaring at me. In addition to any number of wise guys and bikers, four or five street gangs, depending on whom you asked, called Hamilton home. The Parkdale gang and its ultraviolent offspring, the crimson-clad East End Clubbers, had made lots of noise, but the Barton-Sherman gang—drawing its name from an intersection near the steel mills—had gained the most repute for its boldness and sheer savagery.

Oscar flashed his gold-capped incisor. He'd beefed up since his days as an all-city safety and return man, bulging everywhere, skin thick, black eyes set more deeply than ever in a tight mask of pocked flesh. Only the tooth hadn't changed.

"Bobby S," he said, so quick to his feet his startled crew rose in unison and for a moment stood there expectantly. "Where you been hiding, Bobby S? Goddamn, I can't believe my eyes."

"Oscar," I said, holding out my right hand. "What's going on?"

"What's going on?" he said, grabbing my hand with both of his and squeezing instead of shaking it. "I'm with Bobby Doctor, thas' what's going on. How're things in Hogtown, man?"

"Not bad, Oscar."

"I hear you're kicking ass big time at the university. Is this true? I know it's true, Bobby S, Bobby Doctor. I know you're kicking ass somewhere. You're like me. We jus' have to kick some ass, eh? We jus' have to kick some ass or we don't feel right!"

I pulled away my hand. "I'm doing okay, Oscar. Toronto's been good to me."

"I'm glad for you, Bobby. Yes I am! It's a beautiful thing, this thing. But tell me, Bobby—if Toronto's been so good to you, so *fucking* good to you, why you back in town?"

"Just for the summer, man."

"Jus' for the summer, eh? Like a va-*cation*."

He drew his face close to mine with a wheeze of beer and onion: damp black hair hung in tangles over his brow, old and new acne scars scored his cheeks, and a sparse goatee framed his chin. He turned and glanced at his crew, puffed up and waiting with half-open mouths for a sign. The sign they received punctured their expectations, so they glumly retook their seats or drifted off to the bar, glancing back in case he changed his mind.

Oscar wrapped his arm around my shoulder and squeezed. I tried to turn away from him, but he held tight, his smile sharp-edged, black eyes depthless. Maybe time spent in the can explained the hardness. Still no sign of Demarco—I wondered if he'd spooked and bailed.

"So talk to me, Bobby Doctor. Say something beautiful. These donkeys I'm with can barely speak English."

"Ha. Staying out of trouble, Oscar?"

His smile disappeared and he brought a hand to his head as if it were sore.

"What do you mean, Bobby? What does that mean, staying out of trouble? Explain."

"Just saying."

"Jus' *saying*," he sniffed. "People always jus' *saying*. Sometimes jus' *saying* no-thing."

I smiled and held Oscar's gaze. Though we'd been teammates and co-captains for the Cathedral Gaels football team—winning the All-City Championship in our last year—and had played in a regular poker game at Oscar's house throughout high school with other teammates, we were never that close. I respected his football talent but felt less for him as a human being.

Truth was, Oscar had terrorized Cathedral High during his stint there. Everyone would shit their pants when he'd swagger down the halls, even Mr. Mcafee, the hard-nosed, ex-cop principal. But I had never let his antics get to me, and wasn't about to now. His friends were another story. No need to play the hero with them. They'd been on a rampage. That April they trashed Mellows Tavern in the west end after the owner barred them—put the guy in hospital with a fractured skull. And just the week before they destroyed a Tim Hortons in the east end, for some unfathomable reason. Having grown up in the north end with my share of thugs and bullies, I found their brutal and petty agenda was too familiar, and distasteful.

Last summer at Banisters, after a mini-riot, we had tried barring the Barton-Sherman gang, but that didn't pan out. I remember Oscar—flanked by six of his boys—warning me to step aside: "Don't be a hero, Bobby. You got no backup." Sure enough, except for Demarco, my colleagues had deserted their posts.

For the rest of the summer, Barton-Sherman had their run of the place, operating with impunity. I felt like a fucking coward about it, but what can you do? Then in late September, Satan's Choice MC torched it for their own reasons. The owner, Luciano Mercanti, quickly sold the burned-out club to the bikers for peanuts; they refurbished it and reopened as a strip joint still bearing the Banisters name. Business was booming, from the sounds of it. A Black Sabbath tune—*I love you sweet leaf though you can't hear*—thundering from the jukebox jolted my nerves. Hammered guitar chords and cymbals crashed in my ears. I clenched my teeth and rocked my head to the heavy groove. Something inside me, hot, black, metallic, was mounting. I'd heard about roid rage, and had caught a few dark glimpses of it on the football field, where I channelled it into legitimate violence. But there was no telling how it would play out here. Holding my breath, I looked for Demarco.

Oscar gave me a quick once-over. "Fuck me, you're *huge*, bro. I'm training myself."

"For what, the Special Olympics?"

"Ha, funny. Good one, ha," he said, tensing his jaw. "Yeah, Bobby S, make jokes, but you know what, man—that don't matter. That don't matter one bit. You know why? Because you are my hero. You are my hero, swear to God. Cathedral 17, Bishop Ryan 10. Fuck me! Yo, Ricky—see this guy here? This guy won the city championship all by himself, bro. Thas right. This guy was fucking Superman."

Ricky's black helmet of hair and puffy face floated up before me and came to a rest. His eyes were not right—unaligned, the wet black irises trembling like jellies. He'd gained notoriety for jerking off his German shepherd in front of Diamond Jim's Tavern, but his resumé included more typical lunatic acts: beatings, knifings, arson, indecent exposures, sexual assaults. No murders that I knew of, yet. He leaned back and roared with laughter, eyes rolling back in their sockets. Then he abruptly stopped laughing and banged his fist on the table, spilling beer and prompting swarthy John the Greek to darken further.

"Don't you look at me like that!" cried Ricky. "Don't!"

John the Greek was actually from the Azores. Found that out one night at Banisters. He'd shown up drunk and disorderly and I'd barred him entry. When he tried to barge in, I stopped him with a bitch slap to the chops. Did he recall that? Then again, how could he forget? He'd burst into tears. Very odd. Not the guy you'd expect to be comforting before a scrum of gaping bystanders, but that was the case as I led him off to the washroom. That's when he brought up the Azores. He wasn't just crying about the slap, no. Other issues must have weighed in, they always do. I felt pity for him while he wiped himself up in the can, then almost hated him for arousing that pity. No one ever called me on the slap, but I doubt he ever mentioned it to anyone.

Oscar turned and without provocation punched John the Greek in the arm. "Fucking bird!" he shouted, threatening to punch him again.

Rubbing the arm and muttering to himself, John grabbed his beer, moved to another table, and sat there with a pained expression. Sometimes just being yourself isn't enough.

"And stay there, you fucking bird! Where I can see you!"

Oscar had immigrated to Hamilton from Argentina at the age of twelve. When I first met him, he spoke little English. A wild man from the get-go, he'd found a perfect outlet for his energies in football. He had a nose for the ball and the raw speed to turn a game around in a heartbeat. The coaches loved his athleticism and ferocity, and forgave his occasional frenzies and flare-ups. Whatever issues he had off the field, when he strapped on the helmet, he was golden. But after run-ins with the law and several assault charges, Oscar quit school in the middle of his last semester and missed his chance to play college ball, maybe even pro. If anyone had the talent to play pro, it was Oscar. Instead, he'd become a regular at the Barton jail. Only a question of time before he wound up in Kingston Pen.

When he asked me about getting drafted by the CFL, I shrugged. A few scouts had shown mild interest, but it didn't matter one way or the other. I enjoyed playing football and I played the game right, but a football career seemed like a stretch.

Oscar clapped his hands. "Up to me, you'd be first round, Bobby Doctor. First round, hands down. Cathedral 17, Bishop Ryan 10. Thas right, Bobby S."

He was alluding to my last-minute touchdown in the All-City Championship, our last game together, something he never failed to mention whenever we crossed paths, and he wasn't being complimentary. In the last few minutes of that game, I took an interception sixty yards down the sidelines for the winning score, my finest football moment ever. Teammates mobbed me, and just about everyone in the stadium congratulated me—everyone except Oscar, that is, who didn't so much as glance my way. And after the game while we all celebrated wildly in the change room, he sat by his locker unwrapping tape from his wrists and brooding.

I had an inkling why.

Oscar, fastest guy on our team, maybe fastest guy in the league, had a bead on that ball I picked off, that beautiful wobbling duck I snatched from the hapless flanker's hands. Oscar broke on that pass before I did from my linebacker zone. And I don't know how—maybe I had the angle, or simply wanted it more—but I beat him to that ball and likely stole his moment. Maybe if he'd picked off that pass and scored, everyone would have mobbed him; and riding the high, he would have finished his last semester at Cathedral and gone on to a big college in the States, and then maybe on to the pros. Maybe, maybe. Easy to speculate. In any event, he found it impossible to mask his resentment toward me, no matter how he played nice.

Ricky drained his bottle, slammed it down, and stared at me with his strange eyes. I didn't look away. I found him fascinating, repugnant but fascinating, and wondered if he was truly psychotic, or evil, or playing it up for gang status—likely a mix of all three. I had met football players who behaved like they were crazy and who reminded me of him, especially the eyes. They were often bluffing or wired on bennies, but Ricky looked like the genuine article.

He tried to hold the stare, but his eyes betrayed him. He grunted and shook his head in frustration. Then he covered his eyes with his hands. Yeah, not an act when you broke it down. He needed help. He dropped his hands and grinned at me with wide-gapped teeth. He looked like he was about to come over but turned to the approaching waitress, a freckled, gum-chewing redhead. She arrived mouthing the chorus of AC/DC's "Dog Eat Dog"—*Hey, hey hey/Every dog has his day*—one hand balancing a tray, the other probing her green canvas money apron.

"Lemme buy you a beer," Oscar said.

"That's the least you can do."

He turned to John the Greek. "What the fuck are you staring at?"

John stiffened in his chair and flattened his hands on the table.

"Fucking bird doesn't learn, man." Oscar flashed the incisor. "Two Blues for me, Red."

The waitress snapped her gum and winked at Oscar, departing just as Demarco appeared, flexing his arms and swivelling at the waist, bits of tissue paper stuck to his chin, hair slicked back. When I asked what he'd been doing all that time, he winced.

"Mr. Lats," Oscar said, pointing. "Look at Mr. Lats. He can fly, Ricky."

Ricky eyed Demarco.

"He can fly."

"I don't like him," Ricky said.

"Demarco, can you fly?"

"I don't like him."

"Can you fly, big man?"

With his trunk erect and chin raised, Demarco ignored the gawks and jibes, posing as the harmless self-observer. He had played football with us at Cathedral—a blocking tight end who'd caught only one pass his entire football career—but Oscar had never thought much of him. Still, Demarco was no pussy; he could rage like a gorilla when pushed too far.

Oscar and company needed no urging. Mayhem was their forte. They banged bottles and rattled their chairs. Taunts flew. But Demarco refused the bait, keeping his cool, at least on the surface. I glanced at the bar. Nancy had her back to me. She must have seen me come in, but she knew how to play the part. I wanted to talk to her before anything stupid happened.

"Back in a second," I said.

"Wait," Demarco said, grabbing my arm.

I continued to the bar. Demarco was a big boy. If he needed me he'd scream.

Nancy ignored me at first, refilling the maraschino and olive trays with the focus of a surgeon. Behind her, liquor bottles lined the shelves, along with Hamilton Ticats paraphernalia: stuffed tigers and Tiggers, black-and-yellow scarves, banners, toques, bobble-head dolls, and black-and-white autographed photos, one of a spectacled Garney Henley, a childhood hero of mine. Finally she acknowledged me. To her left on a post by the service bar, a set of decorative traffic lights flashed through the sequence: red, amber, green.

"What brings you here?" she asked.

"Nice to see you again, too."

With a head tilt, she pursed her lips.

"I'm back for the summer."

"Big city too big for you?"

"Hardly. Might be working doors at that new bar on King William."

"The Press Club? Nice."

I found myself tongue-tied.

She stared at me, maybe expecting an apology, or an explanation, however lame, for failing to keep in touch with her that winter. But hearing zero from me, she shook her head and coldly moved around the bar to serve a customer.

Embarrassed and somewhat frazzled, I sought out Demarco. I found him seated at a table by the unlit tar-papered stage where bands sometimes played, on a dwarf wooden bistro chair. Bits of paper still clung to his face; rain and sweat had darkened the shoulders and armpits of his cardigan. He fidgeted, jerked his head, tugged his sleeves, and rolled his wrists, radiating profound, excruciating discomfort. I smiled as he twitched away. I'd almost forgotten how much the guy cracked me up. I missed him. I missed his refusal to be anyone but himself.

Snapping gum and rolling her eyes, the waitress brought me a frosty bottle of Blue and leaned into my chest. The top three buttons of her shirt were undone, revealing a delicate gold chain with a heart-shaped pendant, and an inch of freckled cleavage. She had a warm and feminine smell uncorrupted by perfume. Don't lose focus, I told myself, turning away from her.

Oscar raised his bottle and touched it to mine with a loud clink, almost knocking it from my hand. He bent at the waist laughing and dropped his bottle to the floor. It didn't break. He snatched it up spewing and foaming and drained the remaining beer.

"Oh yeah," he said, tapping his temple. "Joey was here, your brother. Left a while ago."

This stopped me. My brother? What the fuck?

Oscar laughed. "What's wrong, Bobby Doctor? You look sick, amigo."

When my mother said Joey was mixing with a bad crowd, I thought she meant the riff-raff in our own neighbourhood, not these assholes. I glared at Oscar.

"What's wrong, Bobby? We used to be bros. That's right, me and you. Like this." He crossed two fingers. "And now you look at me like—what's that look, man?"

"My brother's a good kid."

"Yeah, sure, Joey's a good kid. And you know what, I'll keep an eye out for him if you're worried. Make sure no one disrespects him. I'll tell 'em, you know who this kid is, he's Bobby Doctor's baby brother, and if you wanna mess with him you gotta go through me first." He turned away before I could respond and rejoined Ricky, who was hectoring John the Greek.

Demarco appeared at my side. "Listen to that psycho," he said in my ear.

"Really," I said, digesting the news about Joey.

He wiped his sweaty face. "So how's Nancy?"

"She's fine."

"I can see that."

She wouldn't look my way. Maybe there was nothing there, and I was good with that. As I sipped my beer, I noticed two guys looming at the entrance, a tall, big-shouldered blond, and his shorter friend with tight black curls, both wearing blue jeans, denim jackets, and black T-shirts. The blond looked vaguely familiar. They surveyed the place, then strode up to the bar.

Luigi Fanelli, one of Oscar's cohorts, rose from his table and followed them. Pale and gaunt, with densely tattooed arms, he didn't show well, but I'd seen him fight before and he was a real scrapper. He squeezed beside the newcomers and ordered a drink from Nancy. She handed him a Blue. He paid, returned to his seat, and said something to Oscar that amused him.

"Who are those two?" Demarco asked.

I studied the strangers. "The blond dude kinda looks like Kevin Mulroney from St. Thomas More, but I'm not a hundred per cent."

"Nah, Kevin's shorter."

"Maybe it's his brother."

"He has a brother?"

The freckled waitress reappeared and handed me a Royal Connaught matchbook with a telephone number penned on the inside flap. I smiled at her. She smiled back with a flare of her nostrils and told me it wasn't her number.

"It's Nancy's," she said, starting toward the bar. "Call her sometime."

The waitress passed the two newcomers on her way back to the bar. The dark-haired guy was chatting up a slinky girl in pink with long white arms. Ricky came and stood behind him, fixing his gaze on the back of his head. Then Nancy said something that made Ricky laugh out loud, but she wasn't laughing; she moved to the end of the bar and kept her shoulders turned.

Fox-faced Dino Flex and the black-bearded Mad Dog joined Ricky, crowding the two guys and the slinky girl. Dino leaned to the girl, who after a sharp exchange grabbed her pink handbag and hustled off to the ladies' room. Wide-eyed, the dark-haired guy protested, but the gang members laughed and jeered. Ricky bumped against the blond guy, apologizing with theatrical insincerity. Dino and Mad Dog bawled with laughter. The strangers' faces tightened up.

Demarco looked ill. "Let's get out of here, Bobby."

"Not yet." I had to watch the thing run its course.

Oscar appeared, smiling, gold tooth glinting. He squatted down as if picking something off the tiles. When he didn't stand up immediately, I wondered what the fuck he was doing. He continued squatting for a beat, then with a violent swing of his arms sprang up off the floor and over a chair, floating through the dense pub air in a series of baleful freeze frames before his knees crashed against the blond guy's chest and knocked him to the floor.

The blond staggered to his feet and lunged at Oscar, who deftly stepped aside and clipped him with a right to the jaw that put him back down. Then Oscar fed boots to his head, winding up with each kick and hitting it square. Red stained the blond hair, then more red.

Meanwhile, Ricky and the dark-haired guy stood toe to toe exchanging punches, Ricky getting the worst of it, bloody-nosed and cut above the eye. Then Dino Flex and Mad Dog jumped in, grabbed the guy's arms, and slammed him against a table. While they held him there, Ricky, spitting blood and bawling, smashed his face with hammer fists.

Other patrons fled for the exit, white-eyed in their panic. Someone bumped the jukebox and the needle screeched; then a fire alarm pierced the air to a chorus of screams. In the midst of the stampede, a girl in white go-go boots slipped on a beer spill and hit the floor, convulsing and shrieking until a Good Samaritan grabbed her hand and pulled her out of harm's way.

The manager, a thin man with a perm, slipped out of the office in back with a briefcase, and unlocked a door that led into the hotel proper, through which he disappeared. Demarco started for the entrance. I followed him, almost walking backwards. I couldn't see Nancy behind the bar or among the dashing patrons, but saw a blood-smeared Ricky flip the dark-haired guy to the floor, kicking him again and again and shouting, "What! What!" No answer was forthcoming. The guy was out cold. Oscar and Mad Dog grabbed the blond by the arms and legs and dragged him along the floor. Ricky and Dino lifted the other guy up like a sack but needed the help of John the Greek and Luigi to carry him. Chairs and tables flew as they hastened in a tangle toward the exit.

Demarco and I went up to the street. The rain had stopped; puddles quivered on the drying pavement. Patrons ran this way and that; others stood watching from a distance. Scuffling erupted in the stairwell: Oscar and Mad Dog had the blond sandwiched between them, arms entwined with his. His bloody head lolling, they marched him up the stairs to the street as though escorting an inebriated friend. This impression dissolved when they knocked him to the ground and put their steel toes to work. Luigi joined them. They stomped away, laughing, whooping, their eyes like jewels. Whimpers for mercy drew only more laughter.

It went on. I had to stop myself from jumping in. What I saw revolted me, but the boys were superheated. I'd wind up getting my own ass kicked trying to help two strangers. Not in the program. They kept kicking the guy. When he tried to curl up, Oscar kicked him so hard in the spine something gave and his body slackened.

Ricky, Dino, and John the Greek dragged the dark-haired guy up the stairs and threw him down by his friend, thudding kicks into his body. When they stopped, hands on knees, winded and amused, Ricky studied the limp body, arching his brow. Then he had Dino and John the Greek help him sling the guy across his shoulders, jerking his neck to centre the weight. As Ricky stepped toward the stairwell and the body swayed, he paused to still it. Then he squared himself, bent at the knees, and with a hoarse scream hurled the guy down the stairs.

"Let's get the fuck out of here," Demarco said, striding ahead.

My legs shook as we walked to the Camaro. I stood by the door for a moment before I unlocked it. The silver paint glistened with raindrops; water dappled the roof like mercury.

"Hope it didn't leak," I heard myself say.

"Yeah," Demarco said, dry-mouthed.

The 327 roared, throaty and strong. I revved the engine for a minute and tried to steady my nerves. Sirens wailed nearby. Demarco slumped in his seat, trembling. He wouldn't look at me.

We drove east along King Street in silence. Demarco clenched his teeth and squeezed his thighs. He smelled like a wet, perfumed dog. I thought I was going to pass out. Near Nash Road, I pulled over, lowered the roof, and breathed. A passing red van blared a triple-horn, giving me such a start I almost fainted.

"What's wrong with you?" Demarco asked.

"Nothing," I said, gulping for air.

He looked at the sky. "It might rain again."

"I need air."

We sat there a minute before setting off. My heart rate slowed, my muscles relaxed. The sky was a starless grey mass fringed with orange over the bay where the foundries burned: Stelco, Dofasco, Burlington Steel. Demarco wanted to say something, I could tell, maybe the obvious thing, but he didn't. Neither of us spoke.

We caught green lights all the way to Stoney Creek and were greeted by a mini-traffic jam. Vehicles and pedestrians crowded the corners of Grays Road and King Street in a yellow wash of headlights. A shirtless man with a dog stood by a fire hydrant in front of the Stoney Creek Dairy. For a wet spring night, the place was hopping. Muscle cars packed the parking lot, gleaming and exquisite. A sapphire-blue Corvette with a 454 and chrome side pipes took the ribbon.

We parked and joined the lineup snaking to the double doors. Chatty teenage girls and scruffy, sullen dudes. Older couples arm in arm. A few drunks and roughs. I ordered a strawberry sundae; Demarco, a banana split. He walked around in his damp cardigan flexing, arms fanned out, swivelling at the hips, serious, hard, overcompensating. People stared.

We sat at a picnic table under a green awning on the side property. Neither of us spoke. A stiff breeze whirled some paper wrappers over the moist, matted grass. I blew into my hands to warm them. Demarco relaxed and tucked into his banana split. I stared at my sundae: the whipped cream, the ice cream. The strawberries.

TWO

Soft yellow light filled my mother's kitchen. A vase of yellow tulips trembled on the table as a breeze flowed through the open window; laundry flapped on the clothesline. Birds sang. And it was a sort of music that morning, lovely, lilting, hopeful, though it failed to ease a nagging pang of dread I felt, the sense that something pernicious had been set in motion.

I had slept poorly, tossing and turning all night, my brain replaying the Street Scene brawl on an unremitting Technicolor loop. I'd witnessed beatings before, but nothing like that. I could still feel it in my viscera, still taste it in the back of my throat—acrid, metallic.

Groggy and famished, I battered six slices of bread in egg and milk, fried them in butter, plated them, and slathered on more butter. Then I drowned them in syrup. Not a breakfast of champions perhaps, but it worked for me. I took the plate and a carton of milk out back to the wooden picnic table under the pergola, sat down, and ate.

Wearing black rubber gloves and a scarlet kerchief in her hair, my mother worked a spade at the end of the garden. She glanced at me and waved. I waved back. "Hope you're not planning to dig the whole garden!" I cried. She looked up smiling and said something muffled by the breeze, then returned to her task. She seemed content enough. The spade scraped the earth. I drank from the milk carton. Sunlight speared my eyes.

Five years had passed since my father died of lung cancer. My mother had only stopped wearing black that past Christmas, and she hadn't stopped mourning him. The coke ovens killed him, she'd say, all those years in the coke ovens. Not to mention the two packs of Rothmans a day he puffed for relief from that shitty three-shift grind. So much for seeking his fortunes in Uncle Ignazio's Hammer. By now he would have already dug up the earth so my mother could start her garden. Uncle Giuseppe, her brother, was usually up to the task, but if he didn't get to it soon I would, as much as I disliked the idea. The telephone rang in the house.

After a moment the screen door opened. My brother.

"For you," he said. "Demarco."

I went in. Joey had gone back upstairs so I had no chance to say anything to him. The telephone receiver dangled rhythmically from its wall mount. I picked it up and held it to my ear without speaking. I could hear Demarco breathing.

"You there, Bobby?"

"I'm here. Pretty day out there."

"Yeah. Perfect. What time do you want to meet?"

"After breakfast. Need an hour or so."

"That's fine." He paused. "That blond guy last night—he's in a coma."

"What? You heard it on the news?"

"No, my cousin Santo works at General Hospital. That's where the ambulance brought them. He said the other guy is pretty messed up, fractured skull and so on, but the blond dude's lucky to be alive. And he's not out of the woods yet."

I doubted the cops had investigated or questioned anyone about the scrap, or that anyone had stepped forward. Cops in the Hammer tended to handle violent assaults like hockey fights, and its citizens took the proverb of the three wise monkeys to heart.

"Did Santo say who they were?"

"Westmount boys. Wrong place, wrong time."

"Anyway, let me finish eating. See you in an hour."

I neglected to ask Demarco if he planned to join me at the Press Club doors that summer. Would have understood if he passed.

His old man and uncles worked at Stelco, and wanted to hook him up with a job there. Not an option for me: I hadn't come back to Hamilton to sweat my ass off and die a little in a steel mill.

Joey stood in the kitchen doorway palming the jambs, his undershirt soiled, a sharp body odour jumping off him. He had shaved his head since the last time we crossed paths. A shiner coloured his left eye; his bruised lower lip stuck out. He looked like a cancer patient.

"You were at the Street Scene last night," I said.

He tongued his lip. "Just passed through."

"Yeah, eh? Cool. You're hitting the bars now. Growing up. That's great, Joey."

He rolled his eyes.

"Coincidence. I was there last night! Just passing through, like you."

"I heard."

I stared at him hard, but he averted his eyes. "You heard? One of your *friends* told you?"

He said nothing, scratched his neck.

"They did a nice job on those two pretty boys—beat the pretty right out of them."

"They deserved it," he said, staring at his new white runners.

"What do you mean, they *deserved* it?"

"They were on our turf."

I laughed. What a crock of shit. I glanced at Joey's glaring, unlaced runners; an urge to slap him almost overtook me. It had fuck all to do with turf. Barton-Sherman wasn't battling the Parkdale gang or the Clubbers or anybody from the mountain for turf. They did what they did for the pure rush of it. Violence was their drug of choice.

"Word of advice, little brother. Stay away from those stupid fucks. You think they're your friends? Don't be such a tool. You were raised better than that. And don't let anyone in the north end know you've been hanging with them. Then it won't be me kicking your ass."

"Is that a threat?"

"*What* did you say?"

The white runners drew my eyes again, and I inched closer to Joey, close enough to smell his foul breath. I felt him leaning back, tensing, but still telling me in his way to go fuck myself. I'd always thought he looked up to me, and maybe this was true in the past, but I'd become a stranger. He stepped aside and straightened up with his fists clenched and his mouth affecting a thug-snarl. He'd never been a tough or physical kid, shying away from roughhousing and contact sports. Pushing around my old dumbbells had broadened his shoulders and puffed up his biceps, but that was all I could see, nothing to warrant the attitude. Kicking his ass would have been satisfying, but I shoved past him and returned to the pergola. Joey, Barton-Sherman. Almost comical. Stay calm, I thought. Don't spook him by coming on too strong. I'd bide my time, put him in a slow squeeze. If and when that didn't work, I'd try more forceful tactics.

My mother stopped digging, unrolled the hose, and watered the flower beds. I gulped my vitamins and Dianabol pills with the milk left in the carton. My stomach ached briefly; then I fought back a wave of nausea. Milk disagreed with me—as a boy I favoured the sugary Diamond Beverages delivered in a case to our house every Saturday—but I drank gallons of it to keep up my weight. A bluebottle circled my sticky plate; a cardinal and his duller mate skirmished in the peach tree; grackles scrapped in the Wardens' red maple. Everything was up in the air.

"Ma, I'm going to the gym."

My words fell unanswered as she continued passing the hose nozzle back and forth over the lawn. She radiated calm and content in the sunshine, and opting not to spoil that, I slipped off to the kitchen without disturbing her. I rinsed off the plate and pan in the sink, wiped the counter. Then I went upstairs, brushed my teeth, and threw my gym stuff together. My brother had left his door ajar; he was doing push-ups on the floor. I kicked the door wide open before I skipped down the stairs, and heard him cursing after me.

I stepped outside. The neighbours Mr. and Mrs. Warden sat on their porch, both in tan leisure suits. Pale and tremulous that morning, Mrs. Warden had never looked otherwise. At least the Camaro looked good. I stood there admiring the radiant machine. Circling overhead, dull bay gulls had no truck for a shine like that. One of them blasted the hood, and I ran down with a chamois and wiped away the creamy discharge. The gulls hated beauty. And the Wardens, who owned an old hunter-green Volkswagen parked in the alley that made an execrable sound when started, they hated beauty, too, I surmised from their sneers.

I lowered the roof and climbed in. I revved the engine for a minute, fiddling with the radio until I found a station playing Deep Purple. The Wardens bristled as I drove away.

I drove to the Fitness Academy on Highway 20, a gym I'd patronized since high school. Ned Simic, the owner, welcomed me back with his watery blue eyes and a handshake that rasped like wet sandpaper. An affable, thickset man in his mid-thirties, Ned had once been strength coach for the Toronto Argonauts. Sweat darkened the armpits of his taupe golf shirt; a tarnished copper bracelet encircled his meaty wrist. I released his hand and rubbed my own on my pants.

"You've put on twenty pounds of muscle, Bobby."

"Actually, about fifteen."

"How's your bench these days?"

"Four and a quarter, something like that."

He raised his eyebrows with approval and shuffled back around the white-padded counter. He fished through a drawer and extracted a contract and a waiver for my summer membership. He handed me a silver ballpoint pen and showed me where to sign. Then I signed over a cheque for the fee, quite reasonable by Toronto standards.

"You'll be happy to know I've installed a neck machine," he said.

"Excellent news." I'd be needing a twenty-inch collar before long.

Terry Peters, Barton-Sherman, appeared at the top of the weight-room stairs in grey sweatpants and a Black Sabbath Volume IV T-shirt with chopped sleeves, his flaccid pink arms almost fluttering at his sides. His face projected vehemence, loathing, and a self-confidence I found bizarre. Around his spindly neck he wore a thick gold chain and crucifix, and, tightened to the last notch, an embossed leather weightlifting belt cinched his waist. His black Converse sneakers, at least a size too big, clopped when he moved his feet.

"When did Rupert Brooke start coming?" I asked.

Ned squinted and shrugged. "I'm a businessman, Bobby. Can't afford to discriminate."

"Hasn't brained anyone with a dumbbell yet, has he?"

"No, not yet," Ned sighed.

In the locker room I changed into shorts and a U of T Varsity golf shirt. I rolled out my neck and shoulders and entered the weight room, greeted by the amiable smell of rubber, sweat, and iron. Ah, I felt right at home here. In addition to the shiny new neck gizmo, Ned had added two leg machines, another incline bench, and more full-length mirrors.

A handful of people pushed and pulled in silence; a weak Phil Collins tune whined over the speakers. Nelson "Nipsy" Gomes, a freelance thug of Trinidadian origins, stood before a central mirror grunting and working his traps with a terrible expression. He had metamorphosed since last summer from a stick man to a compact Hulk. His torso strained the fibres of his faded Jack Daniels T-shirt; twitching gnarls of muscle crowded his shoulders; veins wormed his bulging arms. Even at rest, his dense quadriceps quivered with latent power. What impressed me wasn't so much the physique—an asymmetrical, lumpy mess, in all honesty—but that he was still alive. The drugs required to create that body would have killed a normal person.

"Bobby, what it is."

"Long time, Nipsy."

"Yeah, long time. Looking strong, boy, like Hercules. Anavar?"

"Dianabol."

He smiled. "Been favouring Winstrol, lately. You should try it, boss. Thickens without bloating. Hate that bloating. Don't you hate bloating, Hercules? Do some shrugs with me."

"Working chest, man."

"Nah, really?" He frowned and flicked a drop of sweat off his nose. His bloodshot eyes sat close together in the slick darkness of his face. A short neck connected his smooth bald head to a barrelled torso. He sniffed his fingers, muttered to himself, and started another set. Nipsy had done time in Kingston Pen. He used to run errands for some Hamilton wise guys before he got pinched with a sawed-off shotgun in his car trunk and went up for a three-year stint. He liked his guns almost as much as his drugs. He once told me if I ever needed a piece to look him up.

Demarco swaggered in, flexing his biceps while adjusting his headband, a red silk affair more fitting for an ethnic dance or a Shriner parade than a gym, but he looked deadly serious. He could be a drag when he got like this, inflexible, joyless, hearing nothing but his own twisted transmissions. And the man's abortion of style left one blushing. On this occasion he wore a moth-eaten lobster red pullover, high-waisted navy sweatpants splotched with yellow paint or French's mustard, and soiled white canvas runners, no socks, knotty anklebones exposed.

"There he is," I said. "Miss America."

"He looks focussed."

"Needs work in the talent competition."

"True. Can't win without big titties these days."

Without acknowledging me or Nipsy, Demarco approached a bench press. He cracked his knuckles, threw two plates on the bar, and assumed the position, wiggling his buttocks and feet to anchor himself. He warmed up with fifteen slow repetitions. Then he moved off that bench and sat on an adjacent one with his hands on his thighs, waiting like a sphinx for me to do my set.

After ten reps my left shoulder tightened up. I stopped and stretched back my arm.

"You're weak today," Demarco said.

"We'll see."

"Weakling."

The shoulder tightness perturbed me: too much size too fast. Not that I was small to begin with, a natural mesomorph. But steroids radicalized a body. My arms looked like legs; I had an ass like a horse. I'd upped my max bench by a hundred pounds in a year, my squats by almost two hundred, at the same time slashing my forty time by three-tenths of a second. Bigger, stronger, and faster. True, my bones and tendons ached, and at times I felt like I might burst out of my skin, but feeling strange now and then seemed a small price to pay for such mad results.

Nipsy grunted out a set of inclines with two heavy dumbbells, then released them with successive bangs and rose from the bench screaming and pounding his chest. Too much demonstration for that time of day, I felt. Demarco gritted his teeth.

"Did you see Terry Peters?" I asked.

"Yeah, in the locker room with his shirt off, posing."

"Wish I could have been there to witness that. Impressive, I bet."

"Wonder where he was last night," Demarco mused. "Cleanup work's his specialty."

An east ender born and bred, Peters was fifth-generation Canadian with no vowel on the end of his last name, more suited for the white-trash Parkdale gang or skinhead Clubbers than that motley crew of immigrants and immigrants' sons, the Barton-Sherman gang. His favoured status rankled fellow members who considered him a volatile and risk-averse heat source. But he and Eugene were childhood friends, their loyalty ran deep; and with Eugene angling toward a future with the Hamilton mob, Peters proved invaluable as a trusted confidant, an unflinching yes man, and a perfect soldier. His zeal made even the sociopaths on his team blush.

"My brother's been hanging with Peters and his crew," I said.

Demarco frowned but looked away, uneasy discussing Jocy, whom he'd always liked. It wasn't his problem. I pulled my arms across my chest, shut my eyes, and tried to regain focus. After another set, blood engorged my arms and pectorals: the juice was doing its job; you saw the growth with your eyes. Barbells don't lie. Everyone was juicing, even the U of T punter was dropping his pants for weekly testosterone shots. Respectable doctors were prescribing the shit by the barrels, and exotic strains from the States and Mexico could easily be scored on the street. And steroids, worked, this was the thing, they worked. Lifters who had trained clean for years with no progress, within weeks of using steroids had transmogrified into beasts. But all this meant nothing to me: I was fucking strong. That's all that mattered. No need for nuance.

We added two more plates. Three hundred and fifteen pounds now. I banged out eight smooth reps. That was more like it. Demarco struggled with his set, arching his back, shaking out but two assisted reps.

"You're weak today," I said.

"Shut up."

Nipsy clenched his teeth as he shrugged two dumbbells. Veins stood out on his forehead. Demarco watched him intently, perhaps trying to draw inspiration from his efforts. I urged him to do another set but he demanded less weight. Even before the steroids, I'd always bench-pressed more than him. Granted his aims were aesthetic, mine pragmatic. He needed the fine lines and symmetry of a Frank Zane; I needed the explosive strength and power of a Dick Butkus.

Terry Peters reappeared, frowning, seething, his small eyes bright with annoyance. What had teed him off? Maybe nothing. Maybe that's the way he always was. How strenuous it must have been to be so angry all the time. He bent to tie his shoelaces.

"Look," I said under my breath. "He can tie his shoes."

Demarco tried to be serious but snorted a laugh. Peters straightened up and approached us, arms crooked at his sides, nose raised. He stopped and stared at Demarco, muttering to himself. Demarco ignored him and performed another set, his arms almost buckling on the last rep. He sat up disgusted but resigned to his funk. Anyone who lifts long enough can get stale; the muscles get bored; the routine gets routine. As I chalked my hands, Peters performed pullovers with a light dumbbell, yipping with each rep. Then he dropped the weight and jumped to his feet like he'd been stung. He bounced on his toes and shook his pink arms.

"He was eyeing you, Demarco."

"He was eyeing *you*."

"I would've done something about it."

"You're all talk, Sferazza."

After another set, Peters hopped up and did a shuffle, thumbing his nose, jabbing the air.

"He knows how to box," I said.

Demarco said nothing. Peters walked over. He smelled of tobacco, sweat, and something off under that. His head was small, weak chin, snub nose, a wandering eye, hard to tell which one.

"You're Joey's brother," he said to me.

"That's right," I said, ogling his bulging Adam's apple.

"Your brother's a good head."

"A good head?" I chuckled. "Well, I'm glad you think so."

He glared at Demarco. "I don't like your friend here."

"I don't like him either," I said.

Peters turned to the mirror and struck a face-twisting double biceps pose, his eyes popping as though he were passing a compacted stool or being sodomized. He released the pose and slapped his hands on his knees, fatigued by the effort. Then he straightened up and turned to me.

"What's the big pussy's name?" he asked, grimacing.

"Who? Demarco? Hmm. Don't think he heard what you said."

Peters smiled.

"Seriously. He didn't hear you. Call him a pussy again."

"Your name's Bobby, right?"

I said nothing, staring at his throat. I wanted to give it a chop to see what would happen. I wanted to chop him sharply in the throat, with the edge of my hand, and watch. He stood there sneering. I leaned my mouth close to his ear.

"Call my friend a pussy again."

Peters half-smiled. Then he shambled over to the fountain and took a quick drink before he disappeared into the change room.

Demarco stood beside me. "Why are you fucking with that psycho?"

"I have my reasons."

"Or suicidal tendencies."

Sweat inched down the sides of Demarco's face, his mouth fixed in a straight line; one of his eyes twitched. He retied his headband. He didn't get it. I walked to the fountain for a drink; the ice-cold water tasted coppery and made my teeth ache. He just didn't fucking get it.

Nipsy joined me at the fountain. He smelled like sweaty talcum powder.

"Better watch that boy," he said. "He's off. 'Member the Riverside last spring?"

Peters had allegedly taken a baseball bat to an undercover officer's skull in the washroom of the Riverside, a sedate Oakville tavern by the water. The assault put the officer in a coma for six months, and made all the local papers; and though he went around town boasting about his batting practice, no one ever identified Peters as the attacker and he was never charged with a crime. Surprising the cops never straightened him out on their own, you'd think it a no-brainer, much-welcomed, but he operated with a confounding impunity.

We finished our workout. Peters never reappeared, though I mentally filed the incident away for future reference. Sooner or later I'd be stepping around or on that piece of shit again. We showered and dressed and Demarco put on a ridiculous burgundy mohair sweater that he tucked into his skin-tight jeans. In the parking lot he wanted to know the story with Peters.

"Look," I said. "If I need you to watch my back, will you do it?"

He rolled his eyes. "Don't want to worry about psychos like him."

"Who, Tiny Talent Time Peters?"

"You'll be tough until they swarm the joint, then you'll be kissing their asses all summer like last year. Personally, I don't need the anxiety. Have an interview at Stelco next Monday."

I stared at Demarco but he looked away. He knew the very thought of steel mills sickened me. After high school graduation I spent the summer on the nightshift at Burlington Steel, my father's old workplace, as a "hooker," securing and hooking piles of red-hot pipe fresh off a conveyor belt to an overhead crane, a hellish job in a hellish place. I toiled there with unfriendly, unhappy men, scarcely averting death every night. I lost my eyebrows, all the hair on my arms, and melted three pairs of work boots, not to mention all the charred blue jeans. The experience scarred me: I had vowed never to work the mills again.

Demarco led the way in his father's rusty Galaxy 500, with its rear-window nodding puppy, to the Dairy Queen near Ottawa Street. I parked near a mint-condition fiery orange GTO Judge and its 400 c.i. Ram Air engine. It made me warm inside.

At the counter I ordered a chocolate shake, Demarco a banana split with extra toppings, citing a potassium deficiency.

"Sometimes at night when I curl them, my toes cramp."

Demarco's feet, in yellow flip-flops, consisted of hairy toes, knobby corns, and horny, overgrown toenails. I averted my head.

"So you're still going to do it?" he asked.

"Work at the Press Club? Like, did something change in the last couple of minutes?"

"Preservation is a worthy cause, Bobby." He slurped pineapple sauce off his plastic spoon. "I'd like to be in one piece come September. I want to graduate next spring."

"Anyway, that's your decision. I start tomorrow. I'll see what's going on, who he's hired, what kind of schedule he has in mind. Have you been there?"

"Yeah. Tiny dance floor. Gets crowded fast. Lots of ladies."

"I bet, but since when do ladies interest you?"

As I sucked the shake, my straw buckled and a kink in my left shoulder bit me like a parrot. A wave of nausea rose in my throat; I dabbed my wet brow with a serviette. I dumped the remaining shake in the trash, got in the Camaro, and breathed deeply before I started the engine. Demarco stood by the Galaxy 500 grinning like an idiot as two imperturbable blondes in halter tops strolled by, nostrils skyward. He had no idea how ludicrous he looked in that fuzzy sweater, a young man with issues. The blondes snorted off, and I drove away.

I took a detour to the marina at the end of Bay Street. Parked the car and walked to a rocky, garbage-strewn patch near the water's edge. Joey and I had often come here as boys, to skip stones and fuck around. Not that it meant much at that moment. I had no idea why I had driven there. As with so many things back then, my motivations were a mystery to me; I was operating on some kind of kinetic autopilot, at least it seems so now. Rows of idle yachts and sailing craft sat bobbing at the end of a pier. The water resembled pea soup. It had never looked better.

A two-tone blue sailboat drifted by. The flexing sail obscured the faces of the crew and this bothered me as I could hear them speaking. Two male voices and one female. Or one male and two females. What they said was indistinct to my ears but sounded cheerful and frank. As they faded out of earshot, I walked along the shore, toward the steel mills. The air smelled of rotten eggs. It reminded me of my childhood.

A dead grey catfish bobbed on the water's surface, sallow belly exposed, centring a small, trembling oil slick. Gulls hovered overhead, oddly silent. I skipped a stone on the soup, then aimed for the catfish. Missed the first time, but the second pitch caught the head and set the catfish slowly spinning. A gull screamed. The steel mills smouldered away, yellowing the city and its skies.

THREE

I had painted the closet door in my bedroom matte red back in high school and though the room had been repainted several times since then, always in bone acrylic, the door had not. I'd heard somewhere that every bedroom needs a splash of red. White always lapsed; red remained true.

I opened the red door, took out my dark blue suit, and rested it on the bed. I didn't know if the Press Club would issue jackets for the door staff. At Banisters we wore these gold-buttoned crimson things reminiscent of bellhop uniforms. I'd only worn the suit twice: to a wedding last summer and a funeral last winter. It smelled of mothballs but looked intact. I wrapped cellophane tape around my palm and used it to lift lint off the sleeves and shoulders. Then I smoothed the lapels. I slipped on the jacket; it fit snugly. I looked at myself in the armoire mirror and thought I could get away with it for the time being, but I'd need the jacket altered or a new one if Luciano decided not to outfit the door staff. I removed the jacket and struck a boxer's pose in front of the armoire and shadow-boxed until I started perspiring.

Spread-eagled to cool off, I lay on my bed in my underwear and listened to street traffic through the open window as the steel mills emptied for shift change. In a few hours I'd be starting my own shift. As I played out possible scenarios, a sort of pre-game apprehension gripped me: butterflies, clammy palms, persistent yawning.

It wasn't too late to back out of the gig. Nothing was set in stone; I could change my mind at any time. But then I thought of the alternatives, all involving melted shoes and no eyebrows, and any doubts I had were silenced.

My mother and Joey argued downstairs. He was growling at her, really pressing his point until her voice rose decisively. Then Joey stomped up the stairs to his bedroom, and slammed the door shut. This was all recent, all this shit. Joey had always been a good, quiet kid, not prone to mood swings and rages. His age may have had something to do with it; a sixteen-year-old boy is like a monkey with a hard on, not the most reasonable of creatures.

Perhaps that's unfair, as unfair as it is to underestimate how much my father's death had damaged Joey, for it took its toll on all of us. Grief and concern, not to mention economic hardship, had reduced my once vibrant and beautiful mother—whose job at Essex Packers kept us just above poverty—to a shadow of her old self; at times only the warm blue of her eyes reminded me of that lovely woman from my childhood. Anguished and angered by my father's death, I withdrew into my books with a prickly detachment. But as profoundly as I felt my father's absence, more wounding was my mother's sadness, which had no limit. No doubt Joey felt the weight of it as much as I did.

Football had provided me with a much-needed escape, a place to unload my frustrations. When you're angry, bigger, and stronger than your peers—by then I'd had a growth spurt—you can become a bully, or take up sports. Fighting for its own sake didn't come naturally, and beating up weaklings gave me no pleasure, but I'd always liked sports, and by Grade 11 had become a dominant high school footballer. My size, agility, and improving technique, made me an excellent linebacker, and I vented my pain on opponents.

Small-boned, slender-hipped, almost delicate, Joey had never liked football; indeed, he detested it, calling it a game for gorillas. He had played hockey but poorly, without enthusiasm, and unlike me had never found an outlet for his sadness and rage—until now perhaps.

On the way to the bathroom I stopped by his shut bedroom door and pressed my ear to it, listening, hoping he'd hear me rustling about and pop out so we could talk about this situation. He was going through a difficult time, okay. Understandable. Growing up without a father isn't easy. The world can overwhelm you. Relationships can suffocate you. School can be a bore. Rules can box you in. A mother, even a good one, can be overbearing. But hanging with sociopaths wasn't the answer. Would it be that hard to make this point? Was it a fucking stretch? I didn't think so. It should have been easy, after all, an hour's conversation tops, with lots of shouting and laughing, then a hug and a kiss on the cheek. But I held back from knocking. I had to get ready for work.

In the bathroom I washed my face and brushed my teeth. My hair held well with hairspray but sweat poured off my brow and my armpits squelched. Anxiety. No time for another shower. I towelled off my armpits and reapplied deodorant. I studied myself in the mirror. My neck looked unnatural, rising from my shoulders and forming a single powerful unit with my head. I wondered if it made me look ugly, freakish. But muscles were more mainstream in Hamilton, with its well-established bodybuilding and powerlifting cultures, than in Toronto, where they often provoked fear, frowns and puzzled stares or, in certain sectors of town, undesired attention.

Flexing my biceps into rock-like balls, I stared at my florid reflection, and for a moment it wasn't me, not the me I had known at every stage of my life. The figure smiling back with bared teeth and throbbing carotids gave me pause. He looked dangerous.

My mother made espresso and I drank it standing up. She told me the suit looked tight on the shoulders, comparing my appearance to Guido Musitano, a no-necked, barrel-chested paisan with mobster affectations who used to visit my father. She told me she'd pay for a new suit but I laughed and said I *wanted* to look like Musitano. She pinched my cheek and in Sicilian cried, "*Commu si bidru!*" She knew I was working at a nightclub again, but had no idea what that entailed. If I happened to come home with a few bumps and bruises, no screaming, no scenes. She'd gotten used to seeing me banged up from football. At least, that's what I told myself.

I sat in the Camaro for a moment before departing, listening to some soothing George Benson. In the park the Wardens shambled arm in arm around piles of raked leaves leftover from autumn. Their bucket hats worked well in that light. Mrs. Warden looked ashen but this was normal. Abnormal was how ashen Mr. Warden looked, indeed how much Mr. and Mrs Warden resembled each other, almost interchangeable. What did this mean? It meant that time was passing. I glanced at the dash clock. I was late.

Thanks to the Camaro, I made up time, running amber lights all the way to the Press Club. When I got there, Tony Fernandez and Jerome Upshaw stood by the doors in dark suits with gold name tags pinned to their lapels. Across the street, New York, New York the cavernous discotheque owned by a mysterious, obese man from Montreal called Octavio, was quiet.

"What's going on, gentlemen?"

"Not a whole lot," droned Jerome, in his familiar baritone.

Fernandez gave me a manic thumbs-up. "Looking good, Bobby."

"Like the lid, Fernandez. It's becoming."

"Becoming what?" Jerome asked guilelessly.

Fernandez had grown his Afro into a frantic stack, and had lost a few choppers, giving him a snaggletoothed smile and an air of caprice. Jerome, once a sleek, standout defensive end with the Hamilton Ticats, now weighed more than three hundred sloppy pounds and limped around with a bad left meniscus. We'd all worked Banisters together, with mixed results and mixed feelings after the Barton-Sherman fiasco. Seeing them gave me meagre reassurance.

We traded quick updates—Jerome was trying to rejoin the Ticats practice roster even as we spoke; Fernandez had fathered a child with a thirty-year-old ex-stripper—and I went up the short flight of stairs to the velvety black-and-carmine foyer.

Music shivered the walls as the deejay in the blue glass booth by the dance floor tinkered with the powerful sound system. I had to plug my ears with my fingers, but then the bass line shook my intestines. I knocked on the office door; Luciano Mercanti answered, wearing charcoal pinstripes and smoking a rancid cigar. He had aged since last August, his neck like leather, hair thinning, forehead and upper lip pimply with sweat. Rumour had it he was blowing wads on ponies and cocaine, but who was I to judge? He gnawed his cigar and spoke in the staccato bursts of a cokehead, with a habit of emphasizing unexpected words that always threw me.

"Bobby, nice to see you again, come in. Don't mind the mess. How you been *doing*? You look gargantuan. *Eating your Wheaties?*" He held up a finger, leaned out the door, and shouted, "Turn that *music* down, Mimmo!" He looked at me sideways and said, "If that fucking idiot wasn't my sister's kid. Denis from Banisters—remember him?—he's working New York, New York. Octavio's paying him twice what I was. How can I *compete* with that? How can I pay a fucking deejay that *much* and make a profit? So Mimmo will have to do. The kid knows his shit, he does. But he's an idiot. Sorry, Bobby, *you* were saying?"

"I'm doing okay, Luciano. Can't complain."

"Good, good. No one *likes* a complainer."

I entered the wood-panelled office, stepping around a chrome-plated vacuum cleaner positioned by the doorway like a dwarf robot sentry. Red ribbon and silver tinsel dangled from the ceiling: vestiges of a New Year's Eve bash? Or signs of very recent, even kinky festivity? A half-empty jar of Vaseline on a corner shelf gave me further pause; then a musky malodor rushed at me like a punch in the nose and I had to hold my breath for a moment and wipe tears from my eyes. Luciano asked if I was okay. I nodded and covered my nose with my hand.

Stepping forward, around an unsteady floor lamp, my right foot crushed an empty Tim Hortons cup, one of many littering the black shag carpet, and then fell on a blond hairpiece or wig, which startled me. I could find no place to sit. Manilla envelopes and newspapers blanketed a morocco-leather sofa against one wall, and against another a mass of beige folders, doughnut boxes, tile samples, dry cleaning, and other sundry items buried a mahogany desk. There was nowhere to sit or stand.

Luciano shuffled through a pile of papers and told me to be patient while he looked for my file. I had a feeling the file was a fiction. An *Enter the Dragon* poster on the wall behind the desk caught my eye, Bruce Lee looking fierce and fabulous. People used to say he could kill a man without touching him. I never believed that. He had nice moves, sure, good tight physique, and could yip with the best of them. But he weighed a buck and a half. About as much as Joey. How would he have handled a big man who could fight?

On another wall, a gold-framed matador in black and magenta velvet readied his espada for a torquing black bull. Quite moving, in its way, for kitsch.

Under one of the piles, a telephone rang. Luciano cursed and kicked at a pile of newsprint in a corner until the ringing stopped. Then he grabbed a foolscap sheet with figures written on it in neat rows and ran his index finger along a series of sums, mumbling under his breath and wincing. I assumed he was sorting out my schedule, but he could have just been calculating odds and wagers for upcoming races at Flamborough Downs.

"Bobby, here's the situation. Six nights a week. Two bucks more an hour. *Keep* your tips. Here's your name tag. I'll get jackets. Black or navy. I'm working on it. Be on your toes. Don't get crazy. We wanna run a nice club. If things get ugly, do what you gotta do. If someone gets hurt, call an ambulance. If someone gets *killed*, call the cops. I've talked to someone at the cop shop." Luciano smiled and rubbed his thumb and fingers together. "They want to help. It's in their *interest*. Any questions?"

"No." I was going to ask why "the Press Club," but didn't bother. I assumed the building had served the press in a former incarnation, and that was enough to continue with my life.

"And one more *thing*," said Luciano, twitching his shoulder. "No drinking on the floor or I'll can you. Remember last summer? You and Buzzsaw? *None* of that."

"I wasn't drunk that time."

"Yeah, sure."

Booze played no role on the occasion in question; I had smoked debilitating elephant weed with Derek Burke, or Buzzsaw as we called him. Luciano disapproved of all recreational drugs except cocaine, which he claimed gave him mental clarity. I pinned the name tag to my lapel and entered the club, greeted by thunderous speakers:

> Gotta make a move to a
> Town that's right for me ...

I did a walk-around the club, crowded even at that early hour. Girls with massive hair and oily young men in polyester shirts occupied booths by the dance floor, chatting and grinning like beer-ad actors, except their teeth weren't as white. Bursts of coarse hilarity punctuated the convivial, almost festive atmosphere like a sitcom laugh track.

Two girls in tiger stripes and spiked heels shimmied to the illumined dance floor, gyrating their hips but unsure of what to do with their arms—one held them stiffly at her sides, the other bent them into a W with her head—but this didn't deter them. They looked joyful, ecstatic.

> Won't you take me to
> Funkytown
> Won't you take me to
> Funkytown

One of the dancers glanced at me and nudged her partner, who whipped her head around and smiled. Did I know these girls? Maybe from Banisters. I gave them the peace sign.

Unlike Banisters, a discotheque proper, dominated by a disco-lit dance floor, this place had a more intimate ambience, a blend of chi-chi hotel lounge and high-end strip joint, the lighting mellow and dusky, with a Plato's Retreat of shadowy nooks and blackened corners for quiet tête-à-têtes or more passionate encounters. Lush potted plants hung from the ceiling and rubber trees stood in corners; chocolate brown and sugar plum sofas padded the club's perimeter; and in a recess behind the dance floor, black-fabric studio couches surrounded smoked-glass tables.

Tall oak stools salvaged from Banisters lined the cool, brassy bar. The bartenders also came from Banisters: Fat Freddy in tight black slacks and paisley vest, and Carol Fox, as dazzling and remote as Saturn, her perfect breasts and buttocks as unreachable. Even the mildly subversive busboys, Ali and Diego, regarding me with amused expressions, were refugees from Banisters.

Then a surprise. By the service bar, grasping a blood-red glass of tomato juice, stood Demarco. Gaping, lats flexed, sweat beading his forehead, he looked utterly displaced. His black blazer hugged his shoulders and fell short on the forearms; that, and the gold-embossed cowboy boots on his feet, gave him rustic airs unchallenged by the look on his face, or the lack of one.

What the hell was he doing? Then I spotted the name tag on his lapel. I smiled and joined him by the service bar.

"Bobby," he said glumly. "You're here."

"You'll get acidic, man."

"What? Oh, this?" He held up the tomato juice. "I mixed in desiccated liver powder. Hear it's great for vascularity."

"What did you do, bring it with you?"

He reached inside his blazer, pulled out a baggy of reddish-brown powder, and shook it under my nose. "I always come prepared, Bobby."

A waft of dusty rot hit my nostrils. "Yeah, to sicken me. But I'm happy you're here."

Demarco feigned slowness. "What? Oh. I forgot to account for the tips."

"Thought so. Cheap bastard like you. Imagining sawbucks padding your high-waists. Speaking of which, I urge you to invest in a bigger jacket. That garment you're wearing, I don't know. The ventriloquist who gave it up at the Amity wants it back. His dummy misses it."

"You're a funny guy, Bobby," he said, expressionless. "See me busting a gut? See the abdominal wall? Forget football. You'd make a beautiful dollar doing stand-up."

"Anyway, good to see you, Mr. Kadiddlehopper. Would have been a long summer without you, must admit."

"It'll still be a long summer. But it'll be a hot one. Check it out."

He nodded at a towering waitress with pneumatic breasts. Her large blue eyes flinched as patrons barked orders at her; she was terribly new at this, and terribly attractive. The Press Club waitresses wore maroon satin dresses with matching floppy hats that Luciano must have unearthed at a discount bridesmaids shop. But if anything, on this girl, with her doll face, her long neck, and swelling curves, the costume enhanced her toothsomeness, or her toothsomeness enhanced the costume; in any case, one smiled.

"Wow," I said, impressed.

"That's Caesar's kid sister, Felicia."

"Yikes. Good country living, I'm telling you. So blond Jethro's back in the fold, eh?"

Demarco sighed. Caesar Booth, one of the Banisters crew, a lanky boxer from rural Cayuga with a weak left jab and a big mouth, started more scraps than he broke up. I'd heard about his knockout kid sister, but never anticipated this. How could it be? Adoption? A switch at birth? Different fathers, different mothers? Perhaps a torrid quickie with a handsome vagabond, kept secret all these years? The mind could travel far in these matters.

We admired her lines and patent fecundity in breathy silence, until she grew self-conscious and turned to us with a petulant expression. We pretended to be deep in conversation, oblivious to her curves and her unspoken complaint, and with a puzzled look she pushed on.

"Are you a breast man, Demarco?"

He shrugged. "Not as much as you are. They can be a nuisance."

"No, hemorrhoids can be a nuisance."

He nodded. "Our friend Lenny Hutton and his mullet have emerged."

"Thought he was in jail." He'd been charged for torching a variety store in the east end.

"Nah, he got out on a technicality."

Lenny and a bleached blonde in a green mesh dress sat side by side in one of the booths, he drinking a Blue, she a pink cocktail. He lit a match. His shiny blue shirt flashed as he waved the flaming match. The girl laughed. Waddy and Billy Wilson of the Parkdale gang were Lenny's cousins. As he lit another match, his shoulders jerked and his head lolled drolly. Fire tickled him. The girl tongued her drink and giggled. Fire was funny.

"Hope he doesn't get any ideas," Demarco said.

"He always gets ideas," I said. "But you can't knock his joyful approach to life."

Coloured lights swirled over the dance floor. Blondie's "Call Me" started up and several couples lunged from the booths and the aisles to dance, loose-limbed and bug-eyed. Lenny laughed at something the blonde said and slapped the table so sharply the girl's drink spilled half its sticky pink contents. The girl squealed with great animation, shaking her fists by her head like a chuffed toddler. I caught Lenny's steady, leering eye. He winked at the girl, slid out of the booth, and came over to me, pulling up his longhorn belt buckle and shaking his mullet.

"Listen, buddy," he said, in familiar tones. "If Waddy comes asking for me at the door, tell him you never saw me tonight."

"I'll make a mental note of that."

Lenny stared at me to see if I was being straight. I gave him nothing.

"Well, okay," he said. "Thanks. Already talked to Fernandez. How's it going? Haven't seen you around."

"Been away."

Lenny laughed, one of his front teeth dead. "Yeah, buddy. Me too."

He returned to his booth and said words to the girl that made her bend over and shudder with hilarity. He looked very pleased with himself. I told Demarco I was taking a walk-around, and he half-shrugged in his strained jacket, sipping the livered-up tomato juice with a scowl.

The place was filling up fast and I recognized some faces, regulars from Banisters, a few north-enders, football acquaintances. Ran into Nick Pugliese from my peewee days who had quarterbacked our scrappy Stradwick's Argos to a city championship but had porked up since then. He had no nose, only nostrils. His smile stitched shut his close-set eyes.

"Bobby Sferazza—the human projectile. Look at you! Frightening! How are you, my friend? I hear you're doing good things in the colleges."

"Doing okay, man."

"You were always modest, Bobby. Ha ha. Modest. You look the part, though. You look the part. Let me buy you a drink."

"Love to, Nick, but I'm on the clock. Some other time."

Near the service area, Caesar's sister bumped into me and recoiled, knocking into another waitress, the wolfish Paula Marshall, and dumping her tray.

"Sorry," Felicia said in a high-pitched voice. "I'm such a klutz tonight."

Paula lowered her head and stared at Felicia with the tops of her eyes.

"I said I'm sorry."

Grasping Felicia's warm, smooth arm, I pulled her away from Paula, averting carnage. I spotted Ali and informed him of the spilled tray, only to have him mouth the words *fuck off* to me as he skulked off for his broom, the little prick.

Felicia's heaving chest relaxed.

"You're Caesar's sister," I said.

"Yeah," she said, raising her right hand, "guilty as charged.

Hope it's not a bad thing. Thanks for, you know. Thanks. It's my first night, technically. I trained on the floor for a week, but I've never waitressed. And this getup. I feel so foolish."

"You shouldn't. You look fine. I'm Bobby Sferazza. Worked with your brother at Banisters last summer. Weren't you living in Cayuga?"

"Yeah, up on the farm with Mum and Poppa. They sold the farm and bought a bungalow, so I moved to the city. Caesar helped me get the job. Luciano is a very nice man."

A patron in a brown-sugar seersucker suit plopped a toady hand on Felicia's arm. "Hey, babe, get me a screwdriver. Easy on the ice. Two straws." He trained his batrachian eyes on me and licked his lips. "Do I know you?"

"I dunno, do you?"

He pulled back his head. "I *don't* fucking know you."

"Take it easy, pal."

"I'm not your pal."

I leaned close to him. "So get out of my face."

He didn't understand.

I leaned closer. "Get out of my face before I *kill* you."

He opened his mouth but said nothing, a recess. Then, he understood. He stuffed his hands into his jacket pockets and slithered off, glancing over his shoulder once. Felicia smiled uncertainly and moved on.

I joined Demarco by the dance floor, still working on the tomato juice, swinging his head left and right like a dog to the disco beat.

> *People ask me why*
> *I never find a place to stop*
> *And settle down, down, down*

"Think I'm in love," I said.

"I don't play that way," Demarco said. "Gay bar's around the corner from here." Then he cupped his mouth with his hand, leaned to me, and said sotto voce: "Eugene's in the back with Terry Peters."

"What, planning the revolution?"

"What revolution?"

I smiled at Demarco. "Maybe we should get this thing over with right now."

"What thing?"

"This thing that will be a thing, eventually."

"Be objective," Demarco said, wiping a rill of sweat from his cheek. "Let's just keep an eye on them. They're here to have fun tonight. They left the dogs at home."

On the dance floor girls with bare legs and bare shoulders and guys in flashy synthetics shook their hips and spun in the shifting light. Mimmo the deejay did his thing, unleashing an unbroken string of rhythmic beats that kept the dancers edging toward the sublime. A jumpy tune from Kiss—*I was made for loving you, baby*—quickened the pulse of the place. A bronzed zaftig couple squeezed onto the the dance floor, their violent tarantella clearing space as other dancers vied for centre stage, twisters, trotters, acrobats, epileptics. Plastic heels glowed from the floor lights; shiny fabrics swished; musks mingled.

Carol Fox and Fat Freddy poured and shook behind the bar, in mid-season form, Carol's white sharp smile slashing through steam and jungle breath like a machete. Freddy called Diego for a forehead mop as he hopped to the orders of waitresses floating to and from the bar, and without disrupting Freddy's rhythm, Diego sponged him dry with a nurse's touch.

Buzzsaw whistled me over from his post in the back under the EXIT sign, where his ginger hair blazed like a holy fire but his intentions were ignited by Lucifer.

"I've got yellow jackets!" he cried.

"What, no how you been? What's new? What's happening?"

"What's happening? I'm racing like Secretariat right now, buddy. I'm flying."

"Good to hear that. Sign me up for two."

"What about Demarco?"

"Imagine him on yellow jackets."

Buzzsaw sucked his rabbit teeth.

"Do you hear that?" I said. A coach's whistle chirped to the music. He shook his head. "Did I hear what?"

"That whistle. Where's it coming from?"

"I don't hear a whistle, man. What I hear are bells, jingling bells."

Fucking Buzzsaw. I scanned the club for the perpetrator, but Felicia, floating in the aisles like a carnal apparition, distracted me. I followed her, followed her swelling curves, but when she turned around as I drew near, I veered off in another direction.

A Donna Summer number from last season excited nostalgia in the club; the unknown whistle-blower pumped it up a notch in response. Lenny Hutton and his girl in green embraced on the dance floor and gyrated. When the tempo of the song picked up, the whistle kept pace, but Lenny and the girl stayed close, gyrating.

Bumped into Roy Rosati, a north-end friend, decked out in a species of orange jumpsuit and cork-heeled shoes, who'd lost so much weight over the winter at first I didn't recognize him. Then he made the bullshit sign.

"This is what I think," he declared.

"Be objective, Roy."

Roy's face appeared smaller than I remembered it, the bottom missing. Eyes the same bitter brown but lonelier, more deeply set. One hundred pounds of him had vanished since last summer; he'd lost the weight mainly to meet females. I asked him how the mission was going.

"Bobby, I ran seven miles every morning for seven months and lived on a diet of a thousand calories a day. Do you know what a thousand calories a day is? It's malnutrition, that's what it is. Fucking Bangladeshis eat more, I swear."

"But you look good, Roy."

He leaned close. "Bobby. I'm missing half my face."

"You're being hard on yourself."

"You're patronizing me."

"Stop it, Roy." I looked around. "Have you seen Demarco?"

He bared his small beige teeth and told me he'd seen him in the can posing down with Jimmy Lewis, a thug with Parkdale and Clubber ties. "They had their shirts off."

"They what? Bizarre."

"I know. But Demarco is bizarre."

Roy shuffled off, and soon after I located the annoying whistle-blower behind a pillar—local councilman Mario Augusto, wearing a pink sweater tied around his neck and straw shoes with clear plastic heels on his feet—and confiscated the whistle with a stern warning.

"But I want to party!" he protested.

"The whistle dates you, Councilman."

And with that, the matter was settled. I liked to think of myself more as a mediator or an arbitrator than a hired thug. I positioned myself by the dance floor, tracking Felicia. Now and then I'd catch her sneaking glances my way. Other events became a fuzzy backdrop. I had to watch that. Buzzsaw appeared and handed me two shining yellow jackets, which I took with ginger ale. I'd acquired a taste for amphetamines at Banisters. They supercharged me.

The club heated up. Bodies on the dance floor moved in furious rhythm, clinging, merging, dividing, and in the aisles passing revellers made a point of rubbing against one another, a shoulder, a breast, a thigh. Some coupled off and danced in the aisles or writhed as one toward the pulsing shadows of the club.

As strobe lights flickered on, fragmenting the movement into grainy, almost violent still shots, Demarco pulled up sweating and panting.

"Jimmy Lewis is insane," he laughed.

"Heard you two posed off in the can. Sounds perfectly sane to me."

"Jimmy wants to compete in the Ontarios this autumn. He's been working out and juicing like a fiend. He thought he'd dwarf me, but I look okay beside him, I really do."

"And that makes you happy?"

"He gets testosterone shots every week, plus he's on Winstrol.

I hear that's how Waddy won Mr. Ontario. Too much water retention with Dianabol. But if you ask me, Jimmy still looks bloated. He has no cuts, no veins. Needs to up the reps or get on diuretics. Good size, though. Big quads and arms. Whoa. Felicia over there has big tits, except one is bigger than the other."

"Shut up."

Caesar loomed behind us, nodding and grinning like a hog judge at a county fair. He looked nothing like his sister, rougher-hewn, almost ugly with his gaping nostrils, thick brow and jutting jaw. His short blond hair stood on end like the brush of a corn broom and his wide blue eyes jiggled: yellow-jacket markers. He whooped, and slapped me on the back. I told him to take it easy. He went to slap my back again but I stepped on his toe in accidental fashion, and he went hobbling off, rubbing his hair and flinching.

"Where are you going?" Demarco asked.

"Anywhere," I said, bolting through the crowd in a yellow-jacket surge.

Tingles coursed through my limbs as I circled the dance floor; my jaw clenched and unclenched. I twitched and sighed, pushing one foot, then the other, using my elbows for leverage. I almost collided with Paula the Wolf and she showed me her fangs but then started laughing. Fuck her. I kept moving, moving, out of my head, hoping that a brawl would break out, or a drunk need tossing. Or that Terry Peters would pass me and open his yap.

Then Vic Zuccheroni, a faded tough who used to break my balls at Banisters, swerved by with his red-rimmed eyes and stomped expression. One defect of life is that faces often reflect every punch they've ever taken, every kick.

"Hey tough guy," he barked. "I wanna talk to you."

Hmm, talk, talk. Why give this has-been wannabe wise guy two seconds of my time? For an entire summer he did nothing but antagonize and bore me to death. Did I want a reprise? He had on a ruffled yellow shirt, black slacks, tasselled black shoes. Rings adorned his gnarled fingers, the knuckles so callused and prominent they looked like some macabre fashion of glove. After one too many beatings, he appeared twenty years older than his thirtysomething age, but had retained his willingness to scrap, and could go off at any time.

"Tell those two bozos at the front—big black dude, and that Spanish fuck—"

"Jerome and Fernandez, who's Portuguese."

"Whatever—tell those pricks to let in my cousin Roger or there's gonna be trouble. Roger's visiting from Sicily."

"Roger the Sicilian?"

"Ruggerio, okay?"

"Thanks for the heads-up. I'll get to that immediately."

He moved off, pitching hateful looks and cursing hot under his breath. I stared him off; my program lacked tolerance that evening. His small, black zeppelin of antipathy was just that, small. Anyway, I was due at the doors so I walked down and joined Fernandez and Jerome. A sizable lineup had formed outside; as soon as the door closed, someone hammered on it.

"What's going on, boys?"

"You're early," Fernandez said.

I checked my Omega. "No, man. It's time—it's getting hot and heavy in there, and loud. I need a break. Making any money?"

A smiling Jerome limped off with Fernandez, hands in pockets, on his heels.

We were supposed to divide the tips at the end of the night but this never happened. Every man for himself when it came to that, and no one had the balls to complain about it.

I opened the door and the noise of the shouting crowd rushed at me with a furious density that knocked me backwards. As people plunged forward I held out my arms as though fending off charging linemen, but it took threats of dismemberment to repel them. I could taste the crowd's anger and impatience, a bitter soup, but I felt zero empathy for them.

"Why do we have to wait?"

"Because you chose to."

Across the street New York, New York was in full swing. Heavy limousines pulled up to its green-canopied entrance, depositing overdressed roisterers and hedonists, many from out of town. New York, New York wasn't popular with locals, too vast, the music too loud.

A girl in the crowd yelled my name but I failed to locate her. I squinted and saw nothing but floating lozenges of soft colours. A red silk kerchief fluttered: a communist. No freebies here, my friend. Then someone tucked a twenty in my jacket pocket and I let them through to a roar of complaint. I shut the door. No sooner shut than bang bang bang, some bastard back at it. I whipped open the door, hoping to smash an encroaching nose, but the way was clear and the crowd glared at me like a chain gang. Then, as I went to shut the door again, a man in a small-collared pink shirt, black leather belt, tan chinos, and sandals matching the belt, came forward.

"Roger?" I said.

He thought before responding, "*Si.*"

I gestured for him to follow me. He did so timidly, peeking his head around, as some in the crowd bemoaned the blatant unfairness. But is the universe, I wanted to ask them, fair?

When Roger hesitated, I squeezed his shoulder and said, "*Veni.*" I shut the door behind me and informed him in Italian that his cousin Vic awaited inside. That I spoke Italian surprised him. I'd never studied it formally, and asked that he forgive my butchering of the language. He pressed my hand and said that, on the contrary, he detected a charming Sicilian cadence. I told him my folks came from Serradifalco, near Caltanisetta. He said he hailed from Palermo. I wondered how well he knew his cousin Vic; Roger had the demeanour and gentleness of a monk. Then again, he was from Palermo, and looks can be deceiving.

Vic appeared with liqueur shots. Roger took one and Vic thrust another at me, but I refused.

"I'm working, man."

"Lemme talk to your boss about that. Where is that fat fuck anyway?"

"Haven't seen Luciano all night."

"Well, when you see him, tell him I'm looking for him."

The cousins clinked glasses and Vic threw his down with a gasp; Roger dribbled liqueur on his chin. Then Vic put his arm around his shoulder and led him into the club, turning and winking like an imbecile.

My scalp squirmed; tingles raced up and down my spine. I felt like screaming. It took a force of will to hold back. It would have looked bad. I would have been a laughingstock.

Demarco finally came to the front. I asked him if Eugene and Peters were still infecting the club. He said two strippers from Hanrahan's were dancing for them, putting on quite a show. He handed me a stick of Juicy Fruit and I chewed the shit out of it.

People kept banging on the door, pleading, begging entry, but unless a sawbuck or a double came our way we kept it strictly one out one in, and no one was leaving at that moment.

Then Albert and Lloyd, the disco cops, arrived, both freshly barbered and bereft of sideburns. Lloyd, blessed with luminous, slow green eyes, was unwise to expose such flagrant, cartilaginous ears. They made him look unserious. Swarthy Albert had tiny round ears with tapered lobes, the right one pierced, for a tiny diamond he wore. But more than anything, Albert's jaw defined him, masculine, magnetic. And his winged black eyebrows. And his rich black hair and small white perfect teeth.

"Bobby, what's new? Any babes? Yes? No? That new waitress Felicia, hmm. I'd like to corn-hole that, eh. She working, yes? I was here when Luciano hired her. Gave my personal thumbs-up. Told Luciano she'd be good for business. Am I a nice guy or what?"

I didn't answer.

Moistening his lips, Albert fixed his gaze on the foyer. He flared his nostrils as if checking for estrus. His earring twinkled. His uniform shirt, open at the collar, revealed a shark-tooth necklace and a black froth of chest curls, perfumed with heady musk oil. More modest than his comrade, Lloyd stood there staring into space with his hooded green eyes, nostrils and upper lip combatting a yawn.

Albert began to mount the steps, when his walkie-talkie issued a call for backup at the Capri restaurant, not far from the club.

"Lloyd," he said, "did you get that?"

Lloyd's walkie-talkie and his mind must have been switched off, but he managed a nod.

"We'll be back," Albert said.

"I'll be waiting," I promised.

I told Demarco I needed to go splash some water on my face and he warned me to be quick, he wasn't feeling so hot, indeed he looked as turned as Frankenstein.

On the way to the washroom I ran into Felicia.

"Well?" she said. "Are you going to talk to me?"

"You're a busy lady."

"You can do better than that." She fluttered her eyelashes.

I fluttered mine. "You'd be surprised."

With that bridge crossed, I dashed off to the washroom and tried to pee without success; yellow jackets paralyzed the waterworks. I stood there for five long minutes holding my dick like a small dead salamander, and though I felt the urge, the tickle to pee, the pee refused egress, and I tucked the lifeless newt away and zipped up in frustration. Then I washed my face at the sink and wet my hair until it dripped. This felt remarkable. As I dried my face with a paper towel, Terry Peters entered the washroom, wearing a weak lavender suit and several kilos of gold jewellery. His joviality dissolved when he saw me, but he cast his eyes to the floor and disappeared into a stall before I could say anything. I crumpled the paper towel in my fist, and exited with my chest heaving and muscles firing.

Luciano stopped me near the service bar and asked how things were going. Containing my facial tics, I told him that thus far the evening had been devoid of incident and he smiled almost sadly, as if he knew this might not be true by its end.

"Anyway," he said, "I talked to Eugene, and everything is cool. He *told* his boys not to go bananas in here. I *told* Eugene that if they need to vent, New York, New York is perfect, fuck Octavio, fuck Montreal, fuck New York, New *York*."

"That's reassuring," I lied. I'd never had many direct dealings with Eugene, a remote and uncanny figure who rarely spoke and never drew attention to himself, though the actions of his henchmen made his nature transparent.

"So are *you* cool?"

"I'm cool, Luciano." What will be will be, I wanted to say, but I held back. I didn't need to stir up his personal hornet's nest.

When I got to the front door, Demarco looked quite ill, green-tinged and grey-tongued, sweat pouring off his face. He excused himself and trucked off to the washroom. Roy Rosati appeared, puffing a torpedo stogie.

"Already with that thing," I said. "Smoke it outside."

"Whoa there, big guy. It cost me a fin."

"Four seventy-five too much, believe me."

Roy frowned. "Thought you were a man of superior tastes, Bobby. I'm disappointed you find a Robusto as fine as this one repugnant."

"Put it out right now or I'll stick it up your ass."

"You should be more direct, Bobby. Wishy-washiness is a serious character flaw. I've read it in a self-help book. Trust me on this," he said, pushing open the door and stepping outside.

"Ring My Bell" tinkled in the background and I shut my eyes and listened to the words. *The night is young and full of possibilities...* How did the singer know that for certain? Was she psychic? Where was Demarco? His absence worried me. I opened my mouth and let out a roar. Only Diego, sweeping up broken glass from the top of the foyer steps, heard me, and he burst into laughter, hurrying off with his broom and dustpan before I could threaten him.

Lenny Hutton appeared at the top of the stairs. "Has my cousin Waddy come by?"

"No," I said, laughing.

"What's so funny?"

"Do you really want to know?"

He shook his mullet and turned around.

People came and went, faceless, but full of loathing, I could feel it in my nerves. I stopped clicking the counter, lost track of who was in and who was out. What did it matter, in the end? They were just numbers. My pockets bulged with tens and twenties, more numbers. Beefs broke out in the lineup, hissing, spitting, punching. No dodging ugliness. The yellow jackets held me in their electric clutches and I spun on the spot, spouting nonsense, racing. People stared at me, uttering strange things or words that angered me. A woman resembling Evelyn Dick screamed that I was impudent. I complimented her use of the word but still refused her entry. I laughed and laughed but feared I might burst into tears. I struggled to maintain control. A losing battle. People took notice. "What's up with him?" "He's fucked." "He's nuts." That kind of thing. I took it all in stride, with jangling detachment. They were small, these people, Lilliputian.

Finally at midnight, Buzzsaw relieved me.

"How you feeling?" he asked.

"Like I want to run through a wall, but other than that, fantastic."

Buzzsaw bared his choppers and moved his hips to the music.

"Where's Demarco?"

"Saw him in the can."

Gripped by a clammy paranoia, I inched my way around the club, avoiding all contact. Everything tightened up. Everyone looked ugly, vicious. Drawing breaths hurt; my sides ached. I wanted to laugh. I wanted to cry. Someone tapped my shoulder. I violently shrugged and kept moving. Don't fucking touch me! I wanted to tear off my suit and sprint to the lake screaming at the top of my lungs. I wanted to curl up in a corner and shut my eyes.

A raspy-voiced patron with the face of a defecating infant stepped up and asked me a question. I started laughing. I couldn't stop. My laughter reverberated as though it came from someone else, in another part of the club. Its meanness surprised me. The straining patron turned around, crushed, perhaps repulsed, and merged with the herd.

I felt I had to pee or else. Near the washrooms, I passed Vic Zuccheroni and his cousin, double-teaming an older woman who looked like a younger Bette Davis. I left Vic translating Roger's blandishments and entered the men's room warily, avoiding my reflection in the mirror. Under a stall door the soles of Demarco's cowboy boots faced out. I heard him gurgling:

"Ne... never... again!"

"I warned you!" I shouted.

"Blow me!"

When he finished retching, he staggered out of the stall, ashen and shaken, washed his hands and face at the sink, and rinsed his mouth several times. Then he stroked water through his hair and straightened his jacket. No matter, he still looked deranged. He'd have to go with it. I ran water through my hair, checked my profile; I looked no better, perhaps, but no vomit chunks spiced my windpipe. My only real issue was the retentive amphibian in my shorts.

"You're like Jack Palance," Demarco observed. "Ugly but not unattractive."

"Thanks. And I see you've learned your lesson."

"What are you talking about?"

"Des-ic-cat-ed liver powder."

Demarco rubbed his forehead. "Please... don't... I'll start ralfing again."

"Moron."

When we came out of the washroom "Funkytown" struck up again and the dance floor shuddered and shook. Roy Rosati stood by an ashtray stubbing out his stogie. He shrugged as if to say, Don't persecute me. I'm just doing my thing.

Well, I talk about it
Talk about it
Talk about it
Talk about it

I wanted to break his balls anyway because I could, but the tune caught me in its groove.

Talk about, Talk about
Talk about movin

Then I heard a glass crash on the dance floor, followed by shouts and grunts and scuffling. Demarco stiffened. Here we go, I thought.

A commotion of arms and hair erupted, people scattering left and right. Females screamed. I wondered if Peters stood in the middle of the disturbance, or Lenny Hutton, or any of a dozen firecrackers who'd been waiting to go off. I took a deep breath, bent my knees, and clenched my fists in readiness. But as I moved for the dance floor, it grew clear that neither Peters nor Hutton nor any other gangsters or thugs or random amped-up males were knocking heads. I relaxed.

"Two girls are fighting," Demarco said, cupping his mouth sideways.

"Nothing escapes you."

They fought with passion, they fought with malice, cursing and flailing and ripping for all they were worth. Wildcats scrapped with less shredding abandon. Hair and spit flew. Their savagery took my breath away. No one made a move to break it up, no one even thought of it.

The ladies ran out of steam in time, and Jerome and Fernandez delicately moved in. I still hadn't peed, and this concerned me but not enough to try again.

"I always feel like a cigarette after one of those," Demarco said.

"Why aren't you jumping in there?"

"Jerome and Fernandez can handle this."

I glanced at my Omega. "It's midnight, I'm going to the front doors."

Less than a minute after I joined Buzzsaw at the front doors, Lenny Hutton descended the foyer stairs bobbing like a supermarionette to the music, shirt ringed with sweat stains, mullet plastered to his head. His blue eyes burned as he enthused about the cat fight, the first of the season; then he asked me if his cousin Waddy had come by. I let a good five seconds pass before I told him that no, his fucking cousin Waddy had not come by.

FOUR

A black and white cat tapped my toes. My feet dangled off the end of the small lumpy bed. The flat was all angles and slants with criss-crossing shadows, creaking, uncertainty. Someone softly snored under the blanket. I blinked my eyes and tried to piece together the reality at hand. A Telechron Bakelite on the dresser said four o'clock. Not afternoon. It was dark out. I untangled the sheets at my midriff and noticed a rose-shaped splotch of blood. Odd. It took another moment to bring myself up to speed.

The cat backed off when I sat up in the bed. A pale hand emerged from under the blanket, stroked my arm.

"I'm going home," I said.

"Wish you'd stay," said a voice under the blanket. Felicia.

"Need some sleep. Don't think I can here."

She pulled down the blanket, eyes shut. Caesar Booth was her brother. They were from Cayuga. Her left breast was smaller than her right. "We don't need to sleep."

"If I don't sleep, forget working out."

"Take a day off."

Tempting, to a point. Her apartment, the converted attic of a Victorian home near my place of birth, St. Joseph's Hospital, engendered claustrophobia. The bedroom barely held the small bed, the dresser, and a nightstand. On one wall hung a framed rustic scene in enamels: yellow sun with Van Gogh vertigo, porky white cows, menstrual red barn, British racing green hills. On another wall: a blow-up of child Felicia wide-eyed, hands on head. A ratty Teddy bear rested on a rocking chair by the window. Eyeless dolls in velvet and organza occupied shelves in the corner; a bride doll on a higher shelf possessing eyes regarded me. A miniature crystal train encircled the frosted tube lamp on the night table. I wanted to reach out and touch the tiny caboose.

It had been a successful first night at the Press Club. The patrons partied their hearts out and drank themselves into various degrees of delirium without rioting. No real trouble, except for the cat fight, which delighted most bystanders. And, by some fantastic fluke, I wound up bedding the most voluptuous woman in Hamilton, but felt uneasy about it. Working together would inevitably prove problematic, one way or the other. It would be all wine and roses and prickly lust in its first throes. But in time she could turn needy, clingy, batty, stifle my action. Or it could go the other way and I could become the jealous, odious sniveller and ruin my summer keeping tabs on her or raging when others ogled her, and how could they not?

Another photograph on the wall: Felicia and Caesar on the farm in Cayuga, rigid Mum Booth behind them in gingham dress and wire-rimmed glasses. The cat started up again. I turned to my side, cupped Felicia's breasts. The left felt slightly smaller than the other, but they were both big and firm and beautiful.

We climbed out of bed around noon. My waterworks issues had been resolved, needless to say, as the bennies wore off and lust whispered the little newt back to life. Ah, relief. Felicia made coffee in a Bodum. I tormented the cat with a furry spring toy until it grew bored and left the room. We drank the coffee—hot, sweet, and gritty, like the atmosphere in there—on the bed. A Harley-Davidson growled by, trembling my mug, angry, angrier, as it picked up speed.

"Coffee's nice. Strong."

"Mum buys it at Denningers downtown when she comes into the city. They sold the farm but still live in the boondocks. It's German coffee. She's German. My father's English, from Blackpool. He was in the merchant marines. I went to Blackpool once as a child with my family. We stayed by the seaside. People vacation there, but it's not very pretty, and not very warm, but we sat under these striped umbrellas anyway and sucked on salt toffee and watched shivering vacationers in old-fashioned bathing costumes testing the water. Poppa wore this silly cricket cap the whole time we were there. "

"How old are you, Felicia?"

"I turned nineteen two weeks ago, on May 14. I'm a Taurus. My ruling planet is Venus. My stone is emerald. My symbol is— you guessed it!—the bull. It's so true, I can be totally bullheaded, ask my brother. He's a Libra, bad news—well, not always, just in terms of being successful. I don't see him being successful. Do you know your sign?"

"I'm a Leo."

"That makes so much sense, you're so strong, and you're a leader."

"How do you know I'm a leader? I followed *you* here."

She smiled. "That's different. I have what's known as determined energy."

"Determined energy. What does that mean exactly?"

"I think you can figure it out."

She was very pretty, even without any makeup, even with sleep in her eyes, even with the smell of sex and stale cat hanging strongly in the air.

"I hope you don't think... I mean, bringing you here last night."

"You're a pretty girl, Felicia. A sexy girl."

The moment these words left my mouth I felt stupid, but her smile heartened me.

The cat returned with a vengeance, piercing my soles. I shook my legs. Felicia found this amusing. The cat flew onto the bed. I froze. Felicia convulsed with laughter, toothy, gummy, lurid, and unattractive for the first time since I'd met her. That was odd, the possibility of beauty turning on a dime like that into something almost repulsive. Then it dawned on me with a slight shudder how much she looked like her brother Caesar when she laughed like that. I footed the frisky cat off the bed and it leaped onto a stack of hat boxes. The stack collapsed and the cat landed poorly, scrambling to the kitchen, embarrassed.

Felicia stopped laughing. "Satan is a spiteful cat."

"Aptly named, then."

"Caesar, it's his cat. He asked me to take care of it because he's never around. He goes to the boxing gym every single day. I told him he isn't cut out to be a fighter. He has a glass jaw. But he's stubborn as a mule. I don't really like Satan. Not the most affectionate pussy."

I stared at her to see if she was being smart, but she kept a straight face. She looked very pretty again, but I made a note to myself that when laughing uproariously she became her brother. I dressed and readied to leave.

"Call me later?" Felicia said with a pout.

"I'll see you at work tonight, no?"

Judging from her shrug, my answer disappointed her, but at least it didn't make her laugh.

As I exited her place I felt like a porno actor after a long session in the studio. My instrument needed replenishing. At home, I found my mother in the kitchen grinding espresso beans, expressionless. She also knew her part. She churned the iron crank of the wooden mill, then emptied its little drawer into a red metal canister.

"Where have you been?" she asked without looking at me.

"It's okay, Ma. I worked late and then we—"

"First your brother, now you? I can't have this, Bobby. I didn't sleep at all. You were out, your brother was out, and I was alone in this house."

"I work late, Ma. Remember?"

"Were you with a girl?" She glanced at me. "You were with a girl. I know, I know."

She wasn't really angry; more like relieved I'd come home in one piece. I smelled cooking, snooped around and saw on the stove a pot of tomato sauce bubbling away and golden potato croquets sizzling in a pan.

"You want gnocchi today?"

"If it's no trouble, Ma. That sauce would make shoelaces good."

"Let me get you an espresso."

My brother came down to eat in sweaty, hospital-green pyjamas, didn't say a word and wouldn't look me in the face. A cut on his left earlobe oozed fluid; his knuckles were skinned. Blood stained the collar of his pyjama top. He smelled ripe, almost sweet.

"What are you looking at?" he snapped.

"Not much," I said. I didn't look away.

"You're a prick, Bobby. You know that. You talk about everyone else, but you're the biggest prick out there."

"Never mind and eat," my mother said.

"He thinks he can come here and act like my father. Well, he's not my father."

Bowing her head, my mother put down her fork. I wanted to slap Joey. I wanted to wind up and give him one across the chops, open-handed, resounding, like one my father would have summoned in a flash of fury. Before I could do or say anything, my brother pushed away his plate and went back up to his room without a word.

My mother sobbed into a handkerchief as I finished the gnocchi. She hadn't dyed her auburn hair in some time and grey roots were showing. A pang of sadness for her tightened my heart. Feeling foolish, I kept my mouth shut, put the dishes in the sink. She told me to leave them. I'd have to soften my approach with my brother, at least in front of her: she was hurting. Eventually, she made espresso, washed the dishes and, to my relief, brightened up.

Soon after, my cousin Vincenzo showed up with his folks, Aunt Rosa and Uncle Frank. I went out to greet them.

"Bobby, so sorry. I hit the Camaro parking my boat."

"I'll kill you."

"Yeah, everyone's dying at your hands."

Taller than me, with enormous hands and feet, Vincenzo would have made a good offensive tackle, had he played football, but he had never put on the pads. My aunt and uncle, on the other hand, already small people, could now be labelled *little*. Vincenzo kissed my cheeks and squeezed my shoulder until it ached.

Aunt Rosa, my mother's older sister, had brought her a clay pot with a basil plant. She slid a Virginia chocolate bar into my shirt pocket and pinched my arm, a ritual dating back to my chocolate-junky childhood. She sat on a lawn chair, slipped off her sandals, and propped up her swollen feet, while I unwrapped and ate the chocolate bar. Uncle Frank lit a cigarette and studied Eastwood Park with silent curiosity.

My mother emerged from inside, drying her hands on an apron and chirping welcomes. She smiled when she saw the basil plant, picking up the pot and cradling it. "Vincenzo, what do you say?"

"Zia Carmela, your son will get the beating of his life if he's not careful. He disrespected me yet again. He doesn't know the meaning of family, Zia. Toronto has made him superb."

"He has to be taught a lesson," my mother laughed.

"He has to be taught a lesson, Zia."

My mother led Vincenzo inside by the arm, whispering something that made him laugh and turn. Aunt Rosa slipped on her sandals and, urging Uncle Frank to snap it up, followed them in. I stayed with him while he smoked and studied the untended park grounds with slight shifts of his head. The snow fences were gone, the diseased trees truncated, but the park still lacked flowers and the grass looked like peat moss. The air smelled particularly septic that day.

"Look at that park, Roberto. Jesus. What kind of animals are these inspectors, these scientists from the city? What do they expect people to do? What if I wanna go for a walk? What if you wanna to go for a walk, Roberto? How you gonna walk in that sewage? What are they, uneducated? Lay new sod, clean up the trees, eh, why not a few freaking flowers? *Pilamadonna.* Where are the freaking flowers? What park in the world has no flowers? It's almost June, for Christ sake."

His thick-lensed glasses magnified his inquisitive brown eyes, and made him look, depending on your take of him, either like an imbecile or a genius. Brownish blotches covered his scalp. He trembled now, dragged his feet. This was a man who in his prime could, with his head alone, keep a soccer ball in the air indefinitely. Everything had once worked fine and looked fine but life had run him over like a gang of Brazilian dribblers and he wished someone would listen to him about it, but no one would.

"Did you see how Inter finished the season?" he asked.

"No, I haven't been following."

"Those chooches lost to Ascoli 4-2. Do you believe that? Ascoli! What a disgrace. It was probably fixed. All those games are fixed."

Uncle Frank was a big Inter *tifoso*, and a hardcore Toronto Maple Leafs fan, forever indebted to me for scoring him Leafs tickets a couple of times. One day I wanted to fly him to Milan to watch Inter at the San Siro.

After a few minutes Vincenzo joined us, chewing an apricot square and shaking his wide hips in a sort of hula dance.

"Will you stop," Uncle Frank said, annoyed with the movement. "He can be such a ball-breaker. Stop it, you idiot!"

Vincenzo grabbed my wrist and tried to hammerlock my arm, but I powered free and put him in a chokehold. Red-faced, white-tongued, spitting crumbs, he surrendered. Bigger and stronger for most of our lives, he'd always lovingly bullied me; it felt good to give him back some. Uncle Frank smiled mirthlessly. He disliked his son's size, probably thought less of mine. He took a last haul of the cigarette and tossed the glowing butt into the street.

"Now for espresso," he said, rubbing his hands and entering the house.

"Want more of this," I said to Vincenzo, flexing my arms.

He held up his hand. "It's okay, Bobby. I've had enough for one day. You're the champ. Whew. Have to get my ass in the gym. Feeling like a sack of shit these days. Where's Joey? Last time I came over your mother said he was in bed sick with the flu. Is he sick again?"

"Don't think he's sick. Spends a lot of time in his room these days, more than he should. He's going through a bit of a rough patch. Giving my mother grief. Not sure he's even going to school anymore. My mother says he's enrolled at Sir John A. Macdonald, but who knows. No one keeps tabs on him. And I hear he's been hanging with the Barton-Sherman gang."

Vincenzo frowned. "That's no good. What's he thinking? Those assholes crashed Elio Cino's wedding back in April and beat up the best man. Who the fuck does that kind of thing?"

"Beat the shit out of these two dudes at the Street Scene the other night for no reason. Sent them to hospital. One's in a coma."

"You working there this summer, at the Street Scene?"

"No. I'm at the Press Club, over on King William, across from New York, New York. Last night, my first on the job, was pretty quiet. Same crew from Banisters working the doors with me. You came last summer a few times, no?"

"Oh yeah, Banisters. Where I witnessed the riot. That was fun."

"You'll have to come by the Press Club. Busy place, lots of chicks, not as rowdy as Banisters. Eugene Ciccone—the Barton-Sherman boss—was there all night with that psycho puppet of his, Terry Peters. At the gym the other day Peters said Joey was a good head. Can you believe that? Anyway, they behaved last night. But I'm not worried about them."

"You should, uh, be cautious, you know, don't be puffing your chest out. It isn't football, Bobby. These guys are fucking nuts."

"Yeah, I hear you. But this Joey thing..."

Vincenzo smiled and looked me up and down. "But if you get a chance to nail one of those cocksuckers it would be for the better good. They've hurt people."

"They'll get what's coming to them eventually."

"Tell that idiot brother of yours to wise up or I'll kick his skinny ass."

I chuckled. "That'll scare him straight."

"Well, you don't seem to be up to the job."

That said it plainly enough. "Don't worry about it."

We went in. Uncle Frank held court in the kitchen with my mother and Aunt Rosa, reprising for them his well-known lecture on the seat of health, the liver.

"If you don't maintain good liver health, you will sicken and die. The liver? The liver? *Pilamadonna*, here in America everyone dies of infarctas. Why? It's simple. Because of the diet. Mediterraneans eat cheese and drink wine and do not die of infarctas at the same rate, not even close. Not even close. So yes, the heart, the heart is one thing. I know." He tapped his chest. "But the liver, *il fegato*, we pay almost no attention to it, *per che?* The ancient Greeks wrote about the liver. In Italy that's what the doctors worry about, *il fegato*, and for good reason. Remember Nicky Randazzo? He died of cirrhosis of the liver and he never touched a drop of liquor, not even at his son's wedding, and I can say this because I was there."

"Frank," my mother said with a smirk, "we've heard this all before. Drink your espresso before it gets cold."

"But they have learned nothing!" Uncle Frank said to me.

"He stones me," Aunt Rosa said, waving her hand under face with exasperation. "He talks and talks all day about *il fegato* like he's some kind of *dottore*. Nobody wants to hear you, Frank! You predicate! No one wants to listen to an old man predicating. It's a terrible thing."

We smiled at Aunt Rosa's performance. Even Uncle Frank's stern expression relaxed. He finished his espresso and backhanded his lips, eyes twinkling. Aunt Rosa thrust a napkin at him, which he took. He wasn't as impassioned about the liver as he let on. He just needed attention.

Joey never came down to say hello, even though my mother called him a few times. No point in creating a scene about it, but everyone looked concerned.

Later, I knocked on Joey's door. He didn't answer; I waited a moment, then as I was leaving he opened it.

"What is it?"

I told him I only wanted what was best for him.

"How do you know what's best for me?"

"I know what's not best for you."

"If you're talking about Barton-Sherman, enough. I'm not hanging with them anymore."

I tried not to smile; this was progress. "Apart from that, what's up with you and Ma? Things are tough enough for her. At least play the part at home. You going to school?"

He said he had been going on and off to Sir John A. Macdonald but was failing most of his classes and wanted to switch to my alma mater, Cathedral. I warned him they were tough there; the teachers and priests took no shit. He'd have to show up every day and make an effort. Keep his nose clean. Keep a low profile.

"Vinnie's worried about you, worried enough to kick your ass. You didn't even say hi to him today. He's worried, they're all worried. At least put out an effort. If you need something, anything, I'm here. Lay it on me. Whatever you're going through, it'll pass, you'll get through it. At least make it easier for Ma."

Joey listened, nodding, but I felt no warmth coming from him, no understanding. Whatever bug he had up his ass wouldn't be extracted with platitudes and a pep talk. But I left it that, at least it was a start, and he dove back into his shadows.

I went for a jog around Eastwood Park, but the choppy terrain proved impossible to negotiate without risking ankle injury. I returned home and performed calisthenics in my room. Then I ate a frittata with my mother for dinner—my brother had gone roller skating with Charlie Tesser, a neighbourhood kid—and drove to work.

Another quiet evening at the Press Club. A difference of opinion between two drunken endomorphs over a husky blonde in silver lamé ended in an armistice and peaceful expulsion, and the unfortunate outing of our first known transexual, a pretty soul called Sandy, whom we never saw again after that night. Paula almost came to blows with Diego the busboy over a remark he made about her breath, which he compared to rotting meat. A Junior Mint resolved those tensions without further issue, although when I ran into Paula by the service bar she made a coarse sound in her throat.

"You don't like me, do you?"

"I hear you're in university," she said through clenched teeth.

"That's right. Toronto."

"That explains the sharpness."

She left me hanging in an exhaust of minty putrefaction.

From the gangs, only the Wilson brothers, Waddy and Billy, made an appearance, content to peel off their shirts and showcase their muscle-plated torsos on the dance floor. Merry and inventive in their way, flexing and preening, they gave the evening oomph during a lull. But except for this bit of exhibitionism, they comported themselves civilly. At one point Waddy even complimented Demarco on his V-shape, and asked him where he worked out, what kind of back exercises he did, what kind of roids he was taking, and so on. Then he told him Winstrol worked wonders but you had to watch your liver counts. An avid Demarco ate up his words.

Caesar had words with Albert the disco cop about Felicia, his sister, who floated around the club with glowing cheeks and secret eyes, but too many customers, males and females for that matter, were in thrall to her for my comfort. At one point during their exchange I thought Albert was reaching for his gun, but he produced a walkie-talkie and put it to his mouth, while Caesar, with his own mouth open wide, regarded him.

Perhaps the highlight of the evening occurred when Buzzsaw's nose spontaneously started bleeding, a two-pronged faucet of frothing red that neither compression nor ice could staunch, and before he turned the club into a slaughterhouse, Luciano sent him home.

As we were closing up, I called the Street Scene and spoke to Nancy.

"Didn't expect to hear from you so soon," she said.

"You were pretty confident you'd hear sometime though, correct?"

"I was, I'll admit. What's on your mind?"

"Must I be explicit on the telephone?"

"I'm heading home in a while. Quiet night here. No riots."

"Christ, that was messed up. What happened to you?"

"I hid in the staff washroom till everyone cleared out of there. My stupid boss Rico vanished, left me to deal with the cops and the fire department."

"Saw him sneaking out the back."

"Yeah, that's Rico, real prince. A city inspector threatened to close the place down if we don't get some security. It's a basement pub, for crying out loud. We have to hire bouncers? Rico doesn't even want to hire a busboy. Anyway, I'll be home, if you want to come by later. I mean, come if you want. I'll open a bottle of wine. We'll catch up."

"I'm heading out for a bite with the guys."

"I'll be home, Bobby. If not, some other night."

I left it up in the air. A door had reopened that demanded a price for re-entrance. Felicia also hinted that she sought company that night and when I responded that the boys and I were going for a bite, she sulked but took no real issue. Looking at her, at her fraught curves and lines, I wondered if something wasn't wrong with me. What twenty-year-old would make excuses to a girl with a face and a body like that? Maybe the steroids explained it. Maybe that laugh of hers. Never could get used to that laugh.

After work Demarco, Roy Rosati, and I hit Valentino's in the west end, a trattoria that served excellent Italian food till three or four in the morning. A mild night, the candle-lit patio tables were full, and people kept arriving from bars and clubs, tipsy, sometimes quite so. We found a table in the middle of the patio and ordered food from a dark-haired girl with hairy forearms. Demarco and I chose the cheese lasagna; disciplined Roy settled on a mixed salad with oil-and-vinegar dressing, but unconsciously started buttering a roll.

"Roy," Demarco said, appalled. "What are you doing?"

"Oh my God," he said, dropping the roll. "That's more than a hundred calories."

"You still haven't eaten the salad," I said.

"Fuck sake," he said, slumping his shoulders. "Do you see what I'm going through? Do you see? It's torture. You two wolves eat anything you want and still look like Greek gods. I eat a celery stick and have to undo my belt a notch. It's not fucking fair."

"You should go on steroids, Roy." I was serious. That would have solved his problems.

"My dick is very small, Bobby. Obesity made sure of that. All I need is steroid-shrunk testicles to go along with a thimble-dick. You understand what I'm saying?"

Demarco and I laughed at Roy's stone-faced auto-flagellation, but then, arching his brow, he referenced an episode of Demarco's love life that until that moment had been undisclosed to me: a liaison with a member of the McMaster Marauders women's basketball team. Lacking the balls to deny the affair, Demarco confessed it to me himself.

"Rented a room at the City Motor Hotel, that dive near Queenston Circle. Even brought a bottle of Blue Nun and a box of condoms. She arrived a bit late and by then I had masturbated already. Bobby, she's as tall as Caesar, and wears size 14 EEE shoes. I had never been with a woman taller than me. A strange experience. I felt intimidated. We tried to get going, but—"

"He couldn't get it up!" blurted Roy. "She laughed him out of the room. Tell him!"

Demarco's jaw flexed. "She didn't laugh me *out* of the room. Let's get the frigging facts straight. She laughed, yes. But I stayed in the room after *she* left, and watched cable TV."

When I asked if he ever ran into her again he said yes, at the university pub, weeks after the encounter. He spotted her with a posse of her teammates who, upon seeing him, all burst out laughing. But he remained imperturbable. All of the women on the team were very tall, and none truly pretty. If they saw themselves as he saw them, he reasoned, their jollity would have fizzled.

Our food arrived at last and I tucked into my steaming lasagna. What cheesy goodness. Valentino's always delivered. I enjoyed a brief moment of bliss, half-shutting my eyes and sighing. Demarco ripped open a roll and buttered it, then stabbed his lasagna. Roy's salad, a paltry affair, sat limply in a bowl begging for a slab of veal or provolone, a hunk of salami, anything to give it substance, sustenance. Roy leaned to Demarco's plate, opening his nostrils.

"Eat," Demarco half-offered.

"No, I can't. Don't you get it? I can't do it."

"Being skinny hasn't changed a thing, has it, Roy?"

He lifted his head from his salad with a forlorn expression.

"So quit being such a fucking chick, and eat."

Roy hemmed and hawed for about ten seconds, then flagged down the waitress and ordered spaghetti and meatballs, with a side of hot sausage, while pinching two buns out of the basket and buttering them. What a relief: the whole world seemed to sigh. Why fight your nature? If suffering, both physical and psychological, is an inescapable part of the reinvention process, and if denying yourself the possibility of doing that which pleases you most, that which you perhaps do best, is also inescapable, then the process is doomed to fail. And not only doomed but dangerous. It's more than a question of will.

Moments later Oscar and Mad Dog showed up, drunkenly disrupting the patio's sedate equilibrium. Disquiet spread. Some customers got up, tossed their napkins, and left without further encouragement. A few, stretching their necks and peering through slit eyes, wondered what was going on and whether staying was an option. For those more focussed on the food before them, leaving was unthinkable.

Oscar stopped by a table and leered at a buxom blonde in a black catsuit seated with a thin man wearing a periwinkle leisure jacket. Taken by surprise, and conscious of the darkly looming Mad Dog, the thin man froze as Oscar verbally abused his lady, targeting her large breasts and deriding her for dating such a wimp, until she got up and left in tears. Then Oscar grabbed a roll from the basket on the table, bit off an end, and whipped it at the guy, shouting, "Next time butter it, you bird!"

Mad Dog pulled Oscar away from the table, much to the relief of the thin man who sat there quaking with a nauseated smile on his face.

"Next time butter it!" Mad Dog cried with hilarity. "That's the funniest!"

The two stumbled about, knocking glasses and bottles off tables, drawing gasps and mumbles of complaint from the few remaining customers. One unwitting brave heart, possibly from out of town, shot to his feet and, shaking a fist, shouted at Oscar; but when Mad Dog charged him, stopping inches short, the man's legs folded up and he dropped back into his seat, shutting his mouth and casting his eyes downward.

"They're coming our way," Demarco said, concerned.

"Don't run or they'll chase you," I said with a snort. I put down my fork.

Roy stopped chewing his buns as the thugs came close, but only for a moment.

Oscar spotted me and smiled, his black locks hiding his eyes. He swiped the hair from his forehead and took a better look before he stepped toward us. Mad Dog followed.

"Bobby Doctor, wha's going on? Gimme a taste of your noodles, man."

"Maybe he don't want to," Mad Dog said, feigning some sort of brain injury.

Oscar gripped my shoulder. "He wants to, eh, Bobby?"

No, but I gave him a forkful anyway.

"Good stuff," he said, slurping the fork. "Have to get some myself. What do you think, eh? Good fucking lasagna!"

As Mad Dog moved closer, his body odour crowding me, I made myself light in the chair. Mad Dog was actually Marco Santucci, a high school dropout whose older brother, Gorilla Jerry, rode with the Satan's Choice MC. A big boy, Mad Dog was soft in the middle, and softer in the head, a real anti-Einstein. His size and unruly beard made him look formidable, very much like the biker he aspired to be, but to a knowing eye these features failed to mask his vulnerabilities.

"Get out of my face," I told him quietly.

Surprised, Mad Dog recoiled, and took a moment to measure me up, twitching his nostrils and blinking like a bear.

Oscar found it amusing and heckled his friend for annoying me.

"Do you know who this cat is, Mad Dog? You don't wanna fuck with him, bro. You don't wanna go down that road with him."

"He's nothing."

"He's Bobby Doctor, man. You know why I call him Bobby Doctor? Because he sends people to the hospital, ha ha. Ain't that right, man?" Oscar looked at me, smiling.

"He's nothing."

"Don't push him, you bird. I'm warning you."

Mad Dog glared at me with his small black hateful eyes.

Without provocation, without real commitment or passion, he dared to look at me with such rancor—and for this I wanted to rip that ugly beard off his face.

Demarco rested his forearms on the table, fingers agitating. Roy looked on with a mix of horror and glee, not missing a beat as he ate like a famished dog.

What happened next surprised even me. I sprang out of my chair and fell on top of Mad Dog with my hands around his throat, squeezing until his eyes bulged like black cherries and spit bubbled from his lips. Voices shouted above us. Then hands pulled me away from Mad Dog. Oscar and Demarco held me between them, Oscar smiling, Demarco gritting his teeth. After a brief struggle I relented. Oscar massaged my neck. "Take it easy, brother. Take it easy. Mad Dog's hammered. We been drinking tequila all night. He won't even remember this tomorrow. Man, you can move Bobby S. Definitely gonna come and see you play when you go pro. Hey, Mad Dog! Mad Dog! Ah, he'll be fine. He's hammered."

Sweaty and breathless, Demarco said, "Let's go, Bobby."

Mad Dog had risen to his feet and zigzagged his way to the patio fence, which he braced two-fisted as he jet-puked.

Smiling, Oscar clapped me on the back.

"See you later," I said.

"See you later, Bobby Doctor," he said, his smile disappearing.

On the way to the cars Demarco asked after my mental health, and Roy said he had never seen anyone move so fast. "Mad Dog didn't know what hit him," he enthused. Demarco's assessment was more sober. He wondered if Mad Dog wouldn't come back at me for this.

"He's drunk," I said. "Besides, he got out of it with just a tummy ache."

Demarco left his wheels at home but I told him to catch a ride with Roy as I had plans. He wanted to know what plans but I was evasive. The two wandered off to Roy's coppery Delta 88, talking about the incident.

The cool night air refreshed me. I jumped into the Camaro and lowered the window. The silver medallion of the Blessed Virgin Mary on my dash shook: Roy's Delta 88 needed a new muffler. Probably woke up my mother in the north end. The big block rumbled down Main Street toward the city core, waking everyone else. I stilled the medallion with a finger. Then I fired up the Camaro and it shook again. No rest from the sinners.

Driving slowly and digging some Miles Davis on the jazz station, I took Main Street downtown to John Street, got on King and circled Gore Park, where two shirtless men on a bench drank from a brown-bagged bottle. Then I drove east. Went half a block south on Emerald Street and parked in front of a brick triplex. Nestled under the escarpment and lined with old elms and maple trees, this end of Emerald Street needed light. I buzzed number three. The front door clicked open. I climbed the stairs to the third floor and knocked on Nancy's door. She answered in a feather-trimmed red negligee, a sloppy smile on her face. She raised her wineglass, winked, then took my hand and led me to her bedroom.

Thick vanilla candles burned in dishes on the nightstand and the dressing table; a silver candelabra flickered on an ebony pedestal in the corner; a brass candlestick guttered on the windowsill. I sat on the edge of the bed, a canopied queen-size with big downy pillows, took a deep breath, and relaxed.

"Thought you weren't coming."

"We grabbed a bite at Valentino's."

"Hmm, hope you didn't eat too much."

"Hard for me to do that."

"I know, I know, you're a growing boy."

She laughed with a wet mouth and refilled her glass from a bottle of red wine. She asked if I wanted a glass, but I told her I was training hard and trying to stay away from alcohol for the summer. I didn't tell her that roids and booze kill a liver.

"Nothing more boring than a teetotaler," she said.

"I beg to differ."

"You always beg to differ. It's what you do, Bobby."

Her neck was warm, almost hot, as I kissed it. Her hair was damp. The muslin bed curtains shifted as a draft touched them. Nancy whispered something.

She rested her wineglass on the nightstand between two candles. Her eyes closed. The wine trembled in the glass.

FIVE

Nipsy had loaded more than three hundred pounds on the bench press. Last summer he couldn't press it once, now he banged out six reps like nothing—thanks to a nearly toxic regimen of anabolic steroids. He stood up growling, jaundiced eyes bugging, then paced the floor talking to himself and pinching his thighs. Watching him exhausted me, as if that were possible. I was ragged, lacking sleep and rest. Working all those late nights and bouncing between Nancy and Felicia was taking its toll on my body, and my soul.

Demarco did a slow hard set of concentration curls, head contorting, eyes rolling back in a very ugly and funny way. He finished his set and pulled up his sleeves, revealing forearms roped with veins. When Nipsy called him for a spot, he looked like a two-by-four across the head would have been more inviting, but he dragged his feet over to the head of the bench press, and stood there while Nipsy attempted four hundred pounds.

Nipsy balanced the bar over his chest before lowering it, held the bar there for a beat, then pressed it out. He popped up clapping and grinning. His best max ever. He chalked his hands again and added two ten-pound plates to the bar. Demarco waited at the head of the bench, concerned. Nipsy counted to three and took the bar. Then, after a pause, he screamed. Plates clanked and rang. I stopped my set. Demarco held the end of the bar still bearing plates; Nipsy lay on the bench grabbing his right shoulder.

I rushed over. "What happened?"

"Don't know," Demarco said. "Something gave."

"My pec!" Nipsy cried. "It's torn!"

I hustled up to the membership office where Ned and one of his aerobics instructors, a tiny blonde in black tights, were talking. They looked at me with a shared air of annoyance, but when I told them the bad news, Ned slapped his forehead, jumped out of his chair, and followed me to the weight room, muttering about insurance premiums.

"He may have torn his pec," I told him.

Ned shook his head. "I told him he was going up too fast. I told him." He gripped Nipsy on his good side. "Help get him to my car out back. If I told you once, I told you a thousand times—you can't go up that fast, Gomes, you've got to give your bones and ligaments time to catch up. The muscles are too strong. I told you this."

Nipsy's chest heaved, beads of sweat rolled off his face. "It hurts!" he cried. "It hurts!"

We stood him up and helped him out to Ned's hopped-up black Monte Carlo.

"Okay," Ned said, his face and arms bathed in sweat. "I'll get him to St. Joseph's."

Demarco and I returned to the weight room, finishing the workout the furthest thing from my mind. Events like that reverberate well after they pass. One questions motives, methods, ends. Or not, but it takes root in you and you think about it and it grows.

I took a long drink of water, and then let myself sink down on a bench. I dried the sweat from my neck and forehead with my T-shirt to some weak Fleetwood Mac bleating from the speakers. Others studied themselves in the mirrors, beautiful, not beautiful. Demarco persevered: more preacher curls, more hammer curls, more standing concentration curls.

Jon Parson, a rookie linebacker with the Hamilton Ticats, stood near a military press station, resting between sets. A number of Ticats belonged to the club. A redhead with Teutonic thighs, the Ticats had drafted Parson number one that spring out of Western, where he'd captained the Mustangs to a pair of national titles—crushing my Varsity Blues during that run. I disliked the guy but he was holding his own in a pro training camp and deserved respect for that. The *Hamilton Spectator* had run a feature on him in the weekend sports section, citing him as the homegrown answer to the Ticat's recent defensive woes. Demarco, not a CFL fan, offered his frank and unsolicited opinion about Jon Parson.

"He looks like a fucking Viking. Betcha his skin burns in the sun."

"What is your problem?"

"Nothing. Let's go, I've had enough. And you should curb the dogging for a while."

"Blah blah blah, good advice coming from a eunuch."

"You can barely keep your eyes open, you degenerate, like you just ate a plate of spaghetti and meatballs with a bottle of Chianti."

The conversation bored me. I didn't bother defending myself. It was what it was.

We showered and headed to the Dairy Queen on King Street in separate cars. It was well into June now and the gangs had thus far behaved at the Press Club. A skirmish here and there, lots of posing and posturing, but nothing stomach-turning yet. Most folks went to the Press Club to party, to groove, whatever that meant for them, drinking, dancing, sex, drugs, or all of the above. It had gained a reputation as a spirited venue, less flashy but more intimate than New York, New York across the street, with sexy patrons unafraid of a good time. If the odd scrap broke out, it came with the price of admission, and served as a necessary tension-breaker.

Relations with my brother had reached a quiet impasse. He went about his business, I went about mine; we shared meals on occasion without issue; and a delicate peace was maintained in the house. As far as I knew he wasn't mingling with Barton-Sherman or committing break-and-enters or doing other punk things. He was being a typical teenager, moody, self-absorbed, almost narcoleptic, and what do you do with that but wait it out.

Still, all was not rosy. Other gorgons reared their ugly heads. I was jammed up. Not unwittingly, no. More a matter of failing to choose, unable to choose, and yet having to choose, for how could I have said yes and no, or no and yes, when yes and yes was easier? But Felicia had questions; Nancy had questions. Questions about me, questions about them, all requiring answers I did not have, and these questions hounded my waking thoughts, haunted my dreams, and whispered to me when all I wanted was quiet.

Demarco found this side of me repugnant, a serious character flaw—trying to have your cake and eat it too, smoothing the way with greasy lies and vagaries, bullshit and more bullshit. He was old fashioned—the buttoned-up bouquet and candy-box bearer, pining for the perfect moon to serenade his soulmate—when it came to women. I insisted that I'd made no promises, that all parties were willing, but he sucked his teeth at this piece of lameness.

"Enough," he said, and ordered his usual banana split.

I could only stomach a small vanilla cone. The serving girl in stripes smiled at me. Her two front teeth were gapped, like the Wife of Bath. Her name tag, pinned to one of two ballooning breasts, read: Kim.

"Yum. Thanks, Kimmm."

She rolled her tongue. "Want some sprinkles?"

Demarco breathed on my neck.

"No thanks," I said with regrets, and we departed.

"You've lost your objectivity," Demarco said outside.

"She was lubricious."

"She smelled like bubblegum."

"What's wrong with bubblegum?"

"Ask Felicia that. Or Nancy."

"You're passing judgment."

"I'm passing judgment, that's right."

He moved to his Galaxy 500 like a flying wedge in his tight black sweater. I understood his point of view, to some extent. You have to be able to look at yourself in the mirror. Not as simple as he thought. Choosing wasn't simple. And choosing what? Either A or B. But what about C, D, E, and all the others? Nothing was written in stone. Nothing was final, forever. Living in the moment, I failed to see beyond it. Not that seeing beyond it would have prepared me for what came next. Life is like a giant ship. Tough to change course once you're on your way.

My watch had died on me, so I drove down to Sherman Avenue to get it fixed at Sammy's Italian Jewelers. My father had given the watch to me for my thirteenth birthday, just before he got sick with cancer, one of the few keepsakes I've ever permitted in my life. Things would come and go—just about anything and everything you can think of, all temporary, fleeting, ready to turn to shit or dust—but the watch would be a constant.

Sammy's shop had been there since I could remember, though I hadn't visited since my father passed. Sammy was from my father's hometown in Sicily and had sold him the watch, an Omega Constellation with a brown leather strap.

I parked near the Orthodox Church on Barton Street and walked to the shop. People strolled about in the warm and pleasant weather, smiling, their manner easy. Odd that a ruthless street gang came from such a sedate, if rundown, part of the city. A fifteen-minute jaunt from there, the steel mills represented an unpleasant reality, but one that could be mitigated by good living. Immigrants comprised the majority of people inhabiting the modest homes in the neighbourhood, hard-working, stand-up folk who followed the rules and minded their own business. Didn't look like a breeding ground for thugs, but who's to say what generates anomalies like Eugene and Oscar.

When I entered Sammy's Jewelers, little bells jingled above the door. The place hadn't changed since I was kid; my father would bring me there on his Saturday rounds with the paisans. A plump girl in a red floral sundress stood at the counter, pressing a red leather purse to her buttocks. Eyepiece cocked, Sammy hunched over a diamond ring, his unkempt white hair and white lab coat hinting of the mad scientist. On the wall behind him, under a clock with Roman numerals, hung a picture of Aurora blowing a trumpet. A whiff of garlic teased my nose.

Sammy sighed and opened his mouth as if to say something, but shut his mouth and re-examined the ring. The young woman brought her purse to her stomach.

"It's eighteen karat gold," he said. "But the stone is cracked inside."

The girl looked concerned. "What are you saying?"

"I'm saying that the stone is cracked. Period. You want me to tell you stories? I'm not going to tell you stories. Bobby, one second."

I nodded. I was in no rush.

Sammy's message, elementary as it was, had confused the girl. "Tino told me he paid two grand for it."

"Maybe so, but now it's worth three hundred, tops."

The girl verged on tears as Sammy handed over the ring. She slid it back on her ring finger and exited with a jingle. Benny removed his eyepiece, wiped his brow with his sleeve, then came around the counter and shook my hand.

"Bobby, nice to see you. Long time. Your uncle Ignazio was in here a few weeks back."

I nodded toward the door. "You don't always get what you bargain for, eh?"

"You can say that again. Back in town for the summer?"

"Yeah, back for one more. Can't get enough of the place."

"Ha, I was talking about you the other day to a paisan—Jimmy Melfi. Your father used to work with Jimmy at Burlington Steel, back in the sixties. Remember? The Elvis sideburns? Hurt his back working construction a few years ago and collects disability these days. Still has the sideburns. Anyway, when I told him you were at the university in Toronto studying and playing football, too, he said he remembered what a little punk you were, always breaking balls. Look at the size of you now. Your father, God bless, woulda been so proud. *Che disgrazia.* But what're you gonna do, Bobby? We're all waiting in line." He smiled. "Your mother, how's she doing? Saw her at the market about a month ago and she was a little down, a little down."

"She has her good days and her bad days, Sammy. What can I tell you? It's tough."

"Yes it is. And it doesn't get easier for any of us, believe me. My brother-in-law in North Bay has throat cancer. He's had chemo and radiation and they still say he might not last the year. Life is a bastard, Bobby. But at least the weather's nice. And we should be thankful for that, I guess. So what can I do for you, today?"

I showed him the watch. The strap was ripped, the battery dead.

"Ah, that old thing. You still wear it. Nice."

"Can't seem to shake it."

"These things don't go away easy."

He examined it, murmuring to himself, then opened a small metal box on the counter and removed from it a new leather strap. He used a needle-nosed instrument to snip off the old strap, and with a quick clip secured the new one. With another instrument he pried open the hatch, replaced the battery. Then he adjusted the time and buffed the crystal with a green felt square.

Bells jingled. An ancient man wearing thick-lensed glasses entered the shop, tapping a shellacked wooden cane. He cleared his throat and spat into a checked handkerchief, tonguing brown strands from his lips.

"Zi Calo!" Sammy shouted. He looked at me and gestured to his ear. "This is Zi Calo, your father knew him. Zi Calo! This is Giacchino Sferazza's son!"

The old man stopped in his tracks and motioned for me to come closer. Moustaches swept down his jaw. Tar stains blotched the lapels of his brown corduroy jacket. He lifted his hand and I took it, dry, papery, in mine, gently giving it pressure.

"Your grandfather and I fought in Somalia," he said. "Is he still in Serradifalco?"

"He died three years ago."

Zi Calo grimaced, thumbed his ear.

"He died three years ago!" Sammy shouted.

"Well, maybe I'm next. I can't do anything anymore, can't even tie my shoes. Look, I'm wearing slippers." He pointed to his brown velvet slip-ons.

"Convenient!" Sammy shouted.

Zi Calo nodded and wiped his mouth with his handkerchief. Sammy only wanted ten bucks for the band and the battery. He charged me no labour. I paid him and said goodbye to Zi Calo, who was busily stuffing a tarry pipe with black tobacco.

"I fought in Somalia with your grandfather. Say hello to him."

I waved to Sammy, who smiled and shrugged.

Outside the late afternoon sun shone gauzily, the air lacked oxygen. A headache played hide-and-seek behind my eyes. I walked to my car, regretting that I'd worn blue jeans instead of shorts. My thighs were chafing.

On Barton Street near Sherman Avenue, two of the three Slompka brothers, junior flunkies for Eugene Ciccone, who shared the family brow and weasel neck, approached with my brother between them. What was he doing with these winners? I burned to hear his explanation. Thought he'd give me attitude but his face lit up when he saw me.

"Fancy meeting you here," I said. "What's going on, boys?"

Joey gave me a peculiar look. "You know Pauly and Dip."

"That's your brother?" asked the one called Pauly.

"Yeah, that's him," Joey said with the slightest smirk.

Dip said, "You work at the Press Club." He whacked my brother in the back.

I felt my blood rising but said nothing and looked at Joey, who was staring at his feet, in those stupid white runners. When I asked them where they were going no one responded. Pauly smiled and sniffed; Joey shoved his hands in his pockets but would not meet my eye. Then Dip tipped his flabby chin at me.

"Places," he snorted. "We're going places. Your brother and us."

He whacked him again across the shoulders.

"You okay?" I asked Joey.

He winced but said nothing.

"Tell him you're okay," Pauly said.

"Tell him," Dip said, raising his arm to whack him again.

I lunged, snatched his wrist in mid-motion, and wrenched his arm around his back, keeping it straight at the elbow. Then I kicked out his legs and drove him face-first to the pavement, firmly holding the wrist, and leaning all my weight into it.

Joey stepped away from Pauly but positioned himself between us. Not that Pauly was going to do anything.

I leaned down. "Touch my brother again," I said.

"You're breaking my wrist!"

"Touch my brother again and I'll break more than your wrist."

I kept up the pressure until I felt a pop in Dip's elbow. He screeched like a parrot, and when I let the gimpy arm go he rolled around the sidewalk screeching and grabbing the arm. Then I kicked him in the side of the head and he stopped screeching.

Pauly stood there dumbfounded, the whites of his eyes flashing, skinny arms trembling at his sides. When I stepped toward him, he turned around and dashed off down the street with his heels kicking his own ass. I pulled my brother by the shoulder and led him to the Camaro. We got in and I lowered the roof. The sun burned my eyes. I put on my shades, drove slowly up to King Street, and turned east.

"So do I have to ask?" I said.

"Long story."

"I've got all day."

Joey looked straight ahead. "Bobby, I did things for Eugene."

"No kidding. Please go on."

"With Pauly and Dip—I knew them from school. I took machine shop with Pauly, and Dip and I had homeroom together. They introduced me to Eugene and Terry. I had nothing better to do at the time. Ma was driving me crazy. I was bored. I was pissed off and bored. We did a few scores, you know. Small stuff, to prove myself. They run around the streets like psychos, but Eugene's got everyone doing scores, drugs, stolen property, you know. And he does favours for bikers and wise guys, beatings, torchings, shit like that. He's trying to make a name for himself." He stopped his testimony. "Where are you going?"

"Stoney Creek Dairy. I feel like a strawberry sundae. Go on. I'm listening."

"Well, on one of these scores, someone lost a package, or it got lifted, or maybe one of the brothers kept it. I don't know. Anyway, they tried to blame it on me. They say I stole the package or got ripped off for it. They say I'm on the hook for it."

"What was in the package?"

"No idea. Didn't see it, didn't touch it. Dip had it last."

"So where were they taking you?"

"To see Eugene. Well, to see Terry Peters. Eugene never talks to us, even if he's in the same room, even if he's sitting right beside us. Terry always does all the talking. So Terry tells me to meet up with Dip and Pauly on Barton and Sherman and wait for him there. He was going to pick us up and take us out to where Eugene's staying, I don't know where. The guy moves around a lot. I know a few ladies keep house for him but I've never met with him in the same place twice. Terry said he was really pissed off about this thing and wanted to speak to all three of us pronto to find out what happened."

"Pauly can tell Eugene they ran into a bit of trouble."

Joey found this less than amusing. "Eugene doesn't give a fuck if you and Oscar played ball together. Oscar's a soldier. If you fuck up Eugene's shit he's gonna come at you strong. He's already pissed off at me because they told him I took the package. Now this thing with Dip."

"So I guess I'll have to deal with it," I said.

"What do you mean?"

"I'll have to talk to Eugene."

Joey shook his head. "Don't you get it? He won't talk to you, Bobby. You're an annoyance to him. He'd sooner have his boys jump you and put you out of the picture than talk to you. Terry already wants to fuck you up for making him cur at the gym. I heard about that." His face broke into a smile. "You're too much, man."

"But aren't you glad I'm on your side?"

"You'll get us both killed."

"Then we will die well, baby brother, we will die *hot*."

"I don't want to die!"

Joey roared with laughter as I gunned the engine and raced for the amber light at Nash Road. As we flew through the intersection he sat up straight with alarm, hands on the dash, then sat back laughing again when we entered old Stoney Creek.

In the summers of our childhood our father would take us to the Stoney Creek Dairy at least once a week; he loved his ice cream as much we did. And for a brief moment, we were those young brothers on our way for a treat, cruising along Old King Street, its trees heavy and green from recent rains and bursts of flowers beautifying its little shops and boutiques: white, yellow, red. Old-timey couples promenaded arm-in-arm; women with shining faces pushed strollers; and children in crayons skipped and hopped with joyful abandon.

The illusion dissolved when several skinheads in crimson skulked across the road.

Clubbers. Strange to see them around in broad daylight. They kept vampirish hours, conducting their destructive raids on bowling alleys, roller rinks, or pool halls only after sundown. These kids, none older than sixteen or seventeen, could frighten a crowd into white-eyed hysteria; the sight of the jackets alone often sent them herding. But as much as assault delighted the Clubbers, property destruction was their forte, and they could trash a place better than demolition experts, do a more thorough job, not missing one pane of glass or a single breakable object, no matter how trivial or small. Unafraid of the police and arrest, they laughed at the threat hanging over them of juvenile detention, which they mockingly referred to as "junior vacation."

We parked in the Dairy lot and went inside. I felt uneasy and angry about my uneasiness. How could a bunch of punks make me feel like this? Two restless Clubbers waited by the counter for their ice cream, both lean-jawed and snappish as starving dogs. One of them jerked his head and glanced at Joey. He turned to his pal and said something in his ear.

"What was that?" I asked Joey.

"Little beef a few weeks back. It was settled."

My muscles tensed.

"My word, Bobby, it was settled."

I glared at the Clubbers.

"Bobby," Joey chuckled, "you're scaring them."

"Let's fuck 'em up."

My brother's eyes widened.

"I'm serious, let's do it."

"Bobby, what have you been smoking?" He covered his grinning mouth. "I can't believe you. This isn't football, man. They run in packs, these guys. There's more of them around, believe me. Let's just order ice cream."

I took a deep breath and rested my hand on my brother's shoulder. "Okay, let's order ice cream."

SIX

"I have to get going," I called out. Felicia was in the bathroom. I dressed and waited. Satan sat near my shoes. I moved one and he pawed it. I gently pushed him away. He glared at me with a killer's cold green eyes before disappearing from my sight. After a minute Felicia emerged in a white terry-cloth robe.

"What's the rush?" she asked.

"I told you. I've got a picnic today."

"Can I come?"

"It's just family, Felicia."

She sighed. "I like family."

I wasn't prepared to introduce her to my mother. No point bringing a girl around just to bring her. My mother would question my seriousness, question my motives, and my blood ran too hot to pull off a bluff without stumbling, without turning my mother against me. I wanted to avoid complications, for everyone.

"It's a little unfair, that's all. Like, are you embarrassed by me? Am I not good enough for your mother? I wanted you to meet my folks but you refused, you refused and you don't want me to meet your family, and you know what that tells me, that tells me you don't really care about me. You only care about yourself, Bobby."

How could I state my case truthfully? I tried. "I do care about you, Felicia. But what do you want me to say? What do you want me to promise? I don't know what's going to happen down the road. You're a pretty young woman, a knockout. I'm going back to school, in Toronto. I'm going to be busy, it's going to be a busy year for me. You're a dude magnet. I won't be able to compete for your affections; and you won't put up with my lifestyle, my lack of attention, face it. And what if you go to university—and you should—then your whole life will change. Then you won't have time for me. And where will that leave us?"

Tears welled in her childlike blue eyes. I squeezed her hand in mine.

"Let's be realistic," I said.

She pulled away her hand. "I'm just a summer fling for you, a nothing, a fluff."

"And what am I to you, the love of your life? The man of your dreams? I doubt it. We have little to talk about. I study literature and all you read are self-help books or astrology pamphlets. You go on about this determined energy stuff all the time like I have a clue what you're talking about or like I give two shits."

"You're being mean," she said, her lower lip trembling.

"I'm sorry, Felicia. But if you're implying you're head over heels for me or pining away when you're not with me, or whatever, I don't believe you. It's just a reflex, a default response to having sex with me. Don't get me wrong, the sex is okay, we both enjoy it, but I don't think you even like me, not really."

Felicia's bathrobe fell open, baring her stomach and the lower curves of her breasts, the edges of her aureole. More complications. But I had to get going or I'd be late, and I dreaded the inevitable ball-breaking. I went to kiss Felicia but she jerked away from me.

It was bright out. My eyes felt gritty, my mouth like a muddy paste. It took several cranks to start the Camaro. My neglect showed. I promised to take better care of it, and sped home.

"You're late," my mother said, waiting at the front door. "Get ready. Uncle Giuseppe will be here soon."

"I'll drive, too, I have to be at work by eight."

"Never mind, never mind. If you bring your car you'll leave early. We'll get you back in time, don't worry. You need a day with your family. Vincenzo's coming, too."

"Where's Joey?"

"In bed. He's not feeling well. Go get ready!"

Joey's bedroom door was open and he lay on his bed fully dressed, eyes shut. Like his kid self, except for a slight dark tension around his mouth. His hair was growing in and he looked less terminal, but he'd been sleeping a lot, and could have used a blast of sunshine. I glanced at the Mott the Hoople poster over his bed. I had given him that poster years ago and he still kept it around, something I found oddly touching, perhaps a misguided emotion.

It was the Canada Day long weekend, a crime to spend it alone wallowing in a room. When I whispered Joey's name and he didn't move I felt sad. In summers past, instead of cottages and camping trips, my family packed up and went on Sunday picnics at local lakes or nearby conservation areas, and as a kid Joey loved these outings with the clan more than I did. I had half a mind to roust him and drag him along, even kicking and screaming, but I reconsidered. If he was feeling blue, an outing might not have been the best thing. Inevitably he'd have to answer questions—no hiding from the aunts and uncles—and he wasn't up to it. I watched him sleep for another minute.

In my bedroom I changed into red nylon swim trunks and a white tank top. My royal blue flip-flops languished under the bed, where they'd been exiled since last summer. Now I felt excited about the picnic and this surprised me. On paper not the coolest thing to do in the world, but being with my family never came as a chore to me, and I was sure to have a few laughs with Vincenzo. I took one last glimpse at Joey on my way down but he hadn't moved.

I helped my mother take lawn chairs out to the front porch. It was a gorgeous day, dry, cloudless, the air tingly with floral, herbal, and skunk notes. Canadian flags rippled brightly on poles and rooftops. Mr. Warden sat on his porch without Mrs. Warden, bareheaded, sipping from a white mug and staring at a cleaned-up Eastwood Park. On Sundays the Wardens typically got dressed up and attended St. Luke's, the local Anglican Church, for service, then remained in their Sunday best till after lunch, when they often changed into walking clothes and bucket hats and went for a stroll in the park. Mr. Warden glanced my way but made no sign and thus discouraged me from asking about his wife. When my mother muttered that she was probably back in the loony bin, I frowned at her but she shrugged it off.

We'd been living next door to the Wardens for two decades and they'd never so much as invited us in for a coffee, and had only ever given us perfunctory Christmas and New Year's greetings. When my brother and I were children they behaved coldly toward us, or sternly if we got rambunctious within earshot; and they did small, petty things like keep their doors locked and the lights off on Halloween; or they'd refuse to return a ball we knocked into their backyard, or they'd call the police when our relatives came over and things got too loud and joyful. But I suspected that it wasn't personal, that they found Italians repugnant in general. When my father died, they came neither to the funeral home nor the funeral.

So now I felt nothing, not even an atom of pity, seeing Mr. Warden alone on his porch, contemplating the mad mystery that is life, or whatever he was doing. I wondered if the old gal was finished at last, double-bolted in a rubber room. Now he'd be a solo act. Now he'd have to sit by himself, walk by himself, and drive that silly Volkswagen by himself. He had that to chew on for the rest of his days.

Uncle Giuseppe pulled up shortly in his mint-green station wagon and tooted the horn. Why he even drove a station wagon baffled me, since he and Aunt Teresa were childless. But that was Uncle Giuseppe for you, a man not to be profiled. With his trim lean build and busted-nose handsomeness—he'd been in a few scraps back in the day—he reminded me of actor Roy Scheider. I remember the buzz I got the first time I watched *Jaws*. I laughed through the whole movie, pointing to the screen like a dipstick whenever Scheider appeared. Uncle Giuseppe as Chief Martin Brody: *We're gonna need a bigger boat.* Beautiful. When I showed my mother a photograph of Scheider in a magazine, she conceded a passing resemblance, though she insisted that Uncle Giuseppe had better hair. In any event, I never looked at him the same way after *Jaws*.

I carried out a foil-covered tray of lasagna my mother had baked that morning, an unorthodox picnic item but a constant on our excursions. My mother followed with a small orange cooler filled with beverages and fruit. We loaded up the station wagon and boarded. Aunt Teresa gripped my arm as she slid beside me in the back seat. I kissed her cheek. The red paisley kerchief in her hair nipped my nose with perfume.

"I'm glad you're coming," she said. "Wouldn't have been the same without you, Roberto. We never get to see you anymore. So where's Joey?"

"Ah, you know Joey. Not his thing these days."

"Roberto," said Uncle Giuseppe, "your neck's like a mortadella."

"What are you saying to him?"

"Look at his neck, Teresa. Dio. He needs a neck like that for the football. For ramming. Is that right, Roberto?"

Aunt Teresa said, "We used to have two goats back in Sicily, Cicco and Pippo, remember, Giuseppe? They used to ram everything. They destroyed the fence in Papa's *l'orto*."

"I remember them well."

My mother shoved in beside me, squeezed my thigh, and laughed. Her cheeks were red and her blue eyes shone with excitement. It warmed me to see her like this.

We drove to Uncle Frank and Aunt Rosa's tidy bungalow on Belview Avenue in the east end. The neighbourhood used to be clean and solidly working class, but lower elements were creeping in. The houses around their place had gone to the dogs, as my uncle liked to say, many needing paint and plasterwork, some mini-junkyards of broken-down cars, dead appliances, and vicious dogs on chains.

We waited for Aunt Rosa in the station wagon. Aunt Teresa asked my mother if she had put peas in the lasagna. My mother said she had and this information pleased Aunt Teresa. Uncle Frank and Aunt Rosa came down the porch steps laden with foodstuffs, foam cushions for the lawn chairs, bocce balls in a mesh sack, and other picnic items.

"Go help them," my mother said, nudging me.

I jumped out of the station wagon and took the cushions from Aunt Rosa. "Where's Vincenzo?" I asked.

"He went to pick up Uncle Sal," Aunt Rosa said. "They should be here any minute."

This surprised me. Uncle Sal was my maternal grandfather's kid brother. He'd been sick with cancer, in and out of hospitals the past year. He used to be a joyous, boisterous man, life of the party, but the cancer had reduced him to a fragile shell of his old self.

Uncle Frank loaded a green-striped watermelon into the back of the station wagon and lit a cigarette while we waited for Vincenzo.

"Are you sure it's big enough?" I said.

"Your cousin picked it out, that chooch. If my sciatica acts up I'll take a crowbar to it."

Minutes later Vincenzo pulled up in his shit-brown Malibu, honking his loud horn like an asshole and mugging as if for an unseen camera. Uncle Sal looked papery and exhausted. A man drained of all vitality. He waved and smiled at me like a dying pope. In moments we were off.

Valens Conservation Area lay half an hour west of the city, adjacent to the Valens Reservoir, not deep nature but manageable for inner-city Italians. I sat back and enjoyed the mild scenery rolling by, green pastures grazed by dappled cows and ponies, blue enamel silos, red barns, a monastery on a hill. Aunt Rosa handed out mortadella and provolone sandwiches. Aunt Teresa sliced a nectarine with a small bone-handled knife and offered me a piece. It must have been off because it tasted like a potato. Aunt Teresa made a face but said nothing, then discreetly wrapped the bad nectarine in a paper napkin, and clutched it in her lap for the rest of the trip.

At Valens we found a picnic table near a lush tulip tree, a short stroll to the water. The harsh sun troubled Uncle Sal so they wrapped him in light cotton blankets and propped him up in the tree shade with a view of the sandy beach. He looked cozy and content bundled up there, only his little face showing, like a pallid caterpillar. He wasn't long for this world and the idea saddened me.

After we settled in, my mother spread a red-and-white-checked tablecloth on the table, set down the lasagna tray and doled it out on paper plates with simple side salads. We ate.

Other families claimed picnic tables around us. A loud large Italian clan occupied the nearest one: children roughhoused while the men played cards and drank wine from a green gallon jug they kept circulating; several women fussed around the table preparing lunch. A sturdy red-faced man in suspenders barking at the others clearly represented the head of the clan. A well-developed girl in a purple two-piece kept looking over. I tensed my abdominal muscles and flexed my upper body. Then I recognized a guy pulling a beer out of a cooler—Luigi Fanelli.

"What's wrong?" my mother asked.

"Nothing," I told her, but it was an odd moment. I hadn't seen Luigi since that night at the Street Scene. He'd likely been keeping a low profile, as the blond guy he'd assaulted, though out of his coma, still lay in hospital. One never expects to find a violent sociopath caught up in a commonplace family circumstance; and in the end one is always surprised by the ordinariness of it. Even monsters have kin. Perhaps this is unfair. He'd not been raised by monsters. My family and his, to an outside observer, probably looked interchangeable.

Luigi spotted me and nodded. Then he slowly made his way toward us.

As he approached, I felt neither threatened nor concerned, but not easy either. His smile was friendly but sharp-edged. Dark bristles covered his slender lower jaw, under which a pronounced Adam's apple protruded. While his wiry build belied his strength and ferocity, the aggressive tattoos on his forearms—roaring demons and devils and skulls—did not. It seemed a wild dog was nearing us, half-starved, unable to conceal his fangs or his blood lust. Whatever the familial pantomime across the way suggested, I knew I wasn't dealing with a solid human being.

My mother stood up.

"*Buon giorno*," he said to her, with a Neapolitan twang.

"*Salve*," she said, smiling.

"Ma, this is Luigi Fanelli."

"Nice to meet you, Luigi. I always see your mother at the processions. Say hello to her for me. Some lasagna?"

"No, thank you," he said, looking over at his family. "We're just about to eat."

My mother glanced at me and sat down. I walked with Luigi.

"Buddy," he said, "what's going on?"

"Not too much. Family picnic, you know."

"Yeah, me too. Good stuff." He sniffed and smiled with the side of his mouth. "I hear you a had thing there with those meatheads Pauly and Dip."

"They were roughing up my brother."

"Yeah, eh? Eugene's hot, man. They ripped him off—one or all three of them. I told him I didn't think your brother was in on it. He's a good kid. He shouldn't have been with those two fucks in the first place. But it's there, this thing. It's there."

"What was stolen?"

"Can't say. Besides, better you don't know."

"So why are you giving me a heads up? Doesn't seem to be your style."

"What can I say? I'm on probation. Can't mix with Eugene or any of them right now or the courts will come down hard on me. It's given me time to think."

"Oh yeah?"

"Things were getting out of control, you know. Totally fucked up."

"I hear you."

"It's like anything, drugs, gambling, pussy. You can get all caught up in that shit and forget who you are, lose yourself. Anyway, this is a heads up because you're Oscar's boy. Oscar always talks about you, Bobby Doctor, and all that shit. He wanted to talk to you himself about this. But you never know with him. Good thing I saw you."

I wasn't one hundred per cent sold on Luigi's earnest testimonial. What, he had turned the corner since the last time I saw him, braining some poor bastard? He'd taken time to reflect on his bad deeds and had seen the light? Seemed weird. I didn't like it, and didn't feel like engaging him further. But he had more to say.

"Listen, Bobby, no offense about all that. It is what it is. I'm sure it'll get sorted out. Pauly and Dip have it coming to them. Anyway, my sister Connie—she, um, remembers you from Cathedral. I know you played ball there with Oscar. She said you and Oscar were the baddest guys on the team. She said you won a championship game or something, la la la. Anyway, she wants to meet you. She's a fan."

I didn't know what to say. It was queer.

Luigi shrugged and tipped his bottle. "Don't see your brother around."

"He stayed home. Under the weather."

"That's too bad." He returned to his table.

Connie looked over and smiled. Vincenzo squeezed my shoulder. "Everything okay, Bobby?"

"Let's go for a stroll," I said.

"Don't swim now, Vinnie," Aunt Rosa said. "*La corrente.*"

"Ma, we're not swimming. We're walking."

"Always with an answer, eh. Just watch out."

Swimmers and sunbathers blotted the beach, splashed in the water, thrummed. My cousin pulled off his T-shirt, baring a vast, creamy torso squiggled with black hairs. Snug red trunks squeezed his love handles over the waistband: never one for the gym, Vinnie. When I removed my top he stared; I flexed my pectorals and ran my fingers over my abdomen, wondering if I should up the crunch counts. Two stunners on beach towels loosened their bikini tops, one in neon green swelling from the chest, the other in yellow stretching her dancer's legs. I injured my neck admiring them. Then two surfer types pulled up pitching heat, and they grew ugly.

The sand burned; the sadist sun punished its unguent worshippers, pierced their skulls with bayonets of light, sizzled their minds. You want it, you got it, baby. I slid my sunglasses up my sweaty nose and gazed at the blue-green water as I stepped over hot sand, picking out beauties, and there were many. I felt marvellous in my skin at that moment, sensuous, ironic, powerful. My cousin stopped to pick a stone out of his sandal, his face dripping sweat, his shoulders rolling.

"Up for a swim, Vin?"

"Would be cooling."

We plunged in and waded out to our necks; Vincenzo bobbed a few feet beyond me, spreading wide his arms and tilting his broad face to the sun. The water felt cool and gelatinous. I bounced on my toes, fluttered my fingers. Vincenzo went under and moments later re-emerged sucking air and shaking his head like a giant sea otter. He wiped his hair back and snorted out two jets of water and snot.

I lifted my wet sunglasses from my face and shook them off, half-blinded by the knifing glare of the water. Sunlight blurred the figures on the beach. A large bird hovered overhead, silver-black in silhouette. A kid with mirror shades on a dark red air mattress floated by and vanished into the dazzle.

Vincenzo bobbed up beside me. "Who was the tattooed dude?"

"Luigi Fanelli. Barton-Sherman. Not a nice guy. He was there that night at the Street Scene. Get this. His sister wants to meet me."

"But you didn't go over."

"Nah. It kind of weirds me out, you know. To think that Luigi's sister... I don't know. Like I don't have my hands full already."

The eavesdropping sun slapped my neck and traps, pinched

my nose, ran hot nails through my scalp. I went under and propelled myself sideways with my eyes open in the murky water. The bottom was sandy, spongy in spots, weedy in others, with rocks here and there and no fishes as such. I could see only a few feet in front of me. When I came up, Vincenzo went under. Muted voices issued from the beach and picnic tables. Sunlight spiked off the water. I shook off my sunglasses and put them back on. Vincenzo surged up again, wiping his nose with both hands.

"So—Bobby, what about Joey? What's the kid been up to?"

"He's been staying out of trouble as far as I know, keeping close to home. But Eugene thinks Joey and a couple of nitwits he hangs with ripped him off—don't know of what. Maybe drugs. Eugene's been selling bennies by the bucketful for his biker connections. I hear he's been moving coke, too. But I doubt Joey had anything to do with the theft, if there was one."

"Sounds complicated, Bobby."

"It is. I think I'm going to have to talk to Eugene sooner rather than later. If they ever hurt Joey I'd have no choice but to come at them hard. I'd like to avoid that if I could."

Predictably, Vincenzo voiced his reservations. "I hear you, Bobby. Do what you gotta do if it comes to that. But I don't like the sounds of this. They have numbers. And most importantly, they don't give a fuck about anything. How you gonna fight that? What, you're gonna get Uncle Giuseppe to dust off his hunting rifle and join *your* gang?"

"Back in the day he ran with hard guys. I'm sure he'd be fierce. And your dad, man, when that little wop gets going..."

"All kidding aside, have you considered calling the cops?"

"Yeah, I'll get Albert and Lloyd the disco cops to come and save our butts, when their gonorrhea clears up."

Vincenzo laughed but shook his head. "You think it's funny."

"It's not funny, but right now this isn't a police matter. I mean really, what are they going to do? Call everyone in for questioning about some package that did or did not go missing? Ask them if they plan to hurt little Joey Sferazza? Give them a stern warning not to even think about it? That's not going to happen. I'm going to do my best to avoid a situation, but I'll tell you right now, if they cross the line, game's on."

"Yeah, yeah. Be careful, Sonny Corleone. Don't let that temper get the better of you. I know how hot you can get. Think about your mother, too. What'll happen to her? You've got everything to lose, Bobby, not them."

"I'll keep that in mind."

He clapped me on the traps and started for the shore, pumping his arms and thighs and splashing violently. I followed, thrashing, pounding, relishing the brute power in my quadriceps and buttocks. I was about to gain on Vincenzo when he stopped.

"Look," he said.

Luigi's sister had taken to the water with an anemic girl in a navy blue bathing suit. They waded in to their knees, giggling, cringing, their pale hands scooping up handfuls of water.

Vincenzo emerged, primordial, streaming. His feet clapped the sand. I followed him. The girls grew smaller, smaller. Vincenzo enlarged, sprayed, waved.

We returned to the picnic table. Uncle Sal snoozed under his tree, snug, slipping by degrees into the long sleep. The other uncles and aunts played bocce on the wilted grass, the uncles taking the contest far too seriously, and suffering as a result. My mother sliced strawberries, layering the red flesh in tall glasses, then adding chilled red wine. She offered me a glass and I took it to a lawn chair in the shade.

The aunts and uncles tossed the black-and-red bocce balls with soft thuds and clacks. Uncle Giuseppe chased his shots; Uncle Frank tensed and jerked his shoulders watching his. I ate the strawberries, drank the wine. At their picnic table the Fanellis huddled around a large metal pot, jabbing forks into noodles of some kind. Luigi held a Blue and a fork. His sister looked over, also with a Blue and a fork. She smiled. I smiled back.

My eyes wouldn't stay open. I dozed off and dreamed I was playing football. I was running at someone. Beside me I heard breathing, thudding. I lowered my shoulder for the collision. A burst. Then a starry sky above me. People talking. I tried to move. Oscar kneeled at my side, put his hand over my mouth.

"Roberto."

I started.

My mother's face hovered over me. "You were dreaming." She turned away from me chuckling. It took a moment to reorient myself. Dry-mouthed and sunburned, I needed water.

At the picnic table Vincenzo played briscola with Uncle Frank and Uncle Giuseppe. Uncle Frank slammed down a card.

Vincenzo played a card, with less passion than his father.

"Here comes Joe Athlete," Uncle Giuseppe grunted, scooping the trick.

Uncle Frank looked up from his cards simpering. Vincenzo doubled over, pounding the table. The aunts cackled in the background. I grabbed a jug of water from the cooler and drank and drank and drank.

"Look at him," Uncle Giuseppe said. "What's he gonna do with shoulders like that, hoist cars? Face it, Roberto, you're big but you can't move. You're musclebound. You've gone too far. And you're delicate. You were always a delicate kid. So I don't know why you're walking around all tough. Look at him, all tough. Now, Vinnie here, there's an animal for you. Don't let that mozzarella body fool you. He's a beast."

"We're just busting your balls," Uncle Frank said.

"Yeah, get over it," Uncle Giuseppe said, wiping away tears of laughter.

"That's all right," I said. "I'm good. I'm cool. Uncle G, Uncle Frank is winning?"

"What else is new?"

"Tell him the secret, Uncle Frank."

Everyone fell silent. The aunts and my mother sat up in their chairs. Uncle Giuseppe's mouth opened. He looked at Uncle Frank, at Vincenzo, then at me.

"Secret?"

I tried keeping a straight face. I had pushed a beautiful button and was going to enjoy the fireworks it set off

"Frank," Uncle Giuseppe said. "What is this? What is your nephew saying?"

Uncle Frank had removed his glasses and was rubbing them with tissue paper.

"What is he saying? He's lying. I have no secret. Secret, as if."

"Pop," Vincenzo said, "tell the truth now. What are you hiding?"

"It's nothing!" Uncle Frank barked. "Your cousin's making trouble, can't you see? There is no secret. If you want to know the truth, Giuseppe, you are a terrible player. Terrible. And Vincenzo, forget about it. You're a chooch."

Uncle Giuseppe's face reddened. "A hundred bucks says you're wrong, Frank."

"*Pilamadonna*, don't make such a stink about this thing. I don't want to take your money. I'm better, I'm better, smell the espresso. We can play for fun. Let's just play for fun."

"Two hundred dollars."

Uncle Frank slid his glasses back on. "Deal the cards."

Looking sun-stroked, Vincenzo got up and stiff-legged it toward the latrines while the cranky uncles locked horns. I stretched out on a lawn chair in the shade and shut my eyes, happy to listen to them bicker and war over cards. It made the world seem right somehow. Wearing floppy straw hats like three tourists, my mother and aunts nibbled grapes and drank wine under an umbrella with amusement and grace, and that really made the world seem right.

We barbecued at five, as the heat of the day began to lift and a cooling breeze blew off the lake. Everyone had a sun buzz on, wearing dreamy smiles, noses reddened, arms and shoulders baked. Fresh from a rare victory over Uncle Frank, Uncle Giuseppe seized the tongs and took on the metal half-sphere and its smoking charcoal, fanning the flames with a paper plate, squirting extra benzene to accelerate the process, ignoring Uncle Frank's complaints that the meat would reek of petroleum, and that he wanted a briscola rematch. Steaks, chops, chicken, hot and mild sausages, and a quail for Uncle Sal.

The Fanellis had surrounded a huge watermelon. The father figure in suspenders cleaved it open with a large serrated knife. Black-flecked red spilled out. The others grabbed spoons and jabbed and jabbed into the hull of the watermelon, gouging out big chunks and devouring them. Connie turned her head and smiled, spoon in fist.

Uncle Sal nibbled his quail under the tree. I loaded up a plate with charred steak and tomato salad and joined him. He looked up at me with his small wet eyes and smiled. His dentures fit loosely and gave him a skeletal cast.

"Where's your brother?"

"He wasn't feeling well, Uncle Sal."

"That's too bad. He hasn't come to see me in weeks. Tell him I don't have much time left, to come and see me before they put me in a box."

"Ah, don't talk like that, Uncle Sal. You've still got plenty of kick. I was going to call you to help me rout these hoodlums. I need some muscle."

Uncle Sal chuckled. "Okay, Bobby, sign me up."

"Don't worry, I'll make sure Joey comes over this week."

"And you, what's doing? You're a big one, eh. Bigger than your old man and back in the day he was big, especially for a Sicilian. Jesus, you're blocking the sun. Go get me a ginger ale, will you. I'm dying of thirst here."

I grabbed Uncle Sal a ginger ale from the cooler, and one for myself. Vincenzo had squirted hot sausage juice into his eye and rocked back and forth with his hand over it, cursing.

"You okay?" I asked.

"Fucking sausage. Of all things. Why did it have to happen to me?"

"What, you wanted it happened to me?"

"You won't need more pain, Mr. Lobster."

My mother said, "Bobby, you're burned. Put cream on. Look at him, he's burned."

"She's right," Vincenzo said, pressing a wet cloth to his eye, "get some cream on that skin or you'll be crying like a little girl."

"Like you were just now?" I shut my eyes. The sun was strong. Yellow balls spun; then black ones.

There was a loud crash, then shouting. People moving. I squinted in the glaring light. A commotion arose at the Fanelli's. People drew away from the scene both horrified and amused. Luigi stood there with his fists cocked, chest heaving. Connie stood beside him. Their father lay on the ground. His eyes were closed. Luigi looked over at me. Connie looked at Luigi.

"What happened?" asked Vincenzo.

"Don't stare," I said. "I think Luigi clocked his old man."

"No shit—he's not getting up."

"Quit staring. That's what I call good family relations."

Eventually they revived the patriarch with splashes of water, and when he staggered to his feet he seemed to have no recollection of being cold-cocked by his son, and without wasting a moment wiped the blood from his nose and called for the green wine jug, which one of the women happily gave him. He drank from it, then backhanded his lips and the blood still dribbling from his nose.

The sun started setting and I had to get back by seven-thirty if I wanted to be on time for work. Luciano had been busting everybody's chops about lateness. As it was turning into a beautiful evening I felt bad having to drag everyone back with me, but Vincenzo offered to drive me home and then return for the others. With that, I said goodbye to everyone and we departed.

"Pick it up, Vin. I'm gonna be late." Vincenzo glanced at me.

"You're gonna be in a world of pain, Bobby."

"Not you?"

He bared his teeth. "I don't have to wear a suit tonight."

At home I showered and lathered cold cream on my sunburned skin. I had a nice glow on, notwithstanding the pain. What's a little pain when you think you look good?

I hustled to work and arrived just before eight. There was no lineup. Sunday evenings were slow, though now and then a crowd could spring up by surprise.

Fernandez and Buzzsaw stood outside, flipping coins and yawning. New York, New York was closed on Sundays, but a black Cadillac pulled up to its front doors and deposited Octavio and two tall creepy guys in silver suits, who walked up to the entrance and let themselves in. Maybe a Sunday-night poker game. Or a ménage à trois.

Felicia bristled when I said hello to her, but a few minutes later when I saw her horse-laughing at one of Albert the cop's lascivious quips—he was riding solo that evening, Lloyd off sick with a migraine—I resented her for playing the role of the injured party with license to be antipathetic. She could turn it on and off at will. But that was okay. That laugh did not endear her to me—gummy, unrestrained—and to all appearances our thing had run its course.

At the back, Jerome nibbled sunflower seeds, spitting the shells into a cocktail glass, now and then smiling at a private consideration.

"What's up, big man?"

"Not too much, Bobby. It's a quiet Sunday night in summer. Just how I like it. You look robust, relaxed, a bit tender around the nose."

"Just don't clap my back and we won't have any problems."

"You bet, boss," Jerome bellowed. "You bet."

Caesar on the other hand seemed saddled, his movements herky-jerky, his power of articulation clogged. Someone pounded on the back door. Caesar raised the safety bar, setting off the alarm, and shouted hoarsely until the knocker took off down the alley. Then he replaced the safety bar and returned to his Benzedrine-brown study.

I moved past the service bar where Paula the Wolf, hands on knees, barked out orders to a red-faced Carol Fox, and Ali the busboy violently stacked glasses from the dishwasher. I passed Roy Rosati in a cowboy hat and what can only be described as a Nudie jumpsuit, studded with rhinestones, talking to a girl with thick eyebrows and braces on her teeth. He caught my eye and turned a finger in a cheek. To each his own, I thought, sticking up my thumbs.

Vic Zuccheroni stood by a pillar and staring at the empty dance floor. When he saw me he clapped his hands in pantomimed applause, then continued staring.

A lantern-jawed girl with foamy black hair held her arm straight out from her broad shoulder. I wondered if she wanted to shake my hand or arm-wrestle me. Beneath her corded neck, her massive deltoids stretched the fabric of her yellow print dress. Lines heavily drawn around her eyes, and glittery shadow, suggested mischief, danger, perversion. The tiny silver swords swinging from her earlobes reinforced this impression. She pulled back her hand and laughed deeply, her pectorals rising and falling.

"Sorry if I alarmed you," she said. "I was admiring your body, I mean your physique."

"And I was admiring yours," I said, glancing at her teardrop quadriceps and her epic red stilettos. "You must work out."

"I'm a bodybuilder. Placed second in Miss Ontario last year."

"Congratulations. That's impressive."

"Thanks, I'm pretty proud, but I plan to win the next one. Do you compete?"

"Uh, no. I'm a football player." I spotted Demarco, sipping orange juice by the washrooms. "But my friend over there, the big guy, he's seriously into bodybuilding. He wants to compete eventually. Think you two would have a lot to talk about. Go introduce yourself. Tell him Bobby sent you. His name's Demarco."

"I'm Pamela. Nice to meet you, Bobby. Are you sure he won't mind?"

"Nah, it's a slow night, he's bored out of his mind, look at him. He'd welcome the company of a well-built woman."

She walked over to Demarco, calf muscles rippling, buttocks quivering, and to my mild surprise his eyes lit up and he shook her hand and began asking her questions and answering hers with keen bobs of his head and manly gulps of laughter. I felt like Yente the matchmaker.

I lumbered to the front doors where Fernandez and Buzzsaw, seated on two stools with another stool between them, played backgammon to pass the time. There was no lineup. Luciano appeared in a turquoise gabardine suit and told us to close at midnight if it didn't pick up.

"Where you going all dressed up like that?" I asked.

"To see my mistress," he said. "Got a problem *with* that."

The evening didn't pick up and we closed the club at midnight. Felicia approached me as I headed out to my car and told me she didn't want to see me anymore. I told her that was fine, for the best, things were getting weird, but then her chin trembled and she burst into tears.

"Why are you crying?" I asked her.

"I'm sad about this, aren't you?"

"But *you* said you don't want to see me anymore. How does that make you sad?"

"Because. You wouldn't understand. Will you drive me home?"

"Felicia, why don't you get Caesar to drive you? I'm sunburned and beat and don't feel like arguing about anything or talking about anything. I just want to go home and sleep."

"Then go home and sleep," she said.

SEVEN

Next morning, I pulled into the driveway of Rocco's place on Nash Road shortly after ten. Warm, dull, sulfurous: Canada Day long weekend and the city was flagged and chlorotic. Rocco's German shepherd Max came to the driver's door, tail wagging as I climbed out. He sniffed my hand; I scratched behind his ear. Max was getting old, rump descending, coat losing lustre. It happens. I walked to the garage. Max followed a few paces behind, nose to the ground. Rocco was a cousin on my father's side. A certified mechanic, he worked for a Speedy Muffler franchise, but did small jobs at his home. He popped his head out from under the hood of a nondescript green Dodge Polara, showed his grease-streaked face, and waved.

"Bobby and the 327," he said, wiping his hands with a rag. "Come here and let me show you a real power train."

A strong smell of petroleum filled the dark and disordered garage. A calendar pinned to a corkboard over the tool station featured a topless redhead for the month of July with nipples like fingers. I stepped up to the Polara and looked inside the engine compartment. The mammoth cylinder heads took me aback. Rocco smiled.

"Is that what I think it is, Rock?"

"Yes sir. 426 Hemi. The real thing."

"What a sleeper."

"Looks like a family sedan till you peek under the hood."

"Had no idea these boats came with Hemis."

"Trying to convince the owner to sell it to me. But he knows what he's got. He knows. What can I do for you today, Bobby?"

"It's been running rough all week. Got a minute to check it out?"

"Yeah, sure. Let's have a look."

He opened the hood and told me to start the engine. It hesitated, then sputtered and kicked in. He gestured for me to gas it. The engine roared to life. Max growled and barked. I kept the gas pedal down. Rocco disappeared under the hood and emerged after a minute, stroking a finger across his throat. I killed the engine and got out.

"Think it's your plugs."

"You replaced them when I took it off the blocks."

"I know. But these 327s are tough on plugs and points. Let's test them."

He fetched a few tools, a spark-plug tester, and went to work.

Max followed me to the Polara, nudging my knee and looking up with his gold-dust eyes. I reached down, scratched his rough head, and this seemed to please him. I wanted a better look at the sleepy green monster. Had no idea these things came with fucking Hemis. A huge steering wheel, a column shifter, and a green vinyl bench seat contributed to the illusion of roomy domesticity. To all appearances, a vehicle made for the safe and comfortable transport of a large, bland family. But that Hemi under the hood pushed around 500 horses. That was stock, factory-powered, zero modifications.

Rocco called me over and told me two spark plugs failed to fire. He'd replace them in a jiffy. His close-set eyes always seemed to verge on tears. As long as I could remember he'd never looked happy, though I don't think he was unhappy.

After his parents, my father's aunt Maria and uncle Ignazio—he of the boarding house—passed away a few years back, mere weeks apart, he stayed on in the bungalow and did his thing with cars, fixing, restoring, and souping them up. He worked on a '67

Mustang GT for years before he finally took it to car shows and won a few trophies, and then sold it to a guy from Detroit for a bundle. His next project was a cream-coloured '66 T-Bird and he fixed that up, won more trophies, and sold it for another wad. Now he was fixing up a '65 Corvette Stingray that had been in the paint shop getting decked out in metallic gold and gold-flecked black. He thought it would be more beautiful and profitable than the other two. He'd been engaged once—to a girl from Winona with big boobs and a harelip who dumped him for a biker—but after that fell through he never took up with anyone else for any length of time.

He replaced the plugs, did a final point check, and told me to start the car. The engine turned over once and smoothly engaged.

"That's better," I said. "What do I owe you, Rock?"

"A sawbuck's good enough, I barely did anything."

Max barked again as a dark blue Lincoln pulled up. It took a moment for the driver and passenger to crystallize. When they did my heart turned. Eugene sat at the steering wheel, and beside him, with his elbow out the window, leaned a pasty-faced Terry Peters.

"Friends of yours?" I said.

Rocco mumbled to himself and started for the Lincoln. Max kept barking, his tail straight out, ears flat. Rocco tried to shoo him away but Max wouldn't budge and kept barking. He grabbed the dog by the collar, pulled him past the garage and chained him by the fence surrounding the lawn. Max whined and whimpered, then fell quiet.

Eugene climbed out of the car with a cigarette in his teeth. Though I'd seen him countless times, his shortness always took me by surprise. His small dark head just reached my chest. He pinched the creases of his cream-coloured high-waists, smoothed the sleeves of his billowy black shirt, and flicked away the half-smoked cigarette. Peters stayed in the car, staring out with his cross, screwy eyes.

"Hey, Rocco," Eugene said, "I got a problem."

"I told you it might be the timing chain. And I can't do it here, Eugene, not on the Lincoln. You'll have to take it into a proper garage."

"No, no." Eugene gave me a sidelong look. "The car's running fine. Smooth as butter. Whatever you did, you did good. I always tell everybody that Rocco Sferazza's the best mechanic on Nash Road." He bared his small yellow teeth, but it wasn't a smile. "No, I need to have a word with this big guy here."

"With Bobby?" Rocco said, puzzled.

"Yeah, Bob-by," Eugene said with some kind of European emphasis. "I need a word with Bob-by."

"I'm right here," I said. "Talk."

"That's my cousin, Eugene," Rocco said. "Why are you bothering him? And why are you coming here to do it?"

"Take it easy, Rocco. No offense. Your cousin here has stepped on a few toes. People are steamed. I want to hear his side of the story. And, uh, there's another thing I need to talk to him about. Keeping it all in the family, so to speak. Let's walk and talk, Bob-by. Don't mind Terry, we're okay for now."

We walked out to the sidewalk and down the street, past a series of small brick bungalows, each one slightly different than the other. Eugene lit a fresh cigarette.

"Bob-by, you've pissed off a few of my boys."

"Is that right?"

"Oh yeah. They wanted to take care of it right away. They know where you work, where you live. But Oscar, ha. If not for Oscar…"

I stopped walking and took full measure of Eugene. His manner reminded me of a vicious possum. My stomach fluttered and my muscles tingled. I played with the idea of dropping him right there: a crunching right hook to the jaw as he opened his mouth to spout more pseudo-wise-guy nonsense, or a forearm shiver to the throat, all 230 pounds of me. Sensing my building excitement, Eugene glanced toward the Lincoln and Peters.

Max started barking again. When Peters, garbed in an Eastern Block red sweatsuit, climbed out of the Lincoln, Rocco walked up to him waving his hands and chattering. Eugene smiled at me and sucked on his cigarette. He knew that I wanted to talk to him about Joey, not about his members' union beefs.

"Eugene. I don't care what you and your boys do in this shit-hole. I'm out of here end of the summer. But I'm not going to let the likes of Peters or Mad Dog or anyone else push me, my friends—or my brother—around."

"Oh yeah," Eugene said from the side of his mouth. "I almost forgot about that. Stupid Dip, fucking with a beast like you? These guys. He's at St. Joseph's Hospital anyway, the Dip."

"You finished what I started."

"You could say that. Pauly got off lighter, heh-heh. I need him around now that your brother's on the bench. Little Joey. How's he doing? He's decided against a life of crime, eh? But, like his two pals, he's on the hook for some property of mine that went missing."

"I doubt he had anything to do with it. Not his style. What's missing, anyway?"

"Bobby, you're asking the wrong question. Doesn't matter what it was."

"I don't need this shit, Eugene. We can go to war but what would be the point? Let's be reasonable. You have your thing to do, I have mine. What if I made it good? What if I paid you whatever it's worth, within reason?"

Eugene pulled on his cigarette and looked over at Peters, who stood by the Lincoln with his hands flat on the trunk, his head tilted up to watch a passing airplane. Rocco stood beside him, red-faced, talking his ear off.

"The package had bennies," Eugene said. "Black beauties, robins' eggs, yellow jackets, pink hearts. The whole fucking rainbow. High-grade. No joke. I get five bucks a pop for them. There were about 1,200. Figure it out, professor."

"I can't come up with that kind of cash. Besides, Joey shouldn't be on the hook for the whole wad. What if I came up with his end?"

"What do you mean, his end? Someone's gotta come up with *all* the money."

"Yeah, well I'm not paying Pauly and Dip's end. Let's be fair about this. I'll give you two grand. And I need a week or so to come up with it."

As Eugene considered the offer, he glanced at Peters, who climbed back into the Lincoln. Rocco walked over to Max, who had not stopped barking. He silenced him with a cuff. Eugene stuck out his small thick hand. I shook it.

"One week. Two grand in cash and your brother's off the hook."

"If anything happens to him..."

"Keep your own head up, Bobby, is my advice. I can't always control what my boys do. In fact, I have very little fucking control—a problem. And just so you know, I'm weeding out the weaklings, the freelancers, the pigtails. A major housecleaning is under way, but that won't happen overnight."

"You're a man with a plan."

He tapped his temple. "It's all here, buddy." Then he raised his fists. "And here."

Eugene followed me back to Rocco's. Peters sat in the Lincoln with an Eastern dissident's sour expression. I apologized to Rocco and he said not to worry; he was sorry these assholes bothered me at his house. Eugene climbed into the Lincoln and backed out of the driveway, tooting the horn once before speeding off.

"Anything to do with Joey?" Rocco asked. "Eugene mentioned him a while back, asked if I was related. I told him we were cousins but that's as far as the conversation went. I didn't tell you because I thought nothing of it."

"Don't worry about it, Rock. Everything's fine now. And thanks for the fix."

"Anytime, Bobby. Say hi to your mother for me."

"Will do."

He held Rex's chest as I backed out of the driveway.

The new plugs made a huge difference. I floored it down Nash

Road and the engine growled like a tiger. Turned east on Queenston and caught green lights all the way to Stoney Creek. After Grays Road a white 1972 Trans-Am with blue trim cruised up beside me, 455 HO engine. Very rare. No ugly hood bird as with later models. This, the original animal: 400 factory horses. The lucky driver wore gold-framed aviator shades and sported bushy muttonchops. Confident, carefree, maybe high on cocaine. Good for him, I thought as I held up my hand. He responded by gunning his engine and squawking ahead of me. Had he pulled over I would have shown him a close-up of my hand.

On South Service Road I hit the pedal hard and the four-barrel kicked in—pushed me back in my seat and made my cheeks flap. The tachometer nearly redlined. Baby. Eased off the gas and coasted to Fifty Road, where I exited and looped back to Highway 8. My head throbbed. The reality of dealing with a scumbag sociopath sank in. I wasn't sure I'd follow through, even though I shook his hand. Does shaking hands with a pile of shit count? At the time it seemed, short of violence, like the best solution, but not one I relished.

Where was I going to get two grand? I needed to cover tuition and residence fees for the upcoming year—my government loan wasn't due till late August. I only had about a grand at my disposal, and dared not hit my mother for money; she'd ask too many questions. I considered asking one of my uncles, or my cousin Vincenzo—he was my best bet, but still, it would be difficult. I'd have to do more explaining than I desired. Selling the Camaro crossed my mind. What a heartbreak that would be. But I'd get over it. It wasn't my dream car anyway. A 1969 Camaro Z/28, with a 302 engine. That was my dream car. I glanced at my watch: late again. I was in for a reaming but headed downtown in no rush.

I waited in the car for a few minutes before I went up to Nancy's place, almost changing my mind several times. I sensed a coming heaviness, a dark film edging my aura, an excess of chattering, sighing, sulks and painful silences, and tears, dreaded tears, and this killed whatever buzz I felt about us.

She answered the door in a red silk kimono patterned with white characters, crossed her arms on her chest, and after a brief hesitation showed me in. Her hands were very red, as though she had dipped them in bleach.

"Didn't think you'd show up," she said. "In fact, I had written you off."

"I said I'd come."

The curtains in the flat were drawn. An incense stick burned in a red clay holder on the coffee table, releasing a musky smoke that burned my nostrils.

"You don't always keep your word. Not one of your strengths."

"I know. I deserve a whipping, at the very least. It'll take the whip for me to learn how to be a gentleman—to develop character, you know."

Her cheeks were flushed, her eyes soft.

"You're talking too much," she said.

"Just stating my case, your honour."

My hand fell on her hip and I pulled her close. I kissed her mouth, brushed my lips down her neck, kissed her collarbone, loosened the kimono, and kissed between her breasts. I brushed my lips over her nipples and they stiffened. She smelled soft, powdery. She stroked my hair and my scalp tingled. She kissed my throat, my lips. Then she grabbed my wrists and stepped backward, toward the bedroom.

When the back of her legs touched the bed, she let the kimono slip off.

Later, she offered me lemonade she'd made herself, in a frosted glass, with bits of pulp floating around in it and a few pips. I gripped the glass and brought it close to my face. It smelled refreshing. Nancy leaned forward, waiting for me to taste her concoction with the expectancy of a poisoner. When I took a sip and found it sour I said nothing, but she must have misinterpreted my pinched face as a more personal expression than it was, perhaps reflecting how I felt about being there, about her, about life in general. One should never walk through life sucking lemons.

"We don't really do much other than this..."

"Between working, working out, and family obligations, I hardly have time to eat. And you're at the Street Scene five or six nights a week." I swirled the lemonade in the glass. "This is exactly what we ran up against last summer, Nancy. Remember? You can't expect a normal relationship. It's unrealistic."

"It is," she said. "It's unrealistic. And picking it up again after last summer wasn't the smartest thing in the world. I should have known better—I did know better—but it's done. And here we are. And it's okay. It's fine. I can take it for what it is. Still, I have to be honest with you, Bobby, and with myself. As much as I like being with you, I need more."

"Yeah. I won't argue with that."

"Where does that leave us?"

"I don't know, Nancy. I don't know how to answer that."

She sighed. "I think we should cool it for now."

I sipped the lemonade.

So that was it? I didn't think so, as I left Nancy's place. This story isn't over yet, I said to myself, but that may have been my ego yapping, drowning out a tiny voice of reason in a corner of my mind stating otherwise. Except for a few kicks, she had nothing to gain from this liaison, not a damn thing. I wasn't vain enough to think that beyond our physical chemistry I had anything emotionally, intellectually, or financially to offer her. Had I been truthful to her and to myself, I would have admitted that all I wanted was kicks. And that depressed me.

I went to work that evening in a sour mood. I wanted to lose myself. Buzzsaw fed me yellow-jackets and black beauties, the latest in the benny line, and buzzy, very buzzy. I got so wired, so manic, I felt like Don Knotts. And I had trouble peeing; I kept going to the washroom and coming up empty. Dead-salamander syndrome reprised.

At the front doors Demarco asked me why I missed our workout and in a run-on white-tongued barrage I summarized the story for him.

"Tell me I'm wrong," he said, "but you're saddened by this."

"Don't know how I feel. I thought it was just about sex, but I may have been wrong."

"It's never just about sex. You should know that by now. Maybe you do. But I'm glad she took a stand before she lost her dignity. And before your dick fell off."

Demarco wasn't taking me seriously. Perhaps I didn't deserve to be taken seriously, but it's hard to move ahead when you're viewed as a kind of joke.

"This lineup goes around the block," announced Vic Zuccheroni, stepping between Demarco and me in a creamy three-piece suit with a black shirt and a black pouf in the breast pocket. "It goes around the fucking block."

"No one went to the cottage this weekend," Demarco concluded.

"You are sapient," I said.

Vic lit a cigarette, puckering his thick lips around the filter. His high forehead sagged with furrows; numerous scars and nicks framed his eyes. The tiger eye of his pinkie ring blinked. And I don't know if he was talking to me or waxing nostalgic but he went on and on like this:

"When I was your age I used to get into punch-ups every day. Every freaking day some bigmouth or wise guy would break my balls or get smart with me and I'd have to go to work..."

"Shut the hell up," Demarco said.

But Vic wasn't finished. He kept motoring that mouth of his, beatings this, knifings that, pow pow pow, the entire cosmos nothing but a glorious old-school donnybrook.

"Hey, Vic," I said, "whatever happened to your cousin, Roger?"

Vic stopped yammering long enough to ponder my question. "He's in Sicily, where else? He caught herpes in Niagara Falls and said he's never coming back."

After a knock I checked the peephole: Lenny Hutton and a female friend. I opened the door. The lineup groaned. What did they want? I was an instrument, a cipher. How they fit into the big picture didn't concern me, nor how they suffered, with no one to blame but themselves for their pain. Across the street New York, New York bubbled over—folks from Mississauga, Toronto, Woodbridge, Richmond Hill, and Pickering thronged there on weekends, an oddity I couldn't fathom, people driving from those places to the Hammer for kicks. Lenny reached into the pocket of his blue-and-white-striped shirt, pulled out a twenty, and slipped it to me with a wink. It felt warm, and greasy. The girl, in a lustrous blue dress, looked familiar.

"Buddy, this is Marilyn," he said.

"Marilyn," I said extending my hand. There was a night at Banisters.

"I know you," she said, squinting her close-set hazel eyes and pointing a long scarlet fingernail. "Mm. Maybe not."

Without further ceremony Lenny locked her arm and they entered the club. She looked back and smiled. I remembered she had a dog, a two-hundred-pound Neapolitan mastiff with a head like a lion. I wondered if he was still around. I reached into my pocket, pulled out Lenny's greasy twenty, and asked Demarco if he could break it. He scratched himself and produced two clean tens, then made a face at Vic Zuccheroni, who continued gibbering.

"...you guys have it easy. Look at you, two big chooches. You don't even know how to stand properly. Like two punching clowns. Just begging for a beating. You're an embarrassment. Back in the day I used to eat bimbos like you for lunch. Bobby, you think you can take me?"

"Take you where, Vic? To the sanitarium?"

"Don't be smart with me." He made fists and held them under his chin. "You wanna be smart with me. Come on, buddy. Right now. Let's do this thing."

Demarco stepped back as Vic began bobbing and weaving, bending at the waist, flinging lefts and rights into the air. He shuffled, sniffed, thumbed his nose—left right, left right. Sweat erupted on his temples. He stopped his feet and dropped his arms, winded.

"See...what I'm talking...about?" he gasped. "I can still go, man. I can still go. Just say the word and we go like tigers. Like tigers. I'll rip you up. I'll chunk you up, boy. Believe it."

He turned around and limped into the club, head sweaty, pants sagging. I glanced at Demarco and nudged him to shut his open mouth.

"You should choose your friends more wisely," he said.

I stared at him until he understood how much to heart I took his statement.

"You're a prick," he said.

Just as "Funky Town" came on and the dance floor convulsed, the disco cops knocked on the door. Lloyd's green eyes gazed at me placidly, his jumbo ears trembling. Albert's bandaged left eyebrow evidenced the work of a jealous husband, an outraged father, or a brother with other issues. The cold sore on his upper lip had its own sordid history. Not his usual affable self, Albert flashed his baton, slapped it against his palm, and said the place looked overcrowded. I showed him the counter. He pushed it aside and told me to stick it in a hairy place.

"We'd better check it out," he said to Lloyd in his cop voice. He touched his cap and entered the club with Lloyd so close behind him he could have piggybacked a ride.

"What do you think happened to Albert?" I asked Demarco.

"Hm. Maybe he cut himself blowing Lloyd."

The cops kept their visit brief. After they left, two bantamweights in sharkskin suits and skinny ties started scrapping and we let them go until their arms wearied. Everyone enjoyed the spat, even the combatants, whose natures were so sanguine we agreed to let them stay in the club if they promised to behave, which they did. Buzzsaw and Jerome relieved Demarco and me at midnight. The club was seething. I was seething. "Born To Be Alive" pounded from the speakers and everyone raised their arms over their heads, shouting something I couldn't make out, a local catchphrase, a sporty chant. I listened with my eyes clamped shut, mustering all the focus I could, but never did decipher what they were saying.

Strange for me but clearly good for them, judging from their twisted faces: a release. I needed one, too. I felt pinpricks all over my body, and my heart was thumping. I turned left, turned right, dodging patrons rushing to and from the dance floor. Then Felicia assailed me at the service bar.

"We need to talk," she said, her nostrils gaping like hot black eyes.

"Now?" I said.

"After work."

Talk. I didn't want to talk. I was in no frame of mind to talk. It would involve analysis, recriminations, excuses, and lies. Storytelling.

I moved to the back. Rick Zilli, a Ticat linebacker, with an Alabama pedigree, stood by a pillar with his thick neck and flattened face, smooth-talking pretty Sue Allen, Eugene Ciccone's ex-squeeze. Zilli had no idea what he was messing with there, not that it should have mattered, but it did. Too many things were going on that shouldn't have mattered, but did.

I moved on, taking elbows and hip-checks, countering with my own blows, blunt and unforgiving. Under my airless jacket, armpits frothed, rayon stuck to skin, organs and abdomen swelled. But I kept moving, ducking, weaving. The strobe lights flickered on, the music throbbed, but I kept moving until Demarco, palm to sternum, stopped me.

"What's the matter with you? You're pacing around like a psycho." He shook my shoulder. "Listen, Ricky Tartaglia, Mad Dog and John the Greek are here, maybe a few others."

"We should do them," I said, gritting my teeth.

"You've been doing too many bennies."

"Tonight's the night, my friend."

Before Demarco could tell me to cool it, Luciano appeared with next week's schedules, batting his dirty eyelids. He reeked of booze and body odour. Burst blood vessels webbed the sides of his nose. A zit on his forehead glared at me with cyclopean intensity. His pinstriped suit looked slept in, the seams lost, the shirt collar soiled. He was wearing no socks.

"Bobby, anything *ugly* tonight?"

I knew what I wanted to say, what I yearned to say. But I said, "Not yet."

He stared at me closely, as if checking my eyes for signs of intoxication or derangement. He wanted to know Buzzsaw's whereabouts. I told him I had no idea where he was.

"If you see that prick, tell *him* I'm looking for *him*. And what's wrong with you?"

"Allergies."

"Allergies my ass. *Don't* be tricky with me, Bobby. Not with me. I'm dealing with sharks these days. I don't need to deal with a tricky fucked-up doorman. Are *you* fucked up?"

"I'm not fucked up, Luciano. It's smoky in here. It's hot."

"Hell is hot," he said. He handed me my schedule and moved away scratching his ass, scratching his bald spot, then glancing over his shoulder one last time.

Nauseated and pasty-mouthed I went to the washroom to freshen up and there ran into a dog-eyed Caesar complaining of a headache. His sparring partner had tattooed him, he explained, and asked if I had an aspirin. I burst out laughing. Of all the pills he could request. He took offense and left the washroom grumbling.

I walked to a stall, kicked it open, and kneeled down before a toilet bowl as if to pray, not caring how filthy it was. I opened up. Everything came out in a single hot blast, no second acts or dry heaves. It was a one-shot deal. And as rotten as my mouth tasted, I felt disencumbered, euphoric, effervescent. I rose to my feet, cleaned my knees with toilet paper, and then went to the sink to wash my hands. I rinsed my mouth and splashed water on my face. I felt much better after this and rejoined the action in progress.

Nancy showed up near closing time with bloodshot eyes and smudged mascara. She'd been drinking. She grabbed my arm and squeezed it so hard I had to pull it away from her with some force. When I asked her for an explanation she spoke of another brawl at the Street Scene. This time Westmount boys destroyed the place—shut down till further notice by police—and clobbered some patrons, none Barton-Sherman. She was scared.

"Will you come home with me?" she asked.

Aware of being watched, I froze and said nothing.

At the service bar Felicia's face went through several stages of contortion. Her chest heaved. She was about to initiate something ugly, and memorable, I knew it, but I wanted distance from her plan, from its execution, its drama. Bugs crawled over my head and down my spine. I had to move. Nancy grabbed my hands in hers, shouting obscenities, but I broke away and tried to locate Demarco, simply to give myself a diversion.

Nancy followed me on foot, Felicia with hot eyes. No hiding in this fishbowl, no skirting hormonal issues, that is to say matters of the heart, unless I went back into the washroom, into the safe house of a stall, and plunged my head in a toilet.

In time I found Demarco in the back engaging a bloated guy in a tomato-coloured turtleneck with salted armpits: Jimmy Lewis. Nancy chattered away behind me. I don't know what she was saying, nothing good about my character I suppose. Did I feel like being diminished? I did not. Therefore I did not *try* to understand her. Seeing my raised arms, Demarco interrupted Jimmy Lewis and started for me.

"What is it?" Demarco asked, concerned.

"I'm being persecuted."

But Nancy had vanished and Demarco looked at me quizzically until Felicia appeared at my side like a jagged ice sculpture. Then he smiled and turned his shoulders, showing me how much he cared about my female issues. I'd read that you can stop a bad dream by looking at your hands, but looking at my hands at that moment stopped nothing. It all came at me like a well-blocked screen pass. No question of making a play. All you can do is close your eyes and sacrifice the body.

"We need to talk," Felicia insisted.

Need, such a difficult word, such an onerous concept. "I know,

I know," I said without meaning it, for how could I talk when I did not want to talk, or was incapable of it?

As if sensing my need for a lifesaver, Vic Zuccheroni seized my arm and yanked me away from Felicia, Demarco, and the rest of that imbroglio.

"Soft-man," he said. "Let's do it, let's rumba, you and me."

"Not now, Vic."

"Are you backing down? S'that what you're saying?"

I looked at him with both astonishment and admiration. No, I wasn't going to punch him out. It would have given me little satisfaction. But I admired his pluck. It took pluck to make the world go around. We didn't have enough of it. I reached out my hand to shake his and when he put his hand in mine I squeezed. I squeezed until I felt his hand bones crunching together.

I heard Nancy calling me, and Felicia calling me, and Demarco shouting, "Bobby! Bobby! Let go! Let go!" but I wouldn't let go of the hand.

Then, when I saw Ricky Tartaglia vault over the rail to the dance floor and impose himself between a petite brunette and her statuesque boyfriend, I let go.

Ricky rocked from side to side in a sort of jolly jig, thrusting his pelvis against the girl. She wriggled behind her man, but Ricky persisted, coming at her again with clutchy hands. Finally, the boyfriend snapped out of his coma, grabbed Ricky under the armpits, and tossed him over the railing with such ease and perfection the feat looked rehearsed, performed by stuntmen from a movie set, or professional wrestlers. And that was that.

Bending at the knees and clenching my fists, I waited for others to come running, hell-bent on revenge, a natural upshot, but wait as I would no one came.

The big guy and his girl recommenced dancing, elbows drawn, faces cool. Ricky was flat on his back somewhere, seeing stars, the crowd flowing by him, his pals none the wiser.

"Bobby," said Felicia, "I'm talking to you, Bobby."

It made me hate that name to hear it. It made me hate this Bobby creature.

Vic cradled the crushed hand to his chest with an anguished expression, his eyes moist. I felt terrible about that and about Felicia and Nancy, and I owed them all apologies; but I was waiting for a consequence to what I had witnessed on the dance floor, a reaction to the action, some closure, and at that moment they were far from my thoughts: Vic, Nancy, Felicia.

And what about this thing? This event I had witnessed? Had everyone else missed it?

My neck knotted up. I gulped several times as though trying to swallow something stuck in my throat. Everything was off. Everyone looked blotchy, fraudulent. They belonged somewhere else. Who were they? How did they get here? My eyes were playing tricks on me: what was not happening. It felt so wrong. I seized Felicia's hands and she fell quiet. She sensed it, too.

Then, after a moment, Mad Dog charged the dance floor from one direction, John the Greek from the other, and normalcy was restored.

EIGHT

A few days later I tried to call Felicia but got no answer. I felt bad, though perhaps not as bad as I should have felt. Self-pity doesn't count, indeed is distasteful, the sign of a truly polluted soul. What a fucked-up situation I found myself in. I should have admitted my dog status and backed out of everything. I had nothing to gain, nor did they. Still, I thought I'd drive over to Felicia's place with flowers as a token of apology, or thoughtfulness, and leave them at her door even if she wasn't home, perhaps hoping she wasn't.

The big Victorian house was on Jackson Street just under the escarpment; a private entrance in back led up to her attic flat. A humid morning, by the time I climbed the four steep flights of the clanging metal staircase, and knocked on the door, sweat was beading on my forearms. I heard movement inside and knocked again but still no one answered. I peered through the window and saw Satan sitting in the alcove licking a paw. No sign of Felicia. I waited a second, then left the flowers at her door and descended the stairs on my heels.

I decided to drop by Oscar's house and have a chat with him. Joey was still in the dark about my arrangement with Eugene—and it weighed on me. Handing over two grand to an operator like him felt so wrong. I drove down to Oscar's house on Holton Avenue, where we had played many an all-night poker game in high school. He lived with his widowed mother who worked graveyard shifts cleaning offices. She answered the door.

"Roberto," she said, crinkling her black eyes. "It has been so long. Come in, come in."

"Mrs. Flores, how are you?"

"I am fine. I have not seen you for years, Roberto." She had a wooden rosary wound around one hand, the dark fingers of the other hand rubbing the beads; save for streaks of silver in her hair she had not changed. "Come in and let me call Oscar. I think he has finished showering. He tells me you are studying at the university."

"Yes, in Toronto."

"Ah, that is nice. Your mother must be so proud."

She led me through a stifling narrow hall into a damask-wallpapered living room cluttered with French provincial furniture, brass lamps, and football trophies. On the mantlepiece, a votary candle softly burned beside a photograph of a mustachioed military man: Oscar's father. He had died in Argentina before the family came to Canada. Next to him were framed photographs of smiling dark-haired children. Oscar had two older sisters, both married, who lived in Stoney Creek, where they ran a hair salon. I used to have a crush on his sister Yvonne, a dead ringer for Natalie Wood, who would come to our football games with the pencil-necked geek she wound up marrying not long out of high school. Oscar used to flip out when I told him his sister was hot. Mrs. Flores gestured me toward a brown divan that gave not an inch when I sat on it and felt like a dead animal under my ass.

Mrs. Flores opened the drawer of a small walnut side table against the wall and removed from it a yellow envelope. She shuffled into the kitchen, called Oscar's name, and then returned to the living room opening the envelope. She slid out of it an eight-by-ten photograph, took a quick look, and smiled.

"I want to show you something, Roberto. It will bring back memories."

It was a black and white photograph of Oscar and me in shoulder pads, taken after a game during our championship season in which he returned two punts for touchdowns, the second one so dazzling, so audacious, and so beautiful I remember getting a lump in my throat. I wasn't the only one. Oscar could do that. The photograph, which shows us holding each other around the neck with toothy grins, appeared in the *Hamilton Spectator*. I don't recall exactly what the article said, something about the rock 'em sock em twosome from Cathedral High. Striking how much Oscar had changed since then. Except for that gold tooth, conspicuously glinting even in black and white, he looked nothing like his younger self. It never crossed my mind, then, to wonder how much I looked like my younger self.

"Time passes," Mrs. Flores said.

"Yes it does. Thank you for showing me this."

"You can keep it. I have copies. I always meant to give it to you."

She slid the photograph back into the yellow envelope and handed it to me.

Shortly Oscar came up in a white undershirt and grey sweats, his thick arms scarred and inked with generic jailhouse tats, his black hair wet from showering. When he saw me he hooted and clapped my shoulder.

"Bobby Doctor. What's going on, brother? When's the last time you were here, eh? Wanna play some Fiery Cross?"

"Oscar, I need to talk to you."

"Come in the kitchen, Bobby. Remember this kitchen, man? I'll get Mamma to cook up chorizo and peppers."

"I'm not hungry, Oscar."

He looked at me and nodded. "I'm surprised you didn't come earlier. Eugene was going to fuck up Joey. And I could do nothing about that. But other people wanted to see you get fucked up, too, and I said no way, man. Bobby is the goods."

"Enough with that shit, Oscar. I don't live in the past, don't have time for it. I made a deal with Eugene. Said I'd pay him two grand to clear my brother. I don't mind giving it up if it's legit. If my brother fucked up he's got to make good on it. But he's sixteen, can't rub two nickels together. How's he going to make good? So I'm on the hook for two large. Except I'm not shitting my pants, and I'm not handing over a dime if I think I'm being scammed."

"Have a seat, Bobby. Wha's that you have there?"

"A photograph your mother gave me."

"I know which one. I'm much better-looking than you in that one, ha."

The kitchen had undergone changes: veneered pine cupboards, limestone floors, and a black tile backsplash notable among them. A new wooden ceiling fan paddled above us. A few commemorative dishes had been added to the collection crowding the glass cabinet against the wall, one depicting Pope John Paul II. A Kenmore refrigerator had replaced the old convulsive, a source of amusement and anxiety during our poker games. But the blocky oak table that had served us so solidly back then still occupied the centre of the room.

Mrs. Flores entered and fired up the stove, setting on it a cast-iron skillet.

"So, Bobby, you don't believe Eugene?"

"Well, his gofers may have lost some package, but how do I know what was in it? Do you know what was in it, for sure?"

"If Eugene said it was this, it was this. If he said it was that, it was that."

"So he's a plain talker, in other words?"

"You're funny, Bobby. Ha. Two grand, eh? That's not a lot of money. Not really. I know you're in school and all, but your brother chose to get involved. If he can't pay, and you can't make it good, then who pays?" Oscar smiled. "That's the question you have to ask. I don't think Eugene is taking you for a ride. He jus' wants his money. He don't care if it comes from Joey, you, or the Pope over there." He nodded to the glass cabinet.

Mrs. Flores turned to me. "Will you eat with Oscar?"

The smell of frying peppers tickled my nose. "Thank you. I'd love to, but I have to get going. Next time."

"You are always welcome here, Roberto. It seems like yesterday you and Oscar were in school together."

"I know, Mrs. Flores."

"Those were nice times."

"You can't live in the past," Oscar said with a smile.

On that note, I left and drove home. Mrs. Flore's frying peppers had piqued my hunger. I made myself a provolone and pickled eggplant sandwich, with a link of hard sopressata, and devoured it under the pergola and its intertwining grapevines, which were thickening and turning a velvety pale green. In time they would yield blue grapes so tart as to be almost inedible.

My brother came out and joined me. He wanted to know what was going on.

"Nothing's going on, Joey. You're out of the woods. Don't let me hear about you doing scores with Dip and Pauly again or so help me God I'll cut your head off."

"You talked to Eugene?"

"Yeah. Actually, he talked to me. Tracked me down at Rocco's place."

"Are you fucking kidding me?"

"No. Anyway, he's dealt with Dip and Pauly for this missing package of his, and you, my friend, were next in line. I don't know what happened, and I don't want to know. But I'm going to pay him your end of what he lost and that'll be that."

He took this in, pursing his lips and nodding. But he seemed dissatisfied.

"What's the matter, Joey? You look confused."

"Not confused. Not confused at all. How much?"

"Two grand for your end."

"So he's saying he had about six grand worth of pills in the package?"

"That's right. Sound wrong?"

Joey said nothing.

My mother came out with my cousin Vincenzo.

"Look who's here," she said, giving us the skinny eyes.

Joey's face lit up. I struck a Roman salute.

Vincenzo saluted back. "So what are the brothers up to today?

A little heart-to-heart? A little bonding time. Nice. It brings a tear to my eye to see harmony in the family."

"What are you doing here, Icky?" I asked, observing his unshaven face and the egg yolk congealed on his shirt collar. He normally worked during weekdays as a tow motor operator at the Firestone plant.

"Took a sick day," he said. "I hate my job."

"Find another job," Joey said.

"Yeah, brain surgeon at St. Joseph's," he said, opening his hands. "But seriously, I don't have many options. I worked the coke ovens for six months and vowed never again."

My mother unrolled the garden hose and watered her tomatoes.

Vincenzo asked if I was still at the Press Club, he wanted to check it out one night.

"Yeah, I'm still there," I said. "Come down tonight. It'll be buzzing."

"Can I come, too?" Joey asked.

My mother must have heard because she gave him a spritz with the hose and shanked him with a look that told him this would never happen.

"In your dreams," I said. "If we got caught serving sixteen-year-olds we'd be closed down in a heartbeat. So come down, Vincenzo. You'll have a blast, meet some chicks."

"He needs a wife," said my mother. "Not some chicks. What is a chick?"

We laughed and left it at that.

That evening at the Press Club the air-conditioner malfunctioned. A repairman couldn't come till next day so Luciano informed us we had to suck it up. It's not as if the crowds stayed away. High summer; a little steam bothered no one. A good sweat was a good time. But I wasn't dealing with the sultriness as well as everyone else. My blood pressure must have been rocketing; my temples throbbed, my shoes squelched with sweat. I was short of breath and my stomach burned. I wasn't the only one. Demarco walked around with a dripping face that he shook off now and then like a tagged prizefighter. The waitresses and patrons looked drugged and moist, swaying languidly around the club, rocking from side to side, or suspended in place with blank, smeared expressions. Later a fight broke out in the men's washroom between two Portuguese guys in white linen suits and we had to dump the sweaty battlers in the alley where they continued scrapping among maggoty garbage bins, possibly over garment choice. That sapped the lot of us.

Buzzsaw and Caesar, bedraggled and red-eyed from heat exhaustion, waited like abused hounds to be switched off the front doors. Demarco and I were due up but dreading it with quiet passion. Everyone was in a rancid mood, touchy, bitchy, pitchy. Everything verged on anarchy, madness. Those standing in line had no idea how soupy and intense it was inside, how withering, but had they known it wouldn't have mattered. Few who entered willingly re-emerged. I tried to keep cool thinking cool thoughts—Arctic vistas, glaciers, snowy fields. Buzzsaw had served me four yellow jackets that had yet to kick in. I worried about what would happen when they did.

Fernandez appeared, his frizzy hair compounding like a palm tree. "Waddy and Billy Wilson are here," he said. "Luciano wants them out if they take their shirts off."

"Well, keep an eye on them," I said, smiling.

"Come on, Bobby. Don't do me like that."

Shirtless men held no interest for me so I moved on, bumping first into a nubile new waitress with a mournful expression who burst into tears, threw down her floppy hat, and stormed off, and then coming face to face with Vic Zuccheroni, who despite a bandaged hand, and painful memories, refused to reform his attitude. Dressed in a canary-yellow shirt with a thin black tie and bobbing his black-eyed head emphatically, he reminded me of a needy parrot.

"Bunch of pussies," he hissed, gulping gin and tonic. "That big prick Caesar wouldn't last two minutes with me, my word.

Two minutes. I'd break every single bone in his body. Every single bone. Tell me I wouldn't. Go on—tell me."

"Vic, shake my hand," I said.

"You—stay away from me, you. Freaking tricky bastard. Because of you I have to wipe my ass with my left hand, son of a bitch. I have to jerk off with my left hand! Yeah, smile. Someday I'll be smiling and you'll be wiping your ass with your left hand."

"Beat it, Vic." Engaging him did not interest me. After the final yes comes a no.

The yellow jackets started tickling the back of my neck, and mistaking this for insects, I slapped it. My heart galloped. Tiny blue and red sparks lit my thoughts. Someone called my name and I brayed like a jackass. Two black eyes blinked as I reared into a pair of tiger-striped twins, both purring and flicking their tails. Felicia glared at me from the service bar; I pirouetted and folded myself into the turbulent flow churning toward the dance floor as "Funky Town" pounded from the speakers. The drawback of drugs when courage and subtlety are needed.

Won't you take me to
Funkytown
Won't you take me to
Funkytown

Noting the wild surge, I veered away from the dance floor and sneaked over to the bar. I asked Carol Fox for a glass of water. She studied me for a long moment before acknowledging my request. The universe fell into place around her, yet she poured the water indifferently. I smiled, not at her but at the thought of her filling the glass of water for me and feeling so utterly indifferent about it. She had it all figured out. I thanked her for the water but she rolled her eyes and stabbed an ice bucket with a silver pick in response. I checked my Omega: almost midnight, I headed to the front door.

Gotta move on
Gotta move on
Gotta move on

Buzzsaw looked like a drowned russet beaver and Caesar's saturated black jacket released rivulets of briny ooze when he moved. Demarco arrived gripping a glass of tomato juice with wet fingers. I asked him for an update. He shook his head and shrugged. Buzzsaw asked about the yellow jackets. I told him they were fine, but I wanted to top up with black beauties. He tapped two black capsules out of a plastic vial and passed them to me with a secret handshake. I was about to down them when my grinning cousin Vincenzo made a sudden appearance, decked out in a green rayon shirt and high-waisted white pants with a white fabric belt.

"Pleasant surprise," I said, embracing him.

"Yes it is," he said, slapping my ribs. "Time to groove. Demarco, what's happening?"

"Looking pretty snazzy there, Vin," he said, briskly shaking his hand. "Got on your dancing threads."

Vincenzo's bare heels bulged from undersized blue leather clogs that he clopped to the beat of the music. "You know. Summer casual. I save my suits for the office."

"Still at Firestone?"

"You have the memory of an elephant, Demarco."

"Well, when you said *office*, Vin, come on."

"You're a regular *farmaiolo*."

"And you are obviously related to that other comic genius of the twentieth century, Bobby Sferazza. A nice applause for the funny cousins," he said clapping loudly.

Vincenzo started for the foyer steps. I'd need a word with him later. I was pressed. Eugene expected his two grand soon and I was still short a grand. Vincenzo was good for it, but he'd want to know why I needed it, and not accept any old song and dance.

Demarco opened the door for air. The crowd roared and leaned forward like a flagged field. Across the street a lovely herd milled under New York, New York's green canopy, restless in the sour heat, perfumed, coifed, bedewed. Not a Hamiltonian among them,

I wagered. A gold Mercedes eased up to the red-carpeted curb and two ponytailed dudes in pastel suits climbed out, followed by two sybaritic blondes in leather bustiers with atomic bombs for breasts. It was war.

I shut the door, downed the black beauties with my water, and took a few seconds to gather my thoughts. Demarco had unbelted his pants and was re-tucking his shirt with exaggerated swivels of his hips and violent finger-digs. Someone banged on the door and I opened. Two thick-necked guys, one head-and-shoulders taller than the other, in patterned polyester shirts and light flared pants, stood there smiling like aluminum-siding salesmen. Demarco quickly zippered up and with a look of disdain joined me.

"Bobby!" cried the shorter of the guys, thrusting his blunt hand forward.

It was Sam Miller and Johnny Hamm, two of my Varsity Blues teammates. I shook Sam's hand and exchanged a high five with Johnny.

"Sam, Johnny, what's up? Never thought I'd see the likes of you in Steeltown."

Sam's loud laughter sounded forced. With a sheepish look he explained that they were actually partying across the street at New York, New York with some lady friends, but knew I might be working here, so they popped by to say hello and see how I was doing.

"You're massive," Sam said. "Truly. I'll tell Coach Murphy when I see him."

"Looks like a sea of beauty," Johnny sighed as a girl in a silver mesh tube top and peach spandex short shorts joggled by and exited.

"No complaints thus far," I said. "Sam, Johnny, this is my buddy Demarco."

The boys exchanged handshakes, sizing each other up a little. Sam was a second-string fullback built like a baby Ben Grimm. He could bench-press five hundred pounds and had earned the nickname Three Ring Circus for his absurd feats of strength, but slow of foot he played primarily on special teams. Johnny, on the other hand, was a standout, somewhat arrogant tight end, who with his dark bushy hair and fu manchu bore a passing resemblance to Elliott Gould.

"Coming in for a drink?" I asked.

"The ladies are waiting across the street," Sam said. "To be honest with you, they're afraid of this place. They've heard stories."

Demarco bristled. He dismissed Torontonians as a rule. "Meh," he said. "You can't believe everything you hear. There's just a little more action to be had here. Hamilton-style."

"New York, New York is for fruity out-of-towners," I said, drawing smiles from my teammates and a deep nod from Demarco.

"Maybe another night," Johnny said, raising his eyebrows at Demarco. "We'll come down with a few of the boys. Yarmo, Sloth, Zemeredy, you know."

"Yeah, all the hooligans," I said, thinking of the three, milk-fed, diffident teammates they had cited. "They'll have everyone shaking in their boots."

"So camp starts August 25," Sam said.

"Not confirmed yet," Johnny said. "Sooner the better, you ask me. I'm itching to play."

Sam held up two fingers. "We're rated number two in the pre-season poll, behind Western."

"No surprise there," I said. "You know, Jon Parson's inside right now."

"You're kidding," Sam said, stretching his short neck for a peek up the foyer.

"He's here with a few of the Ticats. I see him at my gym all the time."

"He made the Cats?" Johnny said. "That big prick. He almost cracked my hyoid bone two years ago with cheap shot to the throat. Remember that, Bobby?"

"He's a pussy," Demarco said. "Shoestring tackler."

"Anyway," Sam said, offering me his blunt hand again. "We gotta get back. Nice to see you, Bobby. You're gonna do some damage this year, I know it."

Johnny clapped my shoulder. "Yeah, see ya in a few weeks, Bobby. Stay healthy. We need you one hundred per cent to stop those Western bastards."

They departed and Demarco shut the door with a sour expression.

"What's the matter, big boy?" I asked.

"If I told you it would only piss you off so I won't tell you."

"What if I said you're pissing me off anyway?"

But he was right. Those Toronto guys were a little too light-footed and white-eyed for Hamilton. Being decent football players, who could mix it up fine on the playing field, I found their fundamental timidity discordant and hard to stomach, but it was what it was. Being tough on a football field didn't always correlate to the streets.

Moments later Fernandez rushed down from the foyer and told us that Waddy and Billy were acting up. Luciano wanted them kicked out.

"Tell Luciano to kick them out himself."

"Just telling you what he told me," Fernandez said.

"And you just tell him what I told you if he asks again."

"He won't like it."

"Life is full of disappointments."

On the dance floor Waddy and Billy Wilson boogied with the tiger twins. Shirtless Waddy bared the sculpted torso that had won him several provincial and national bodybuilding titles. His abdominal muscles looked like briquettes; striations rippled his symmetrical deltoids and smooth, round hard pectorals. Inflated upper arms tapered into slender forearms and thin, almost feminine wrists, ending in shockingly tiny hands. And on his small feet he wore a delicate type of boxer's boot laced up at the ankles.

Less defined than his brother's physique, Billy's no less impressed, vast across the shoulders with narrow hips and quads like casks.

"They're just dancing," I said. "They're not causing any shit."

"They dance good," Fernandez said with a nod.

The brothers dipped between the twins. Waddy's black hair dripped and his upper body glistened like wet brass. Billy's shoulders see-sawed as he bent from one twin to the next.

"You tell them to leave," I said. "I'm not doing it."

Fernandez shrugged. He wasn't going to do it either.

Rick Zilli, Jon Parson, and a few other Ticats stood at the bar scoping out the crowd, moving to the music. Zilli said something to Carol Fox that made her laugh out loud and caused Jon Parson to blush in florid blotches. Zilli pounded the bar top, his flat face tipping back with open-mouthed guffaws. I recognized another player, Jerry Anderson, a slim-hipped strong safety with a nasty reputation on the football field. The other two, a tall ebony dude with a sinewy neck, and a big bearded lineman who looked like a lumberjack, were unknown to me. Strobe lights flickered: "Ring My Bell" jingled on, and the dancing intensified.

In the washroom I rinsed my face off with cold water. As I was drying myself Diego the busboy entered and said he wanted a word. He was feeling low and needed a couple of yellow jackets. I told him to talk to Buzzsaw.

"Buzzsaw said he had none left."

Really? That sounded odd. "I'll get them for you," I said. "Two?"

He nodded with a dark smirk, and reached in his pocket for money, but I told him to pay me later. When I exited the washroom my cousin stood by a pillar dancing with himself.

"Why don't you get up there, Vin? Look at all the ladies."

"Almost too many."

"Home in on one and go to work. It's not brain surgery, cuz. Most of these girls want to hook up, or at least dance the night away. Accommodate their fantasies."

"Easy for you to say, Romeo. I'm out of practice."

"By the way, Vincenzo, I need to talk to you about a loan. I know this isn't a good time or place, but I'll give you more details tomorrow."

"Whatever you need, Bobby. Let me know."

I left Vincenzo by the pillar probably wondering why I needed a loan. He was tight with his money, understandable when you work like a dog for it.

Albert and Lloyd surprised me, patrolling the bar as suave civilians, their élan lifted wholesale from Crockett and Tubbs, including the sockless loafers. I wondered if they'd gone undercover; but when Albert, in full enchantment mode, started chatting up Felicia, and Lloyd laconically ambushed a girl in a satin zebra romper with a herd of black hair, I knew that safeguarding the city tonight had been struck from their itinerary.

Buzzsaw came by on his way to the can.

"What's this about a shortage of bennies?" I asked.

"Don't wanna corrupt the kiddies."

"So you have a couple of yellow jackets for me?"

"You're worse than Caesar," he chuckled.

When I ran into Diego again he admitted that Ali, a virgin to bennies, also wanted to try one. I cautioned it might not be a good idea but he shrugged it off. Someone tapped my shoulder and I whirled around ready to defend myself.

"Whoa," said the dark-haired girl standing there. "Didn't mean to startle you."

"The heat makes me jumpy."

I needed a moment to take her in: sleeveless white pantsuit with gold buttons, gold snake armbands, rich brown hair tumbling to her shoulders, large gold-hooped earrings. Her chest swelled under the zipper of her costume. A tiny crucifix on a thin gold chain asterisked her cleavage. She smelled warm and feminine with a hint of the kitchen. I still couldn't place her.

"It's crazy in here tonight. Is it always like this?"

"Pretty much. Have we met?"

"Sort of. At Valens Park. Remember? You never did come over to say hi."

"Ah, yes. You're Luigi's sister."

"The one and only. I thought, since we weren't formally introduced—"

"Sorry, I forget your name?"

"Connie." She reached out her hand and shook mine with a warm pressure, looking me in the eyes. "Are you okay?" she asked.

My eyes were vibrating. Unless hers were. I was far from okay, sweating from every pore and yet almost shivering. I cited heat stroke as the culprit. Connie nodded as if this were perfectly normal, and without missing a beat informed me she had come to the club with a gang of feisty bridesmaids from her cousin Antoinette's bridal party. A girls' night out before the wedding next week. Ho ho, you know how the ladies get on such occasions. When I asked about her brother she scrunched up her nose.

"He got pinched a few weeks ago. He doesn't learn. He's in Barton waiting for a hearing. You saw what happened with my father. Disgusting, I know. He's washed his hands of Luigi. But let's not talk about him. Let's talk about Cathedral High." She smiled and shook her shoulders.

"Glory days."

"I was your biggest fan, Bobby. Bobby Doctor—that's what Oscar called you. It was so funny. Bobby Doctor. Luigi said you were a big mook and that he could kick your ass, but I always laughed at him. You can't kick Bobby Doctor's ass!"

My face flushed. "I had some good years at Cathedral."

She sighed. "We all did."

A clammy hand clapped my neck. Roy Rosati, wearing a cowboy hat, and starting a beatnik beard. A change of direction for him. Not a bad idea.

"Roy, I want you to meet Connie Fanelli."

"Nice to know you," he said, pressing her hand, then hastening away.

"Forgive my friend, he lacks the social graces."

She rolled her eyes. "Not the first time someone split when they heard my last name."

"Your brother has quite the reputation."

"Like I said, I don't want to talk about him." She forced a smile with her small white teeth. "So I hear you're studying law or something at U. of T."

"No, not law. English. Don't really know what I want to do yet. But not law."

"I'm thinking of going to McMaster. I should have went last year but I needed to make some money first. I'd like to get into law eventually."

When I heard my name being called from the back I felt somewhat relieved; Connie was lovely, but at that moment cloying. I promised I'd catch up with her later and skipped off.

I passed Ali. His eyes shone like a lemur's and he trembled all over, but he smiled and gave me a hearty thumbs-up. Then I spotted Diego sweeping up debris in a corner with great energy, speeded-up and herky-jerky like an old silent movie, and when he saw me, he also smiled and gave me a thumbs-up.

I returned to the back where Fernandez was locked up with a guy in a black suit snorting and bowed over like a small enraged bull.

Caesar and Buzzsaw appeared just as the guy punched Fernandez in the jaw and knocked him down. Caesar tried to grab the guy's arms but he whirled around, almost coming out of his suit jacket, and caught Buzzsaw with a right to the face that sent him sprawling into a stool. I jumped behind the guy, slapped a full nelson on him and squeezed until he folded over. I held him while the others regathered their senses.

"Open the back door," Buzzsaw cried, a flap on his cheek bleeding brightly.

Caesar removed the safety bar and opened the door, which led to a back alley. I worked the guy to the door and pushed him outside. He had strong shoulders and tried to break free but I had leverage on him and squeezed his neck so hard he squawked.

"Relax, buddy. Just relax." I squeezed until he stopped resisting.

When Caesar and Buzzsaw grabbed his arms I let go, figuring we were done, and turned to go back in. Before I got very far, Fernandez flew out the door like Bruce Lee. While the other two held buddy by the arms, Fernandez squared up to him and unleashed a head-snapping roundhouse kick to his jaw that opened his chin. Then fists smashed his face.

They held him up and worked on him like that until he collapsed in a heap, but Fernandez wasn't quite done. As the guy struggled to get up, he kicked him in the face, then kicked him in the ribs, reefing hard. Buzzsaw joined him, shaking his head and grinning as his kicks connected. Then Caesar took his turn, flinging out his arms for balance, face calm, his blows economical.

I stood by the door, detached, indifferent. I wanted to tell them to stop, or at least part of me did. But another part of me watched it as some kind of violent theatre, the participants following a script. And yet I had to say something, I knew I did, I felt a weird obligation to intercede, but my mouth opened and nothing came out. I said nothing. I shut my eyes. All I could hear was the drama of thudding blows and the guy's breath escaping in grunts and whimpered half-cries. But after a while he made no sound.

NINE

Felicia answered the telephone on the nightstand. It was light out, birds chirped and rustled. She spoke in a low voice, her pale naked back to me, then listened for a minute, said goodbye, and hung up. She ran her hands through her hair, put them under her breasts, and tilted her head to the right. Against the wall, the long curve of her body appeared in grainy silhouette, with her heavy breasts casting their own pendulous shadows.

Satan leapt on the bed, claws unsheathed, but I gently shooed him off. He padded by the hat boxes and tossed a scornful look over his shoulder.

"You have to go," Felicia announced with a huff of panic in her voice.

"I'm on my way."

Strapping up her bra with side-to-side heaves she said, "I mean, you have to go *now*."

"I'm going, I'm going."

"This was a bad idea."

"It wasn't mine."

I grabbed my clothes off the dressing chair, pulled on my briefs and pants but didn't bother with the socks, and left the shirt un-buttoned. Shoes on, I exited, carrying my jacket and the socks, hoping Albert the disco cop wasn't waiting to pump my ass full of lead. Sharp barbs of sunlight jabbed my eyes and I staggered half-blinded to the Camaro.

When I got home Demarco's Galaxy 500 lay in front of my mother's house like a beached scow, he and Roy inside it with their flip-flopped feet up on the dash, wearing yellow sun visors and reeking of coconut oil.

"Where the frig have you been?" Demarco asked.

"Who are you, my mother?"

"Speaking of which," Roy said, "she was out here a few minutes ago. Nice lady, your mom. Very funny. She said you were working the night shift, with a wink."

Oh great, I thought, my mother has boarded the mockery float with the other comic geniuses. She didn't bat an eye anymore when I stayed out all night, took it for what it was. But now, before my friends, she felt empowered to mock me.

"Hey, big boy, wanna go for a cruise," Demarco said in falsetto.

"That persona becomes you, Tonino," I said.

"Thought you might like to head down to Hutch's," Roy said. "Catch some rays, check out some chicks."

"Guess what?" Demarco said, "that guy they beat up last night, those idiots. Turns out he's Johnny Papalia's nephew."

This was news. Johnny "Pops" Papalia had been an enforcer with the Bonanno crime family, and though his star had fallen in the mob universe, he still carried a lot of weight in Hamilton, enough to get somebody whacked if it suited him.

"Anyway, the guy was bombed out of his head," I said.

"Even worse," Demarco said. "Maybe Pops will want to come down on all of us."

"Be objective. What's he going to do, get us all tommy-gunned because of a beat-off nephew?" Not beyond the realm of possibility, but remote. Nevertheless, someone would face the music for that beating.

"Come on," Roy said. "Let's hit the beach."

"Give me a few minutes, I need a shower."

"You certainly do," Demarco said, pinching his nose. "Unless it's the bay."

In the house I avoided my mother, and tiptoed up to my bedroom. I undressed, and performed one hundred push-ups on the floor. By the last one, my trembling arms looked like vascular hams. Catching myself in the armoire mirror, I experienced a moment of distinct estrangement. Those arms, that puffy face, those bulging eyes, the taut skin, and those veins, those alien veins pulsing like tentacles under that skin. Not normal, eh? No, not normal. I took a cool shower and dressed, out of sorts.

When I came down, my mother was out on the porch humouring the boys again.

"What's so funny?" I asked.

"Nothing," Demarco said, covering his mouth.

"Don't look at me," Roy said. "Meow."

"What was that?" I said.

Roy and Demarco snorted with laughter but kept mum.

My mother was more forthcoming. "They laugh because I told them when you were a child cats scared you."

"Is that true, big guy?" Demarco said. "Pussy cats? Little kitties? Meow and you went running to your mamma?"

Roy studied me. "It's embarrassing, Bobby. Terrified of cats. A big bad linebacker like yourself. What if your opponents discover this?"

"They'll start a big Tom at quarterback."

"They'll throw mice on the field to lure local cats."

"Shut up," I said. "I hang out with you pussies, don't I? We going or what?"

"Meow," Demarco said.

"Keep it up, fuck-face."

"I finally figured out that his violent streak is really just fear."

"Makes a lotta sense when you think about it," Roy said.

"We're going to the beach, Ma. Be back for dinner."

Averse to boat rides and ridicule, I insisted we take my car. After a mild protest the boys agreed. Demarco sat in the front seat, his skull propped on the headrest, his bulky grey sweatshirt already damp. Roy stuffed himself into the back seat, not Chevrolet's greatest appointment, and lamented that his life as an obese man had been easier. Then he would have been granted the front seat automatically, for instance. Instead, the broad Demarco prevailed. And the desiccated man, shoulder blades conjoining, sucked it up for the team. That's what the desiccated man does.

The engine turned over crisply and roared to life. My mother waved us off.

We drove to the lakeside strip known as Hutch's. Muscles were out in force, both human and machine. A souped-up baby-blue El Camino burned long smoking streaks of rubber on the asphalt. A group of ferrety Clubbers in red bandannas thronged around a backfiring matte-black Nova SS, now and again coupling off for feisty skirmishes that ended when one went down or other members interceded.

Someone had parked an astonishing orange Superbird complete with a Daytona spoiler right in front of Hutch's Grill. Black Sabbath's "War Pigs" hammered from its windows.

Generals gathered in their masses
Just like witches at black masses...

It looked unnatural sitting there, that thing, with that wing, extravagant, satirical.

Wearing their colours, Satan's Choice MC thundered up and down the strip on glaring choppers, as truculent and lordly as great white sharks, apex predators with no enemies and no scruples. Glistening bodybuilders in neon tank tops vainly promenaded, preening and puffing self-consciously, rubbing oils and creams on themselves or on each other, admiring and scorning rivals in turn with sharp stares and sneers and soto voce sarcasm as sibilant as a schoolgirl's. Clubbers openly mocked the shining hulks but kept their distance, now and then scattering in giggles when a big man took offense and lumbered toward them.

"Hyenas," Demarco said, eyeing the Clubbers with disdain, perhaps because he numbered himself among the beautiful-bodied targets of their jibes—unwarranted when their only raison d'être was to perfect the human form. In contrast, the Clubbers contributed zilch to society, and to human achievement. They existed only to injure, mock, and destroy.

"I hear they torched Queenston Lanes last week," Roy said. "Beat up the owner and his mentally retarded son, and burned the place to the ground. No eyewitnesses, so the cops couldn't touch them."

"D'you know any of them?" I asked.

Roy shrugged. Demarco said he only knew Tar, Jimmy Lewis's kid bother. Tar was a bucktooth mulatto dude with an unkempt Afro and pale green eyes. The loudest of the pack, he brayed with laughter and harassed everyone he passed.

"Look at him," I said.

"Yeah. Jimmy says he's brain-damaged from eating lead paint."

Everyone has a story. I parked the Camaro in the lot near the go-carts and we made our way to Hutch's and its growling hubbub. Polished choppers ripped back and forth, a canary-yellow dune buggy sputtered by, and a candy-apple-red '67 Mustang with a chromed blower ticked and strained down the strip like a Funny Car, stalling out several times. Tattooed dudes with shaved heads and dead-eyed pit bulls on chains strolled around self-importantly, now and then allowing the dogs to test their teeth. The air smelled of gasoline and charbroiled meat.

"I could kill a couple of burgers," Roy said.

"Me too," Demarco said, his face studded with sweat.

"Aren't you dying in that sweatshirt?" I asked. But this was routine.

"He's embarrassed of his body," Roy said.

"With good reason," I said. "He looks like a freak kite."

"Ah, shut up, both of you. You wouldn't get it even if I explained."

"Like Tarzan not having a beard?" Roy said, his own scruff lacking substance.

Demarco shut his eyes and shook his head. "What the fuck are you talking about?"

"Bobby!" someone cried from the patio.

Wearing a straw hat and a yellow mesh tank top, Buzzsaw waved from a table, his mealy arms lacking definition, the skull and crossbones inked on his left shoulder self-inflicted. Beside him his kid brother Perry fidgeted with a red transistor radio, and across from them sat a guy unknown to me with a stupendous moustache.

"Check out all the pussy," Buzzsaw said. "Meow."

Demarco and Roy exchanged a look but I glared at them.

"Aren't you dying in that sweatshirt?" Buzzsaw asked Demarco.

"Why don't you blow me?" he replied.

Buzzsaw winced. "What's wrong with him?"

"Eh," I said. "You hear about that guy you idiots dummied last night?"

"No, what? You were with us, too."

Buzzsaw's buck teeth shone with spittle. I waited for him to take back what he said.

"No, right. It was me and Caesar, Fernandez, and..." He glanced at Demarco.

"I was at the front doors," Demarco said. "Say otherwise."

I got close to Buzzsaw. "That guy was Johnny Papalia's nephew."

Buzzsaw's leporine smile vanished. Concern whitened his eyes. He glanced at his brother, toying with the transistor radio, then he stooped to his slouched mustachioed friend and said something in his ear that made him sit up straight. In moments the apprehensive trio departed.

I took the table while Roy and Demarco went to order food. I told them I wanted a chocolate shake, nothing to eat, as my stomach was off. Hutch's lacked a liquor license but people openly poured mickeys into soft drinks; pot and hash burned. Two emaciated blondes in bikinis at a nearby table sniffed a yellowy powder off a pamphlet with a rolled-up ten-dollar bill, failing to respect the temples of their bodies. Soon after they were cheerful in their totalism.

Roy and Demarco returned with the food and went at it like dogs, pausing just to breathe. I warned them to slow down, not for their sake alone but for mine, as I found this voraciousness nauseating. My chocolate shake tasted chalky and I blew what I'd sucked of it back down through the straw into the cup, which bubbled.

Hot hissing ensued; I looked over and saw the black Nova SS spewing smoke and steam as several Clubbers scrambled away from it.

One of the girls doing lines stood up too fast and fell, striking her head on the edge of the table with an ugly thunk. Her big eyed friend looked ready to bolt. But the fallen girl picked herself up, apparently uninjured, though trembly and pale. They staggered off soon after that.

"What are those bastards doing now?" Demarco said.

A group of Clubbers had confronted two guys in pastel golf shirts and pressed shorts. They yelled at them, pointing and pushing, perhaps outraged by their apparel. The duo tried to keep moving but the Clubbers had no intention of letting them go. They continued yelling, crowding them, pointing. Punches flew. The two guys dropped, then the kicking started. Tar Lewis led the assault, expending more energy than all the others combined, kicking one of the victims, then the other, with sureness and satisfaction.

People at the tables, those not blinded or befuddled by the sun, gasped and cried out, and clearly experienced horror, but no one moved a muscle to help.

I watched for a few more seconds, then shot out of my seat so suddenly Roy dropped his hamburger and Demarco knocked over his soft drink. And then, without thinking about what I was doing, or what the consequences of my actions would be, I leaped over the short fence barricading the eating area and charged the Clubbers.

"Enough!" I shouted. "Enough!" But they continued kicking with mindless insistence. I aimed myself at Tar and drove my shoulder into his midsection with such force he wheezed as he hit the ground, and writhed there, voiceless and bug-eyed like a big fish out of water.

Another Clubber stepped up to me but before he could throw a punch I chopped his throat with the flat of my hand and he dropped to his knees gurgling. Another charged and I gave him my left side and hooked hard with my right, clipping his chin and knocking him down, but at the same moment something hard, metallic, walloped my right ear. The blow stunned me; I saw stars and wheeled around clutching my head, touching my ear where the blood gushed hot and wet; I reeled and almost fell, but panic, instinct, told me not to go down. Blood splashed my shoulder.

A roaring crowd amassed around the melee. As I struggled to regain my composure, Roy and Demarco appeared. Demarco restrained the Clubber who had struck me in the ear and flipped him to the ground, where he clawed and screeched like a wildcat until Demarco smashed an elbow into his neck that silenced him. I turned to Roy, entangled with two grunting Clubbers, and slammed one in the side of the head with a hammer fist that rocked him sideways and buckled his far leg. He went down grabbing his knee. The other took a well-timed kick to the nuts from Roy and loped off like an ape-man, cupping his crushed jewels and bellowing.

Holding his side, face perverted with pain, Tar stood off at a safe distance beside a fleshy blonde in an orange bikini top with an Ocean Stripe Beach Towel girdling her hips. The girl rubbed his shoulder and spoke gentle words, but Tar would not be comforted.

A police car pulled up and two cops hopped out adjusting their hats and batons.

"What's going on here?" asked the taller, red-faced one.

The Clubbers had already vanished into the crowd.

"Just a little punch-up," said a wide man from the patio in a blue luau shirt, his similarly attired friends voicing unanimity.

The shorter cop asked me if I was okay. He had a long nose and very wide hips.

"I'll live," I said, pressing my ear with the tank top.

"Better get that looked at, it's bleeding."

"Okay, folks," the tall cop said. "Show's over."

"Move along," said the other one.

One of the original victims, forehead gashed, turquoise golf shirt splotched with blood, bobbed his head about searching for the culprits, shouting. "Charge those cocksuckers! I want to charge them!" His clothes and his belief in the system betrayed him as a non-local. But the now-sweating officers, given the hot, breezeless day and the hormonal vagaries and impulsivity of youth, showed no interest in pursuing the matter further. No one was maimed or killed, after all. Not a choice time to chase down spirited punks or burst into flames trying, but the perfect time to indulge in a very cold beverage, on a patio if possible. They perfunctorily asked if anyone recognized the assailants. Someone mentioned the Parkdale gang but others booed that person down and identified the Clubbers as the culprits.

"Most of those bastards are juveniles," the tall cop said from the side of his mouth to his long-nosed partner, who nodded either in agreement or to acknowledge, without necessarily gathering the nuance of the statement, that he was paying attention.

The officers took down names, or at least went through a pantomime of doing so, for when I told them mine they both looked as if I had poked them in the eyes and they didn't bother asking me how to spell my last name; the shorter one merely scribbled a few letters down with his stubby pencil and told me to move on.

"You need stitches," Demarco informed me as he eyed the injured ear. "I can see the cartilage. What did he hit you with?"

"Don't know, felt like a hunk of metal, maybe a rock."

"You took off so fast, Bobby," Demarco said.

"And what?"

"Be objective," he said.

"I'm trying. But the blood is poisoning that."

"What the frig is wrong with you? Now we have to keep six with those fucks—they came to the Press Club the other day and when Jerome and I turned them away they said they'd be back to shut us down."

"Did they shut you down?"

Demarco handed me a tissue to wipe my ear. "No, not yet."

"Then shut up. I'm going to St. Joseph's to get this ear looked at. You guys coming?"

Neither said anything, so without wasting time I drove to St. Joseph's Hospital. After a two-hour wait in Emergency, a sallow intern stitched my ear and told me to leave it uncovered.

"It'll heal nice in the air," he said.

Roy said, "The scar will always remind you of this summer."

There'll be more than that to remind me of this fucking summer, I thought, and led them out to the Camaro, regretting that I hadn't asked for pain pills. I told Demarco I was passing on our workout, but that I'd be at the bar that evening. I dropped them off and drove home.

My mother questioned me about the ear, which she examined with a painful tug. I told her I collided with Demarco horsing around at the beach, no big deal. She didn't believe me, but had I told her the truth she wouldn't have believed me, so I might as well have told her the truth.

I ate and had a nap. I awoke from a dead sleep in a sweat. I was late.

Still groggy, I ran a cold shower and stood under it, bracing myself until I was fully awake. I dried off and dressed. As I went down the stairs, Joey exited his room and said he wanted a word. I told him I was running late, to make it quick, but sensing my impatience, he said not to worry, he'd talk to me tomorrow.

Heart in my throat, mind a static field, I gunned it to the Press Club. When I arrived the lineup stretched down the block and a snarl of glossy limousines and muscle cars roared and honked for egress. A chic horde under New York, New York's green canopy spilled onto the street, where two red-lit police cars bleated sirens to urge along a stalled stretch limousine and a swatch-capped tow-truck driver hooking up a small red Firebird. A man in a double-breasted chauffeur kit stood by the limousine, indicating the international gesture of futility: arms to heaven. Lacking empathy, the officers fed into his suffering by personalizing it, peppering him with abuse and threats. The tow-truck driver, pulling a lever, looked on indifferently: he had his job, they had theirs.

At the front door Buzzsaw foamed at the mouth with Benzedrine frenzy.

"Jesus fucking Christ, where've you been? Fernandez didn't show. Don't know where the fuck he is. Tried calling him but got no answer. That cocksucker. See that lineup? We're too full. If cops come by we're screwed. Thought you weren't going to show. I heard Papalia's sending someone to see me and Caesar. We were named. We were fucking named!"

"You're kidding me. What are you doing here, then?"

"I'm gonna stay at home, with this? It's not that hard to find me. Here or there. At least if I'm here...d'you think I should go?"

"Where's Caesar?"

"In the back with Demarco. He's not worried. Thinks it's bullshit. Doesn't believe the guy was Papalia's nephew."

"Where's Jerome?"

"He went to the can. Should be back any second. He's been gone awhile. If you see him tell him I need him up here. Okay? Tell him. Luciano was looking for you earlier and I told him you were in the can. He's probably still looking for you."

As soon as I entered the club I saw Vic Zuccheroni in a black suit, black shirt, red tie, nuzzling a drink by the washrooms. He looked old standing there, defeated. When I passed him he lifted his lip and tipped his glass toward the dance floor where a few large men were dancing athletically and whooping it up. I recognized Rick Zilli among them, wearing a patterned green silk shirt with puffy sleeves, unbuttoned to the waist, the redhead Jon Parson, and a handful of other Ticats, including Jerry Anderson, the hard-hitting safety. Surrounded by a heaving bevy of ladies, they were having the kind of time you lift all them weights for.

Zilli was dancing with pretty Sue Allen, and when Kool and the Gang's "Celebration" came on, they slowed it down to a sensual hug, rocking from side to side, Zilli with his hands over her ass. He held her tightly against him even when "Ring My Bell" rang in and everyone around them roared.

"That will not end well," Vic said with a pull of his cigarette.

"What d'you mean?" I asked, but I knew what he meant, I knew, and contented myself to watch it unfold like a minor Greek tragedy, though no goats would be sacrificed. Jon Parson, who hailed from these parts, should have told his teammate that shameless showing-up like this seldom went unchecked in Hamilton. It was only a matter of time.

Felicia swooped by with a tray full of drinks and pleasantly but viciously asked how I was doing, though she didn't wait for my response. I wondered how things between her and Albert were going. Then again, I tried not thinking about it. They'd been seen around town and that was enough. The rest merely led to teeth-grinding, cold sweats, apocalyptic visions.

Fat Freddy and Carol Fox pumped out the Singapore slings and piña coladas like machines, both of them dead-eyed, mechanical, joyless. I worried about the conditions of their souls, but not at length; my damaged ear was throbbing. Diego and Ali frenzied like hebephrenics to and from the service bar, dropping things, giggling, screeching, and quarrelling incoherently—walking deterrents for Benzedrine abuse and overexposure to Lipps Inc. Jerome stood by the deejay booth, dark hands folded at his waist, his face contemplative. Perhaps he had reached a psychological impasse. It happens.

"What's up, Jerome? Buzzsaw's waiting for you. Unless you want me to up-front. I don't mind. Think I know what's going on."

He blinked his soft, almost pretty brown eyes. His face could have easily been an obese woman's. "Last night. What they did was wrong. They gonna pay the price. Oh yeah, uh huh. Fernandez got smart. I talked to him. Said he ain't coming back. He's got a kid. Caesar's playing the fool because that's all he knows how to do. And the sharks, they're here. Mad Dog and Terry Peters sitting in a booth with a pair of strippers, and your friend Oscar in the washroom snorting coke in one of the stalls. I'm no cop. I don't care what people put in their noses or their veins. But something's going down tonight and I'm wondering which way I'm gonna go."

"It won't matter. Wheels have been set in motion. I'll go to the front if you want." I touched my ear.

"Cut yourself shaving?"

"Something like that, Jerome." I looked at his nice face. "Jerome, why the fuck do you stay in this town? Just for the football? Still chasing that dream?"

"Uh huh, still chasing that dream. Still think I can play when and if my knee heals. As for Hamilton, man, I'm from a place called Guntown, Mississippi, haha. Don't know how much you know about the southern United States." He smiled. "But I like Hamilton just fine. I like this town just fine. I plan to stay if I can. There's some bad people here, sure, but there's some real good people, too. Real good. Can't be too hard on this place if you've lived in worse."

Jerome had silenced me. I felt a little embarrassed.

"I'll go to the front," he said. "I'm not Buzzsaw. Watch yourself, Bobby."

"Thanks, Jerome. I will."

"And get that ear treated. Looks nasty." He ambled off to the front, looking over his shoulder once and shrugging.

Demarco and Caesar slouched under the EXIT sign in the back like two Lurch understudies. Caesar's mouth looked stuffed with cotton and his bloodshot eyes jutted like bird embryos from their sockets. How many bennies? A dozen? He gibbered on—about cement roofs, cement shoes?—but I listening to him hurt my head and I turned away. I walked with a sweaty-faced Demarco, his eyes jerking left and right. The paranoia bug had bit him, too.

"Where have you been?" he asked. "Fucking place is a madhouse."

"Oscar and company are here, think I know why. I expect others to join the party."

"What are you talking about?"

"See those Ticats on the dance floor?"

"Yeah, that big mook Jon Parson and Rick Zilli, I see them."

"That blonde molesting Zilli is Eugene's ex."

"So what? Eugene dumped her a year ago. He doesn't care about her."

"That's not the point."

Demarco failed to see the big picture. Unless I was wrong. But I doubted it.

Moments later when John the Greek appeared, his right eye bandaged, joined by the third Slompka brother, George, whom they called "Gorgeous" because of his long blond hair, and Luigi Fanelli, whom I hadn't seen since that day at Valens Park, and then Ricky Tartaglia, eyes whirring merrily, and a handful of other Barton-Sherman gang members, wearing blue plaid work shirts and steel-toed boots—when they calmly, almost casually materialized, I didn't panic. I didn't rush up to Demarco and cry, Look out! Or go warn Luciano that his club was about to be trashed. Or tell Carol Fox or Fat Freddy or one of the waitresses to call the police. I did nothing.

By now Sue Allen's hands had found refuge inside Zilli's green silk shirt, pawing his six-pack, scratching his hairless chest. "Funkytown" came on, and I'd heard it so often over the course of that summer it gave me vertigo.

Gotta make a move to a
Town that's right for me...

And the usual tumult ensued on the dance floor, as this was still a crowd favourite. Zilli and Sue Allen performed a piquant bump and grind, drawing stares from dancers and observers alike. The other Ticats also danced away, and when Ricky Tartaglia and Mad Dog turned and twisted onto the dance floor, and Oscar popped up by the railing with Gorgeous George, Dino Flex, and Luigi Fanelli at his flanks, and Terry Peters eased up to the deejay booth in a shiny blue suit holding two beers and dancing by himself, I held my breath and counted to ten.

Won't you take me to
Funkytown
Won't you take me to
Funkytown

Then someone, hard to say exactly whom, cold-cocked Sue Allen with a punch to the face that knocked her down. Obscured by the writhing bodies, the puncher maintained his anonymity. Meanwhile Zilli hopped around with his arms raised like a man set on fire. Odd. Then, in a moment of blinking horror, I real ized that Zilli's shirt, his dazzling green shirt, *was* on fire! As he thrashed and groped to get off the dance floor, everyone continued dancing, blocking his way.

> *Well, I talk about it*
> *Talk about it*
> *Talk about it*
> *Talk about it*

But Zilli was on fire, at least his shirt was, and he wanted off the dance floor. As he blazed through the crowd for the rail, waving his arms, knocking over dancers, he tripped, and in a billow of bluish smoke fell down, his screams penetrating the dense wall of music and voices.

Everyone continued dancing, even Zilli's strapping, clapping teammates, oblivious to his condition, his pain, his panic, unfamiliar with his screams—which intensified as a dark ring of legs closed in on him and started stomping, at first glance as if to put out the fire, to stomp out the flames shooting up from the shirt. But as only charred shreds of the shirt remained—the fire already extinguished, either by the fall and Zilli's subsequent thrashing about, or by the rapid combustion of the green silk—the stomping served another purpose.

Eventually the other Ticats clued in to the violence raging nearby; they could smell it, feel it in their testicles; and when they pushed through the crowd to confirm what they sensed, they were surprised to meet resistance.

And I was surprised how easily they went down, these professional athletes, these men who understood leverage, who could deliver bone-crunching blows with great velocity and violence, who were trained and conditioned to get up even when knocked down. But these athletes had never been trained or conditioned to be stompcd.

Gotta move on

Gotta move on

Gotta move on

Demarco showed his eyes above the fleeing crowd, now alert to the score. Run, run, but which way? Toward the dance floor? Toward the EXIT sign, an alley to safety if not freedom—there is a difference. Twitching Caesar loomed, swaying his long body like a sick giraffe. He wanted to curl up into a ball and go to sleep or have someone carry him off to a safe, dry place. Not Demarco; he like me felt removed from the theatre, up in the gallery somewhere.

Where was Buzzsaw? Quivering wherever he was. And with good reason: a man, even a young freaked-out man can think it through, can see it unfolding in his mind's eye: there, that's how it will happen, I'll be busy, unaware, distracted, doing a thing, whatever, and then...not doing it, not doing anything. Then what follows follows, not good no matter how softly you play it out. But all this worry aside, it wasn't Buzzsaw's turn that night, not that night, earmarked for Zilli and his error of judgment. Stomped into whimpering solicitude, *please stop please stop please stop*, so much for his Alabama manliness.

All rushed for the exits, save a few perverse souls, who could not help watching men being stomped. The music fell silent and the deejay killed the dance-floor lights and then only sounds of stomping echoed through the club, in a sort of contrapuntal rhythm, like carpenters nailing down the floor at a new build.

Crouched in the middle of the dance floor—blue suit shimmering, face fired with glee—Peters had Sue Allen pinned under his knees, and was pouring a bottle of beer into her mouth, the flow flashing in the dimness. She kicked and screamed beneath him, and when he finished pouring the beer he pulled back his arm and slapped her hard across the face. By then I was moving, picking up speed, high-stepping over toppled stools and debris. As Peters closed his fist and raised his arm to strike her again, I drove at him with high knees, timing it so that my right knee crashed into the side of his head as I arrived. I caught him hard in the temple and he flopped over so motionless I thought I'd killed him; then, after a moment, he stirred his legs and moaned.

By now the stomping had stopped and anyone left rushed for the exits. Bodies sprawled darkly across the dance floor, some moving, trying to kneel or stand, others immobile. Intermittent murmurs and groans punctuated a sort of dripping, ticking silence.

Peters gurgled and twitched. I turned him on his side. A worm of blood oozed from his scalp. Even injured he was unsympathetic. I checked Sue Allen. Conscious, she slumped by the rail, touching her red cheeks and bloody lips. I helped her up and walked her to the service bar.

A dozen cops arrived on the scene, batons drawn, among them Albert and Lloyd. Albert wasted no time consoling a shaken Felicia, whom he wrapped in his jacket and whisked off like a kidnapper, unnoticed by all but me. One officer approached and asked if Sue Allen, gibbering hysterically now, was okay. When I said she had taken a few shots to the face he took her gently by the arm and escorted her to the front.

Another officer, with horn-rimmed glasses and a sardonic disposition, asked me what the hell had happened here. I said I wasn't sure, but it seemed like a vendetta thing, a statement someone had made, a process, a synergy.

He asked me if I was being smart and I told him I didn't know how to answer that.

"Looks like the work of the Barton-Sherman gang," he said, sidestepping my issues.

"You could be right about that."

"Who are the fallen?"

"Ticats, Rick Zilli among them."

The officer's eyebrows jumped, then he tried not to smile. "You mean to tell me those bastards did this to Hamilton Ticats?"

"Looks like."

"No wonder they suck. Can't even whip a bunch of street thugs."

It was refreshing, such honesty. The world could use more of it. As I moved for the dance floor, curious to see the aftermath up close and personal, Demarco grabbed me by the arm and ushered me to the back with urgency.

"Stay here," he said, darting glances. "You don't want Peters seeing you."

"Why not?"

Demarco smiled.

"Wonder if anyone else saw it."

"Mass confusion, dim lights, you know, unlikely. But rats are always watching. You don't know they're watching but they are." He tapped his temple. "Thought you'd do something stupid, and you did."

"You know me too well."

"Your ear's bleeding again," he said, handing me a bar napkin.

"Think I can grab a couple more stitches from those guys?"

Ambulance attendants rushed in and ministered to Zilli and his battered teammates, with the exception of the lumberjack lineman, who tottered about raging with a bashed-in nose, bleeding all over the club, knocking over stools and rubber trees, refusing medical assistance, and generating friction with the officers eager to question him about the incident.

"How the fuck do I know who they were? I didn't get a good look at them! They came out of fucking nowhere!"

"Calm down, sir. We know you're excited."

"Don't call me sir! I'm Ed Georgovich!"

And when big Ed Georgovich, right offensive tackle of the Hamilton Ticats, an Eastern Conference All Star, grew belligerent, spraying everyone with blood and waving his arms like hairy truncheons, the officers had no choice but to manhandle him and drag him handcuffed to the station. And as no one identified any of the attackers, big Ed Georgovich, busted nose and all, was the only person arrested that night.

Another officer, a silver-haired sergeant with polished steelies for eyes, wanted a statement from me. I told him that I saw Sue Allen get assaulted but never saw the perpetrator; that I saw Rick Zilli with his shirt on fire but didn't see who set it ablaze, and that I saw Barton-Sherman gang members on the dance floor but couldn't say for certain which of them were there or which one was doing what to whom.

"It was crowded, sir. Hard to make out anything. Is Zilli badly burned?"

"Nah. Whoever did it used lighter fluid and the shirt went up fast. But he took quite a beating. Might have a fractured skull. Where's your boss?"

"Good question."

Luciano, nowhere to be seen, must have bailed earlier. Sooner or later he'd have a lot of questions to answer.

I caught Jerome's eye as I exited the club and he shook his head, as if disappointed. Maybe Guntown, Mississippi, didn't seem so bad now.

As Demarco and I walked toward the parking lot, a black cat crossed our path. We watched it disappear under a red van.

"Don't say it," I said.

"I won't," he said.

TEN

Next morning my mother roused me from a restless sleep—
flashing with snapshots of Zilli's green silk shirt ablaze—and told
me Uncle Sal had passed away during the night. It took a few
seconds to process. Then I hugged my mother and shared a quiet
moment with her.

As inevitable as it had seemed—Uncle Sal had been dodging
the Dark Angel for months—the news struck me deeply; and
as I watched my mother sobbing intermittently that morning,
bending her face to her hands and shaking, or staring out the
window with tears streaming from her eyes, a lot of old pain re-
surfaced, compounding the sadness, layering it so that it was ex-
haustive, and inescapable. And yet as sad as the whole business
is, as overpowering and debilitating, death and the experience of
mourning a particular death always comes off a little surreal—
off kilter, perhaps melodramatic or indulgent—and thus hard to
swallow, like something happening in a far-fetched movie, or a
disquieting dream.

Family and friends filed into Friscolanti's Funeral Home to pay
their last respects. Uncle Sal had been well-liked, a bit of a rake in
his heyday, a nimble dancer with an exquisite head of hair that had
held up until the radiation treatments, who had never married,
or fathered any children, but whose good humour and warmth
had touched many: in fewer words, a stand-up guy. Dozens of rich
floral bouquets surrounded the casket, a smothering superabun-
dance of colour and fragrance. Tears flowed.

Uncle Giuseppe pulled out a monogrammed white handkerchief and dabbed his eyes and nose. His black suit fit him loosely, aged him. I squeezed his shoulder, but this gave him faint comfort. Uncle Frank stood beside him weeping wholeheartedly, face in his hands, shuddering with sobs, his manner childlike and inconsolable. Watching those men weep saddened me more than the death itself. My mother and my aunts mourned beside us in familiar black; they refused to let go of Sicily in this regard. Black it would be for months now. My mother had only recently stopped wearing black for my father. Both my grandmothers wore black their entire lives, as did their mothers and grandmothers. My brother, wearing black clothes, black shades, had been crying all morning. He had always been Uncle Sal's favourite.

Tiny and stiff in his navy blue suit, with the faintest peaceful smile ghosting his face, and his waxen fingers clutching a rosary and a prayer card with a picture of the Blessed Virgin, Uncle Sal looked nothing like the Uncle Sal I had known.

"At least he won't suffer anymore," Vincenzo said.

"That's right," said Aunt Teresa, crossing herself. "His suffering's over now."

"He looks strange," I whispered to Vincenzo, recalling with an inward shudder how my dead father had looked in his casket, like a puffy effigy of his animated self.

My cousin, perhaps inappropriately wearing a chocolate-brown suit, shushed me with a finger across his lips and then stood there with a straight face, but how could he ignore the obvious? That wasn't the Uncle Sal we had known, in that casket. Uncle Sal, the dancer, the ladies' man, the inveterate bachelor.

Death is final. Uncle Sal no longer existed.

"When I die I want to be cremated right away," I told Vincenzo, and this almost caused him to smile. "Seriously, I don't want to be put on display like that."

"But people have a right to say goodbye to someone they cared about. This is more for the living than the departed."

"Don't see what difference it makes. He's gone. That's not even him anymore. Going through this charade doesn't change the essential fact."

"So what are you gonna do?" Vincenzo asked. "Launch a protest, stage a strike of some kind? Let's see what your mother has to say about it."

Lacking a good response to this, I stalked off with him sucking his teeth behind me.

But as much as I found the occasion hysterically contrived, I enjoyed running into relatives and paisans I hadn't seen for a while. My godfather Tony DiStefano, whom my father loved like a brother, teared up when he saw me. We exchanged a warm embrace. He had taught me to walk, according to my mother, or at least I took my first shaky steps to him. He used a cane now, wore hearing aids in both ears, and trembled. He asked me why no visit for so long and I told him about my studies at the University of Toronto, which he heard as the University of Torino, and he began to drone on about Torino, where he'd been stationed with the Italian military when he was nineteen. How time flies! He lamented his declining health and the cruelty of existence and said he'd be joining Uncle Sal before long. This made me sad for that fading generation.

Joey wanted to step out for air, and Vincenzo and I joined him, though exiting the crisply air-conditioned funeral home proved misguided. The afternoon sun beat down its hazy golden hammers, softening the street so that everything sagged, bowed, drooped, dripped, storefronts, street lights, telephone poles, awnings, asphalt.

We removed our jackets, flung them over our shoulders, and lumbered to James Street, or little Sicily as it's known, a short stretch of sundry shops and café-bars just south of the old CNR station—a late Beaux Arts beauty and one-off in a city bereft of truly significant or interesting landmarks—Uncle Sal's old haunt. We crossed James Street, walked half a block south to Bar Italia, and entered breathless into its air-conditioned, coffee-tinctured confines.

The white-haired barista, Domenico, smiled when he saw us, and with unconscious formality buttoned up his red paisley vest. "Look who it is, the Sferazza boys. What brings you to these parts? You're not Sicilians, are you? You're of the Mangiacake people. With names like Bobby and Joey, what should a simple man like me think? You might as well be Wally and Beaver, eh? Now if Roberto and Giuseppe entered like proper gallants, I'd hug them and kiss them on both cheeks twice. But, ah, I have my scruples, boys."

"Very funny, Domenico. I'd swear a hint of polenta is creeping into your accent from following Juventus all these years."

"Your uncle Frank, the big Inter fan—we knock heads every time we see each other. People laugh out loud—look at the two *terroni* arguing over those northerners."

"I've always followed Palermo," I lied. "I'm a patriot."

Domenico waved dismissively. "You—you always hated soccer, said it was for sissies."

"It still is, Dom. It still is. Eh, you remember my cousin Vincenzo."

"Of course, with a strong name like that. It sings. Vincenzo, *bello*, how's your father, he doesn't come to James Street anymore now that he lives in the east end. It's not as if he's up on the mountain or in Stoney Creek."

"The old man hardly drives anymore, Dom. He's become a crank, You wouldn't want him around here anyway, he'd just break your balls."

"But that's exactly why I want him to come!" Domenico said with an operatic arm drop. "You say ball-breaking like it's a bad thing! Anyway, we're all getting old. I've got grandkids in high school. I can't believe how the years have flown by. When I think about it I want to cry my eyes out. I remember when we all came here from Sicily with nothing but busted suitcases. We had respect back then. And went out of our way to show it. Nowadays people are like dogs. They shit whenever and wherever they want."

"The world has changed," Vincenzo said. "But it's always changing, Dom."

As if to illustrate how bad things had gotten, Domenico picked up a *Hamilton Spectator* and flipped to an article, TIGERS TAMED BY THUGS, reporting that several Ticats—among them import linebacker Rick Zilli—sustained serious injuries yesterday evening in a brawl at an undisclosed downtown Hamilton nightclub. "You see," he said, slapping the paper. "No respect for nobody."

"That was last night—at the Press Club," I said, startled by the article, as it drove home the reality of what I had witnessed. "I was there."

"You were there?" Vincenzo said.

My précis of the donnybrook—a well-planned ambush, really—provoked a mix of horror and laughter. The idea of a street gang thrashing professional football players, among them one of the more hard-nosed defenders in the CFL, amused them. But Zilli's flaming green shirt drew the strongest reactions, and would in future tellings. That the article in the *Spectator* failed to mention the story's most vivid detail amused me.

"Did anyone get charged?" Joey asked.

"Nobody got charged. Nobody could say for sure who did what."

"The usual story," Vincenzo said. "Omerta of the masses."

"No one wants to be a snitch," Joey said under his breath.

Shaking his head, Domenico poured out four shots of Napoleon brandy and we drank to Uncle Sal, sharing a moment of thoughtful silence afterwards. Then he refilled the glasses and we drank to the Ticats, hoping they'd recruit tougher players.

"Anyway, Vincenzo," Domenico said, "Send my greetings to your father, we shared a lot of laughs back in the day—and your mother, too, such a nice lady."

"I'm sure he'll come by someday. Maybe I'll bring him around."

Domenico leaned to my brother. "And little Joey, Jesus Christ, last time I saw you your father, *buon anima*, was carrying you in his arms. You were a quiet baby. Not a peep. He'd bring you in here and you'd never cry or complain. Not like your brother there. What a pain in the ass he was. Look at him now. I bet he's a bigger pain in the ass than he ever was."

"You don't know the half of it," Vincenzo said with Joey nodding confirmation.

We ordered espressos and Domenico engaged the Gaggia classic, surrounded by Italian flags and tricolour banners, posters of mighty Juventus in their storied zebra stripes and modest Palermo in pink, postcards from Cefalù and Siracusa, ornamental carts from Agrigento, liqueur bottles with sugary trees in them, family portraits old and new, and a gothic-lettered homage in parchment to Leonardo Sciascia, the Sicilian writer.

"How old was your uncle?" Domenico asked.

"Sixty-eight," I said. "Retired from Stelco three years ago after thirty years there."

Domenico shook his head. "Ah, that's a shame. He was a dancer back in the old days. Sharp dresser with the scarpini and double-breasted suits. The ladies would line up to dance with him at weddings and at the old Modjeska Hall galas."

Joey lowered his head; his shoulders jerked. Vincenzo gently squeezed his neck.

"What are you gonna do?" Domenico shrugged. "We'll all get there eventually."

None of us could disagree with that.

We finished our espressos and started back for Friscolanti's. Dark clouds had moved in, blotting out the sky and pressing down. The air felt hot and metallic. A gust of wind rattled the trees, blew around bits of paper and debris; an empty pop can clattered under a red pickup truck. Lightning crackled in the distance, followed by low rumbles of thunder. My temples throbbed.

Vincenzo walked like he had pebbles in his shoes. Joey ducked his head and plunged forward pulling his lapels. A speck of dust struck my right eye, causing it to tear up and spasm. Stopping to dab the blinded eye with tissue paper, I thought I heard Vincenzo calling my name and looked up—he was walking toward Friscolanti's with his back to me. I called him but he kept walking. "Vincenzo!" I called again, but he kept walking. What the hell.

An electric darkness swept through town, gritty, turbulent, but when Eugene Ciccone's dark blue Lincoln pulled up across the street from Friscolanti's, I sensed that a summer storm, one that would shower us and blow over, that would offer a reprieve from the heat, wasn't the only thing on its way. Something else was hurtling toward us, more malevolent than a mere turn in the weather. And I had no idea how prescient that impression would be: that a storm was upon us owing nothing to the clouds in the sky.

Eugene rolled down his window, sucking a toothpick and wearing an oily smirk.

"What do you want?"

"Take it easy, big boy," he sneered. "I come in peace."

I gestured for Vincenzo and Joey to hang back.

"Sorry about your uncle," Eugene said. "I hear he was a stand-up guy."

"Yeah, and now he's not. But you didn't come to pay your condolences. If you're here for the money, I don't have it yet."

Eugene spit out the toothpick and snapped his fingers as though something important had occurred to him. "Hey, d'you hear about those Ticat pricks? Funny, eh. Big tough football players. Not so tough without their pads on."

"Yeah. I was there."

Eugene turned his face to me, the edges of his mouth twitching. "You were there, that's right, that's right, I heard. Eugene knows all, heh-heh. He has eyes everywhere. But what does Bobby know?"

"To be honest with you, Eugene, I only saw shadows."

"Shadows, eh? And no flaming shirt?"

"Saw the flames, not who lit them. Okay? Now about that other thing—"

"That's all right." He looked straight ahead, hands on the steering wheel. "Tell your brother he's off the hook."

It took a moment to digest the message. And it didn't sit well. Something, maybe the hard look on Eugene's face as he turned to gauge my reaction, told me it wasn't good news. He was an individual uninterested and incapable of bearing good news to anyone. I had to know why Joey was off the hook.

"The matter's been settled," he said, sucking his teeth and glancing at Vincenzo and Joey, who now stood behind me. "Back up?" he asked with a smirk, and rolled up his window. He gunned the Lincoln and pulled away from me as the rain started falling, big heavy drops that drenched us by the time we reached Friscolanti's white-columned entranceway.

We dried off in the washroom with paper towels and emerged like three greasers with sweating sickness, Vincenzo's brown suit reeking like a bog-drowned dog, Joey's teeth chattering in the air-conditioned chill. We spent several heavy hours greeting mourners. I told Vincenzo to forget the loan, that the matter had been resolved, but that I smelled a rat.

"Maybe he found the package or whatever."

"But turning down an easy two grand—I mean, I was going to give it to him. Seems out of character. And something else happened last night besides the Ticats getting whipped. I knocked the snot out of Terry Peters."

Joey stiffened. "You did?"

"Yeah, fucking guy was beating up this chick on the dance floor. Don't think anybody saw me. The lights were killed. I doubt Eugene knows about it. But I'm not sure. Didn't get a good read off him. What do you think he's got up his sleeve?"

"Who knows, Bobby."

My mother interrupted our pow-wow. "Why do you look so serious, standing over here?"

"It's a funeral home, Ma. Uncle Sal..."

"I said serious, not sad. What are you up to?"

"Zia," Vincenzo said, "we're reminiscing, that's all."

My mother half-smiled and drifted back toward the casket. We returned to our posts by the door, greeting visitors. The common theme: Uncle Sal had his flaws but was a stand-up guy. The ladies loved him but he never married. He died childless but loved.

Ah, Uncle Sal. The man had treated me to my first hamburger. When I was seven or eight he loaded my brother and me into his big silver Cadillac and drove us down to Burlington Beach, under the Skyway Bridge, by the old arcade, where they sold food and drink out of this baby-blue wooden shack. He bought us hamburgers, fries and chocolate milkshakes, and we ate them near a rusty, decommissioned Ferris wheel. I remember how lurid my burger looked, bright mustard and relish and ketchup, with a thick slice of tomato and a thicker slice of onion; and I'll never forget how incredibly good it tasted, and how I would have eaten another had it been offered. But I also remember how acridly I burped that onion up for the next two days. Funny what sticks with you. I wondered if Joey remembered that. It must have been his first hamburger, too.

Later, at Nancy's, after a meal of honey-garlic ribs and rice, and a bottle of red wine of which I actually drank a glass, I reminisced about Uncle Sal.

"Were you close to him?"

"Sort of. A bit crusty, Uncle Sal. Not the easiest man to talk to. My brother was his pet. When Joey was a toddler, Uncle Sal would babysit him during the day. He worked steady afternoons at Stelco, so he didn't mind. He'd take him to the swings at Eastwood Park or hike him around the marina on his shoulders. He was childless, so he doted on Joey, bought him all kinds of shit, and Joey reciprocated with lots of love and respect."

"Aw. He must be taking it hard. When is the funeral?"

"Tomorrow."

Nancy stretched her warm legs across my lap and wriggled her neat, painted toes. All she had on was a grey sweatshirt.

"Don't you like this?" she asked.

I smiled. What was there not to like? The sex, the food, the conversation, the ease with which we passed the time? Nancy had even started reading a few books I'd recommended, *Tropic of Cancer*, *The Great Gatsby*, *The Sun Also Rises*, and could talk about them in detail—bones in whale cocks, chauffeurs in robin's-egg blue, three martinis at lunch and four bottles of wine. But as much as I enjoyed these brief breaks from the larger flow of my life, that's what they were: intermissions, not the play itself.

That encounter with Eugene weighed on my mind: he wasn't being straight. It reminded me of an obvious passing situation on the football field. Ready to backpedal into my defensive zone at the snap of the ball, anticipating a forward pass, I detect something in the quarterback's eyes that tells me he plans to run a screen or a draw or some other tricky play instead. What is it exactly? Hard to say. A self-conscious cloaking?—I will act like this is real when it is not; in other words, I will act *too* seriously, *too* straightforwardly, when in reality this is nothing but a feint. This is where you earn your stripes as linebacker, sniffing out bluffs, and counterattacking with force. And with these alarms blaring in my head, a buzzy restlessness took over; I needed to keep moving, not to find anything, not even to escape anything, but to keep moving for its own sake.

"What's on your mind?" she asked.

"Lots of things."

"Anything to do with me?"

Yes, in a way. Yes, of course, in a way, she was on my mind, but other things prevailed. She found this depressing, but what could be done about it? I made excuses. Uncle Sal's funeral was at eleven next morning and I needed to talk to my mother and get my rest and blah blah blah. Nancy rolled her eyes, and with a sigh of resignation showed me the door.

My mother and Joey were sound asleep when I got home. The house felt like a sauna and sleeping proved futile in my airless bedroom or on the living room couch—encased in sticky vinyl from the 1960s—and the basement was so damp and drippy as to creep me out, so I put on shorts and went for a night run.

For an hour I ran laps around Eastwood Park, which had been finally cleaned up to a presentable green with flowers aplenty, the air foggy and foul but cool from the suspiring bay and shaggy trees.

Its usual starless charcoal mass, the sky heaved and sighed, and crickets resounded in flinty multitudes. I thought about Uncle Sal, here one day, gone the next. Uncle Sal, you up there? Hope you're well. Keep an eye out for Joey. Keep an eye out for him.

I ran a dozen sprints on the re-sodded soccer field, performed jumping jacks and squat thrusts, stretched my hamstrings and quads until the mosquitoes swarmed me, then jogged home.

As I walked to the house I noticed Mr. Warden on his porch. He was by himself, in a damp undershirt, white hair plastered to his forehead, eyes fixed on a point in the distance. I stood there as the sweat cooled from my shoulders and mosquito bites started itching, waiting to see if he would give a nod of recognition, a blink, a grunt, but he continued staring at something in the bay, or at some further remove.

ELEVEN

We buried Uncle Sal at Holy Sepulchre Cemetery on the out-
skirts of Hamilton, where my father and maternal grandmother
lay at rest in a family plot; and after Uncle Sal was in the ground
and the other mourners departed, I took the time to visit with
them. My mother had arranged flowers from her garden and votary candles by the headstones. The smell of dry earth, grasses,
and burning wax filled my nostrils. I knelt down and said an Our
Father because I didn't know what else to say. I was as bad at com-
municating with the dead as they were with me. A gloomy man in
a charcoal-grey suit and white felt gloves passed me and continued
up to the mausoleum. With bags under his eyes, and in need of a
shave, he looked a bit off. I wondered if he was a mourner or just
a depressed cemetery employee.

A few plots remained for my family, though not enough for
everyone. The aunts and uncles joked about who would get there
first and who'd wind up being buried alone somewhere else,
something I found less amusing than they did.

The foundries plumed majestically into the soaring blue sky,
burning, forging, refining. Their exhaust parodied clouds. But the
thought of them, of their industry, like the thought of a funeral
plot reserved—or not—for me, made me glum.

I looked across the lake at the radiant CN Tower, piercing the sky-
line, puncturing its vast blue balloon, and I felt hopeful, if not cheerier.
After hanging around for another twenty minutes—not before
the lugubrious man wearing white gloves exited the mausoleum

and passed by me again, this time sniffling—I drove home. On the way I listened to Frank Zappa's *Apostrophe* on the tape deck, but after Nanook ate the yellow snow I switched to FM jazz radio. Some delicate Bill Evans was playing; my blood pressure dropped.

My mother had asked me to join the family at Aunt Rosa's for dinner, but I needed a break from the sorrow. Joey must have been off on his own somewhere, he wasn't home. When I called Demarco to cancel our scheduled afternoon workout he expressed condolences for Uncle Sal and asked if I was booking the night off work. But I saw no reason to stay around the house all evening, brooding by myself.

"I'll be there," I said. "I need the distraction."

"Okay. I'll still be hitting the gym if you change your mind."

"Do some incline presses for me, will you?"

"Yeah, you bet. See you tonight."

I ate a salad of tomatoes, cucumbers, and basil from my mother's garden, showered, and before work took a cruise along Burlington Street in the Camaro with the roof down. Thursday night in early August, warm and rank, everyone dragging their asses, even dogs, even cats, the sulphur-tinged city neither here nor there. Someone had wrenched open the valves of a fire hydrant, but abandoned it, and it sat there gushing without meaning. A few blocks east of my house, three burly Satan's Choice bikers stood before the old Essex Meat Packers plant smoking and talking, their hogs in an orderly row beside an orange pick-up with a stove in back. One of them said something that made the others burst out laughing. They all looked like they belonged.

I drove up the treacherous Jolly Cut to the escarpment, parked on Concession Street near a lookout, and exited the car. The road was sticky underfoot, the air rank with skunk and rotting vegetation. A dead black squirrel lay near the curb, its body so intact and unmolested it looked asleep. Wispy mosquitoes droned through the shadows, now and then touching down on my hair or brushing by my face. One bit my hand but died bloody when I flattened it. Crickets chirred from the depths behind the safety fence, a sheer drop down the rock face. A red van rumbled past, due west, bearing two bearded men in baseball caps. Together they glanced at me, then looked straight ahead. Perhaps I didn't belong. The van disappeared around a corner.

The setting sun sank like a red hot air balloon; the carbon black of lengthening shadows crept across the city. The dirty jewels of the downtown core glittered below, waiting for night, full of light, full of promise; spectral ships moved through dark bay waters bearing coal, iron ore, cocoa beans, and pelletized rubber; the foundries flared—I thought of Uncle Sal: thirty years and *poof*— tainting the sky, firing the ink of the bay. Such busyness at close of day, such industry.

Once upon a time Hamilton, "the Ambitious City," competed with Toronto for prominence on Lake Ontario. But that was long ago. Things had changed. I was looking at the past.

I arrived late at the Press Club. Not much of a lineup what with the recent troubles. New York, New York, on the other hand, thus far free of major incidents, continued to enjoy teeming dance floors and endless lineups of people waiting for hours or paying through the nose to get inside. When I knocked on the Press Club doors a strange guy in a pinstriped navy suit answered. He glanced at my black jacket and name tag and nodded me in.

"Hi, I'm Tommy. Luciano hired me to take the place of the Spanish guy."

"Nice to meet you, I'm Bobby. Fernandez isn't Spanish."

"No? Anyway, you're posted at the back with the bodybuilder guy, Anton."

"Tonino. Demarco. We call him Demarco."

Tommy shrugged. He didn't care one way or the other. His big brown eyes, bulbous nose, oversized jaw, and half-smile gave him the air of a comedian about to crack a joke. I asked who was manning the doors with him.

"Buzzsaw. Fucked off an hour ago. Seemed nervous or upset about something."

"I'll tell him to get back here," I promised, and went in.

When I saw Demarco, he was so wide-eyed and pallid I thought he'd popped bennies.

"Bobby, did you hear about Luigi Fanelli? He was shot in front of his house."

"He was what?"

"Shot dead. Shot in the face, right in front of his house."

The news gave me shivers. I recalled what Eugene had said to me at Friscolanti's, about cleaning house. But did that include someone like Fanelli? Or was his murder unrelated? And I had to wonder how Joey and I fit into Eugene's grand scheme, or if we did at all. There was always a chance I'd been giving Eugene too much credit and that he was nothing but a sick fuck with no plan whatsoever.

Felicia approached me already chattering, her urgency equine, but I could made out nothing she said—her words rushed, the music loud—and needed a moment to think, so I walked away from her in mid-rant and sped to the washroom, where I occupied a stall, buried my face in my hands, and thought.

So Eugene was purging. But why shoot Fanelli right in front of his own house? Wasn't that recklessly brazen? Was it meant to send a message?

Then again more than one person could have wanted Luigi dead. He had hurt people all over the city. He'd been in and out of jail, may have made enemies inside. Or when push came to shove his old man put his foot down. Pure speculation. Only one thing you could say with certainty: there was a new game in town.

When I went back out I ducked Felicia, but moments later her brother accosted me.

"What is it, Caesar? You look unhealthy. Everything okay?"

"I heard something. I was going to ask you about it."

"You mean what happened to Fanelli?"

"I know about that already," he said irritably. "I mean Johnny Papalia—I talked to Fernandez on the phone today. He heard that Papalia's not too happy about what happened here. His nephew's gimpy from the beating. Can't walk right, dizzy spells, talks to himself. Buzzsaw said he's been getting a lot of wrong numbers calling his place. He's spooked, afraid to go home, afraid to be here. Fuck, I don't know what to think. Should I take this seriously? I mean, would Papalia, you know... "

"I don't know, Caesar. The way things are going right now, I don't know what to tell you. You probably *don't* have to worry—but if I were you I'd keep my head up. Anything is possible in this town, you know that."

Caesar wasn't reassured. He shoved his hands in his trouser pockets and walked away mumbling to himself. Finally I spotted Buzzsaw in a booth, chatting to a slim brunette with long red fingernails. He looked ragged, inflamed.

"Taking a break?" I said.

He shot out of the booth with a scalded and guilty look on his face.

"It's okay," I said. "I understand. But that new guy Tommy is alone up front. He doesn't have a clue."

"Tommy's a moron." He licked his chapped lips. "Mind spelling me?"

"I can do that. But you can't hide back here all night, Buzzsaw."

His look told me that he could sure as fuck try. Unprepared to fight back, to stand up for himself, he exercised his only option. One way to go, I suppose, the way of the worm. I left him to the slim brunette, cautiously scratching her nose.

Roy Rosati, fuller in the cheeks than he had been all summer, bearded, and wearing a vintage Aloha shirt as large and loose as a muumuu, stood by a rubber plant, stogie in mouth.

"It's not lit, okay?"

"Didn't say a word."

"I take it you heard about Fanelli. Terrible thing. Now tell me again that was his sister you introduced me to that night."

"Connie. That was his sister, all right."

"Unbelievable. How life goes sometimes. Don't look now, but—" He pointed to a woman in a clingy white cotton dress with permed black hair and shoulders like bowling balls.

"That's Pamela," I said. "Demarco's friend."

"You mean squeeze. You'll hear rutting sounds any moment now."

"They've been seeing a lot of each other?"

"They've been working out together." Roy smiled and sucked on his cigar. "I hear she's a hermaphrodite."

"Demarco's a hermaphrodite."

He stood under the EXIT sign in back with his arms folded across his chest like Charles Atlas. "Funkytown" came on earlier than usual, a desperate move to rouse the moribund crowd, but we'd all grown immune to its groove and it failed to excite anyone's pulse. Except for a few diehards, the dance floor was empty.

> *Gotta move on*
> *Gotta move on*
> *Gotta move on*

"It's coming to an end, my friend."

Demarco's arms came down. "The Press Club?"

"No, the whole thing, the whole scene."

I meant all of it, the summer, the era, my time in that town, it was all coming to an end. At least it felt that way to me. Getting out in one piece still needed doing, but the dying fall had begun. The 1970s were behind us. Disco music and the human ear's tolerance for it had peaked. Platform shoes had fallen from grace, along with musk colognes and chest hair. Stetsons and cowboy boots began to stud the landscape, even in northern steel towns. Whispers of a new and horrible sexually transmitted disease circulated. Cocaine was nudging amphetamines off the charts as a stimulant of choice among partiers and clubbers.

"Demarco, your squeeze is here."

"What do you mean, my squeeze?"

"Your new workout partner."

"Now hold on a sec. Pam's serious about bodybuilding, committed. She inspires me."

"I'm glad for you, Demarco. You don't have to be such a weasel about it."

"Well, I know she's not for everyone," he said, lurching off to find his new soulmate.

"Weasel."

Vic Zuccheroni stood alone by the bar with a drink in his hand, wearing a jacket of raspberry felt and a black shirt and tie. I avoided his eye in vain; within moments he appeared beside me, nearing his face to my neck.

"Soft-man," he said, so darkly tanned his teeth looked fluorescent. "I wanna tell you something. But I want you to keep it like this—" He pressed an index finger to his lips, showing me exactly what he meant. "See what I'm saying? Nobody must know this. Nobody."

It had been a grim enough day; needing to be humoured, I summoned the patience to listen.

"I'm moving back to Sicily," he said, looking behind me to check that no one knelt there, eavesdropping. "My cousin Roger invited me to stay with him in Palermo. We've talked about opening a trattoria there for years and I think now's the time to make a move. There's nothing left here for Vic Zuccheroni. That's right. Ciao ciao, Steel Town. Been here since '65. Came here from Sicily at sixteen with a one-piece of luggage, a punk kid. Now I'm a man. I've made money here, fucked women, and fought the toughest men in the city. I've kicked ass and, yes, taken a few beatings, but I'm still standing, still looking good, still fierce. I can still rock'n'roll, soft-man, you know. Don't have to tell you. But I wanna go out on top. Know what I'm saying?"

"I think so, Vic."

"What's the matter, Bobby? Aren't you excited for me? Palermo's an amazing city."

"Sorry, Vic...we buried my uncle Sal today."

He looked at me, puzzled. Then he frowned. His next move took me by surprise. He leaned over, wrapped his arms around me, and gave me a tremendous hug. When he pulled back, tears welled in his eyes.

"Sorry to hear. When I lost Uncle Giacomo, my father's kid brother, back in Sicily—dead ringer for Sal Mineo. Remember Sal Mineo? Handsome. When Uncle Giacomo died—they were digging for Greek antiquities near Palermo, when there was a collapse of some kind—he got buried alive. I cried for a week straight."

I asked him when he planned to split for the old country and he said as soon as his papers were in order. A few near-deportations for various charges had held things up, but if all went well he'd be gone by autumn. An unusual moment—the first time Vic had dropped the wise-guy act and spoken to me like a regular human being; but then I realized it was the first time that I had ever listened to him as a human being.

Then, while I was still flushed by my exchange with Vic, Luciano arrived with a bucket of reality to cool me off. Tieless and needing a shave and a haircut, he had a cold, or was coming down from an eight-ball junket—judging by his rheumy eyes, scabby nostrils, and off smell. He stopped to have a word with two of the newer, wide-eyed waitresses, and with Paula the Wolf, who threw her tray on the bar counter and stalked off to the staff room. Then Luciano sent Fat Freddy home, who took it better, claiming he looked forward to hitting the sack early for a change.

When Luciano sent Diego home instead of Ali, a skirmish ensued, with Diego hurling vague accusations of corruption and dog-fucking at his colleague, who, taking offense, threw a beer-soaked towel at his face, which sparked off a chest-to-chest shoving match that thumped on for a good minute before Jerome came by and, clasping their skulls like bocce balls, pulled them apart. Luciano, too defeated to reprimand them, promised Diego that next time Ali would go home first. An equitable, rational solution, but Diego's emotions, running *caliente* as they were, caused an unwarranted and exhausting prolongation of the scuffle.

Fed up with Diego, Jerome flattened his hand and delivered a sharp chop to the back of his neck that quieted him. The dazed busboy left rubbing his neck but bearing no grudges as the fire in him had cooled.

"That's Tommy, my sister's *kid*," Luciano said. "Why is he up front alone?"

"Any relation to the deejay?" I asked.

"That's my *other* sister's kid. Now tell me what the fuck is going on."

"Buzzsaw's not feeling well, I'm on my way."

"He's a good *kid*, a bit slow, but well-meaning. My sister begged me to give him a *job*. She got *sick* of him hanging around the house. Do me a favour and show him the *ropes*, you know. He's green. He's never worked doors before. I don't think he's very *tough* either. The way things have been around here lately, I don't want to see him get into a *beef* first night on the job."

That was nice to know. A dim-witted wuss. Exactly who I needed to back me up when, say, the Clubbers came rushing the door with baseball bats. I went to the front and Tommy was standing there with his hands folded at his crotch and his eyes closed. If I wasn't mistaken, he appeared to be snoozing.

When I cleared my throat, Tommy's eyes opened and that half-smile materialized. I thought he'd make a wisecrack or witty excuse for himself—I suffer from narcolepsy, man—but he didn't. He said nothing. He just looked at me dully, sniffed, and snapped his eyes shut again. I found this unusual and annoying but not surprising. Had he pulled out a ceremonial sword and started dis-embowelling himself, and then asked me to cut off his head—that would have surprised me. I assumed my position across from him and actively prayed the evening would fade away gently, without incident or ugliness. This turned out to be vain and misguided.

The first malodor arrived in the form of Lenny Hutton, bravely wearing a fuchsia shirt, and flanked by the tiger twins, showing off their stripes and pipes in leather bustiers, garters, and black stiletto heels. Lenny shook my hand but slipped me no money, which did not break my heart. He offered me instead a few lines of coke.

"Not into coke," I admitted. My one experience had caused me nosebleeds and diarrhea.

"That's okay, more for me and the gals, meow." He nudged my shoulder. "Looks like things have quieted down here, buddy."

"Yeah, Lenny, looks like."

"Well, I'm planning to perk things up," he said, clapping his hands twice.

The twins took his arms and they strutted into the club like hired entertainment, Lenny raising his arms, the girls kicking their heels. They wasted no time invading the dance floor and delivering like pros, writhing and grinding, spinning and dipping, with occasional sprints to the can to powder their noses, but no one else joined their little party. It was almost as if they were dancing with no music, and looked strange doing it.

At around midnight, Albert the disco cop arrived, out of sorts, and unaccompanied by his partner in crime, good old Lloyd. He wanted a word with me.

"Let's walk and talk," he said, leading me outside.

A carnival atmosphere prevailed at New York, New York: balloons, horns, flashing lights, and a frisky, silky crowd filling the air with chatter and laughter. Even a joker on stilts clopped about wearing Mad Hatter headgear and red elephant pants, showering the crowd with glittery confetti and pamphlets, likely shilling for a club promotion. At least some folks were having fun. I stared at the cheery spectacle with envy.

"Bobby," Albert said briskly. "I want to talk to you about Felicia."

"Okay." I assumed he knew, whether via his own diligence or Felicia's confession, about our clandestine encounters. "Let me start by saying, I'm sorry. I'm sorry about all this, Albert."

He leaned back to better look at my face, perhaps to see if I was serious.

"What are you sorry about?"

"Sorry for cutting your grass. Had no idea you two were hot and heavy. There were still unresolved feelings there. No more. And you shouldn't be angry with her. It's on me."

Albert said nothing to this and continued walking. It only occurred to me then that he might not have known about my trysts with Felicia. Where was he going? What was he thinking? What did he want? Even with his jaw set and the veins in his neck bulging—what does that mean in the way of tells?—I failed to get a read on him. He kept walking, heavily bringing down his heels. His scuffed shoes lacked their usual black dazzle. He smelled of stale cologne mingled with a tang of body odour, and another sour, unidentifiable note. His uniform needed pressing, fingernails buffing, and his sideburns crept like tarantulas from under his cap.

When we turned a corner, not far from the cop shop, he continued walking, and in a darkened section of the street came to a stop. Uncertain of his program, I slowly advanced toward him but stopped a few feet short, in front of a closed diner with a Labbat Blue neon sign buzzing in the window. A moment passed. Albert's breaths came short and quick. Bolting crossed my mind. When he whirled around reaching—I thought—for his holster, my heart turned. For a second it looked like the Bobby Sferazza story was about to come to an abrupt and unheroic end, but at that moment Octavio, the corpulent owner of New York, New York, emerged like a leviathan from the shadows, flanked by two leggy goons wearing identical silvery suits.

"Hey, Albert," he said gruffly. "Been looking for you. We need to talk."

"Not now, Octavio, I'm having a conversation here."

Octavio shot me a contemptuous look with his small piggy eyes and sucked his short grey teeth. The flabby flesh impressed by his shirt collar looked like a surreal neck brace. His shiny black suit jacket, an enormous garment, could have cloaked a small family. And yet his feet, in supple black moccasins, were very small, and he moved with odd grace and nimbleness for a huge man, like an ex-athlete or dancer. His partners, easily passing for twins from afar but at close range markedly dissimilar, stood there like professional sneerers. One had a gruesome case of acne, scattered over his neck and face like buckshot, the other a cloudy glass eye, made more obvious whenever he looked sideways and the glass eye trailed. Between these two handsome bookends, the voluminous Octavio seethed.

"Now, Albert. I want to talk to you *now*. I've already talked to Lloyd."

"You talked to Lloyd?" Albert said, nonplussed. He touched the brim of his cap.

"That's right, I talked to him. And he's not happy."

Albert turned to me and quietly said we'd talk later.

"I'm not interested in her anymore, if that's what this is about."

He looked at me darkly. "We'll talk later, Bobby."

As I walked away I wondered what kind of jam Albert and Lloyd were in. Rumours swirled about this Octavio guy, about his connections to the Montreal mob, how he had a City Hall bigwig in his pocket—Councilman Mario Augusto had been blowing his whistle at New York, New York all summer, but the finger could have been pointed at anyone. You hear all kinds of shit. In the end, it's all part of a story that can never be completely told.

When I got to the Press Club, shouting and commotion issued from behind the door. I knocked and a red-faced Demarco opened up.

"What's going on? I heard—"

He shook his head. "Where you been, man?"

"Talking to Albert the cop."

When I stepped inside, Tommy was flat on the floor with blood oozing out of his mouth and nostrils. I stared at Demarco, trying not to smile.

"What happened to him?"

"A gentleman came to the door asking for Buzzsaw, and when genius over there said he was the one and only, the guy cracked him in the beak with brass knuckles."

I'd never heard of such a thing in these parts. "You're trying to tell me someone actually busted his face with brass knuckles?"

"That's what Tommy said."

It sounded ridiculous.

Luciano rushed down the steps, almost tripping on the last one, and exploded in a frothing rage, cursing the stairs, the bar, his family, the universe, and God. Once he spat through that inventory, he redirected his ire at me.

"Told you to *watch* out for him, Bobby. Told you he'd never worked *door* before, that he wasn't a fighter, that he was *green*. Was I talking to myself? Tell me I wasn't talking to *myself*."

"Albert the cop wanted a few words and pulled me outside."

He dismissed me with a double wave and stalked around the entrance, glancing at his bashed-up nephew and wringing his hands.

Everyone stood there like sweating statues, powerless to move or speak.

Luciano lit up again. "Did *somebody* call an ambulance? And where is that jackass Albert anyway? When you really need a cop, he always *fucks* off. When he's hounding your waitresses it's another *story*. What the fuck happened here! Somebody please *tell* me what happened!"

"This guy came to the doors and asked for Buzzsaw," Demarco said. "Tommy said he was Buzzsaw and the guy clipped him with some brass knuckles."

"Brass knuckles?" Luciano cried. "Who the fuck carries brass knuckles around *these* days? It stinks. I'm telling you, it *stinks!*"

When Albert appeared at the door, Luciano greeted him with a torrent of abuse and pushed him outside to fully vent his feelings. Demarco and I exchanged a look and shrugged. What are you gonna do? Grit your teeth and bear it. I felt an iota of pity for Albert. There must have been a good reason why he let Luciano chump him like that.

Minutes later an ambulance arrived. Two attendants heaped Tommy on a stretcher and wheeled him away. Never saw the guy again.

Shortly, Oscar and Mad Dog showed up, red-eyed and twitchy, wired on something, their clothes soiled and reeking of diesel and vomit. Oscar's hair was a sticky black mass, and bits of white matter specked his chin. Blood and filth crusted his knuckles. Odd, and touching in a twisted way, was the Cathedral High championship ring on one of his fingers.

When I said Oscar's name he looked through me.

Reeling, mouth agape, Mad Dog held himself against the door frame. He mumbled and pushed away from the frame, glaring at me with those red eyes and making low sounds in his chest. My heart pounded like a piston; I bent at the knees and tensed my core.

Big Jerome rumbled to the doors, and when he saw Oscar and Mad Dog he was so put off I thought he'd bail, but he took a deep breath and flanked me.

"Everything okay, Bobby?"

"Everything's okay. What can I do for you, Oscar?"

He tipped his head forward, laughing and licking his dry lips.

Mad Dog shifted his feet, muttering, and when I turned to him Oscar tried to slip by me, but I grabbed his arm and hammerlocked it behind his back, then wrapped my arm around his neck and held him.

When Mad Dog lunged forward, Jerome met him with a forearm shiver to the chest that stopped him on the spot and left him pop-eyed, grabbing at his sternum with a childish look of hurt. Mad Dog wisely decided to save Jerome a workout.

I held Oscar until he relaxed—and he wasn't really resisting—then I let him go and stepped back. He didn't rush me, but stood there with his hands at his sides, wearing a sick smile.

"Sorry about Luigi, Oscar."

He shook his greasy hair, laughed to himself, then slowly raised his eyes to me.

"Luigi? Luigi was scum, man. He was nothing but scum."

This was unexpected.

"We're gonna go in and jus' look around. Okay, Bobby? You don't mind, do you? Fucking guy." He looked at me sideways, squinting, licking his lips. "Cathedral 17, Bishop Ryan 10. Tha's right, Bobby Doctor. Tha's right, my brother. Superman, Super-man."

"Enough, Oscar."

"It's never enough! Ha! Never!"

I tensed up and readied my fists, expecting to come to blows with him at last—it was time to resolve this thing, whatever it was—but his shoulders slumped and he cast his wrecked eyes downward.

"I know you, man. I know you," he said, more to himself than to me. Then he clapped Mad Dog on the back. "I know this fucking guy. He won't bother us. He won't bother us. Come on."

I was going to stop them, and maybe I should have, but a snapshot of Oscar and me on a football field flashed through my mind. I'm looking over my shoulder at him as he shouts out coverages and beams that gold-tinged smile. *Make a play, Bobby Doctor. Make a play...* And in an instant, memories of Cathedral High and golden autumns and twilight practices and Blue and White Days and pep rallies and flying all over the field feeling more alive than you've ever felt—it all came rushing back to me. No matter how I tried to distance myself from those memories—seeing Oscar, the finest athlete I'd ever known, the fastest, most agile, most cunning and savage, reduced to a gibbering thug, disarmed me.

So I let them in. And within minutes, after trying to molest the twins, they clashed with Lenny Hutton. Oscar and Lenny squared off by the dance floor exchanging blows, while Mad Dog stood by gaping. To my surprise, Lenny held his own, avoiding Oscar's wild swings, and chopping up his face with short sharp punches. But they say the punch you don't see is the one that knocks you out, and Mad Dog's unforeseen sucker punch came out of nowhere. Lenny went down like he'd been shot.

And then I thought the kicking would start, but Demarco and Caesar grabbed Oscar, Jerome and Buzzsaw grabbed Mad Dog, and without too much fuss threw them out.

TWELVE

Then the call in the night comes. The one that takes your breath away, that guts you. I remember getting a call like that when I was fifteen years old. At three in the morning, May 3, 1975, the telephone rang, waking me from a deep sleep. I was in the house alone with Joey. He was eleven at the time, a puny kid with these skinny arms and big brown eyes, afraid of his own shadow. My mother had spent the last few nights at St. Joseph's Hospital, keeping vigil at my dying father's bedside. When I answered the telephone Uncle Giuseppe spoke. All he said was "He's gone," and at first in my sleep daze I didn't know what he meant, or who he was talking about. Then it clicked, and I realized that my father was dead.

This time the telephone rang at two in the morning, and the call came not from Uncle Giuseppe, but from Charlie Tesser, Joey's north-end chum.

"Bobby," he said. "Joey's been hurt."

"What you mean he's been hurt? How bad?"

"We got jumped, Bobby."

What was this? My brain refused to take it in; all that registered was a profound sinking feeling. Dry-mouthed, I asked, "Where are you?"

"At a phone booth here at Gage Park, near the main gates. Joey's in the parking lot. He's hurt, Bobby. I dunno what do."

"Stay calm, I'll be there in a minute."

"Hurry, he's bleeding bad."

"I'm leaving right now, Charlie."

I probably should have called the cops or an ambulance, but I wasn't thinking straight, I wasn't thinking at all. My conscious mind had shut off; my movements became automatic. I threw on shorts and flip-flops and flew out the door shirtless. The Camaro wouldn't start at first; I banged the dash so hard I cracked the plastic clock face. Then it caught and I floored it out of there, burning rubber.

Praying no cop would pull me over, I sped along Burlington Street to Gage Avenue, running two red lights, then blasted it south to Gage Park.

Charlie stood by the telephone booth near the front gates, his jeans torn, blood crusted on his forehead. I pulled over to the curb and jumped out. Charlie approached, limping badly, his jean jacket splotched with blood. I asked him where Joey was and he said in the back parking lot. I told him to get in the car but he had trouble standing. His right knee was fucked up. He put his arm around my shoulder and I eased him to the car, then helped him get in. A cut under his scalp oozed blood. I gave him a wad of tissue paper to press on the wound, and as I drove around to the parking lot he told me what happened.

"We got jumped, Bobby. Two guys wearing ski masks. They had baseball bats. One of them hit Joey in the face. One of them nailed Joey, out of nowhere. Right in the face." Charlie's chin quivered. "Never saw them coming... They were... But I got away... I ran." He covered his mouth and muffled a sob.

"It's okay, Charlie."

"I was going to... I hope..." But his emotions got the better of him; he put his face in his hands and wept.

"Take it easy, buddy," I said, squeezing his shoulder.

When I turned into the parking lot, Charlie looked up.

"Over there, Bobby, by the bushes."

As I pointed the car toward the dark bushes and flashed my high beams, I saw no signs of Joey. Then two white slashes grew distinct, and I realized they were those stupid running shoes of his sticking up. I got out of the car and started for him, but when I saw he wasn't moving my heart sank; and when I glimpsed his face, I was so sickened I turned away.

They'd made quite a mess of him, left eye socket shattered, nose pulped, mouth a mash of flesh, blood, and pearly stubs gleaming in the high beams. Blood flowed from a head gash. My legs shook; I fought back tears. But Joey was still breathing, and when he opened his right eye in the sticky muck of his face, I realized he was conscious. I had to recompose myself, and focus.

My flip-flops slid in drying blood as I stepped around him for a look at the rest of his body. Blood greased his denim jacket and jeans, and darkened his white T-shirt maroon. Hard to tell if his legs were hurt, but he flexed them when I put my hands on his knees, and he brought them up as if to make himself more comfortable.

Unsure how safe it was to move him, I made a quick decision: waiting for an ambulance was out of the question. I was going to take him to the hospital myself.

Joey tried to say something but I shushed him. He held out his right hand, the fingers angled oddly, and to my horror, I realized they had been broken at their bases. I tried not to look at them as he continued holding up his hand.

And he kept trying to talk but something was blocking his throat. I held his forehead and probed his mangled mouth with a hooked finger, pulling out tooth fragments and phlegmy clots of blood. A thick welt bulged beside his Adam's apple, but no blood issued from it. They hadn't cut his throat, but maybe he'd caught a bat there, or was stomped when he was down.

"Joey, I'm gonna help you to the car. I have to get you to a hospital."

His eye opened and he nodded, but his throat was still blocked.

"Don't talk, Joey."

Precious seconds passed. Despite my best efforts to keep cool, panic set in. So much blood covered his clothes that I couldn't grip him, and had Charlie help me. We carried Joey to my car and eased him into the front seat. I tucked a chamois under his head. I must have been quite a sight climbing into my car shirtless, freaked out, smeared with blood. I could smell the blood, that's what I recall most vividly. The sweet, almost metallic *smell* of my brother's blood.

On the way to St. Joseph's Hospital I ran more than a dozen red lights, almost getting clipped by a transport truck at one intersection, and just missing an ambulance at another; and then I found myself in a drag race with a hopped-up 1969 Barracuda for several blocks, ending only when buddy blew a hose or a gasket and pulled over to the curb spewing steam. Charlie, sitting in the back with his banged-up knee and his traumatized soul, must have suffered another good fright on that trip, white as a sheet when we got to Emergency.

Joey had lost consciousness, and with all the blood, and the obvious severity of his injuries, staff attended to him promptly, and wasted no time seeing Charlie, who continued bleeding from the scalp, and sobbing. They were prepared to assist me as well—after Charlie verified I was Joey's brother—but I told them I wasn't injured, that the blood on me wasn't mine.

A male nurse handed me a towel and a green scrub top, and directed me to the nearest washroom, where I cleaned up. I knew I'd have to answer questions, and make a telephone call I dreaded with every fibre of my being; but when Joey's age was discovered, and Charlie reported how they'd been injured, I'd have no choice.

Police were called. And I called Uncle Giuseppe because calling my mother was unthinkable. He took the news in stride, as if he had been expecting it after Uncle Sal's death, that bad news always came in bunches. I told him to tell my mother that Joey had been in an accident, not to tell her he'd been jumped, as if it made a difference.

Uncle Giuseppe probably dreaded the idea of breaking the news to my mother as much as I did, but she was his kid sister, and I had enough to deal with at the hospital.

The police asked a lot of questions, and didn't sugarcoat their hostility, not to me necessarily but to this whole gang thing and anything remotely gang-related. After more details of the Ticat assault had surfaced in the media—Rick Zilli missing the rest of the season due to injuries sustained in the beating raised eyebrows—Hamilton city councillors demanded an inquest into street gangs, and the creation of a task force. In the meantime, they advocated an aggressive, zero-tolerance police approach—admitting to laxity in the past, if not corruption—to stem the wave of violence. Luigi Fanelli's shooting death had driven home the message: action had to be taken before things got out of control. Under this kind of heat the police had donned their prick masks and were taking no shit.

Once he had his head stitched and bandaged up, and his knee X-rayed and wrapped, the police grilled poor Charlie until he was drowning in tears and snot and begging for his momma. And they asked me more questions than I cared to answer, in a manner I found both blunt and disrespectful. Why was Joey out so late? Who is his legal guardian? Is he a gang member? If not, who would want to hurt him? Is he on any drugs? Has he been in trouble with the law before? Questions that I answered briefly for the officers—I don't know, my mother, no, I don't know, no, I don't know—and thus not to their satisfaction, but that left me thinking long after the officers let me go. Especially who would want to do this to Joey.

That's the question that badgered me: who did this?

A list came to mind—first up Terry Peters, and puppeteer Eugene Ciccone. And as obvious as they seemed, upon reflection, their involvement was unlikely. The Clubbers fell a close second, and they specialized in bat work, though Charlie made no mention of crimson jackets. I wracked my brains for other possibilities. Maybe it was random. Or Charlie was the target. Or maybe someone from the bar, a patron I had turned away at the doors, or tossed out, or insulted, someone like that was trying to get at me by nailing Joey. But that was weak, and I let it go. For a moment I even toyed with the notion that Albert the cop was behind it; but if Albert had wanted to fuck me up, given his beef, he would have likely taken a more direct approach.

When I asked one of the officers if an arrest had been made in the Luigi Fanelli murder, he thinned his eyes and demanded to know my interest in it.

"He's an acquaintance. Our mothers know each other from church."

"Too bad Luigi wasn't more God-fearing," he said, pausing perhaps for a laugh, then clearing his throat. "The case is still under investigation."

I thought about Connie, Luigi's sister, and how profoundly transformed her reality must have been, a few weeks removed from that beautiful day at Valens. Even if your brother's a thug he's still your brother, the one you loved as a child, the one you never stopped worrying about.

Poor kid. Life can be such a bastard. And I thought about Luigi, the few gentle words he had exchanged with my mother, his scruffy slightness, and I felt strangely sad. But then I remembered his old man sprawled on the ground, and that look on Luigi's face—focussed, bright, almost cheerful—when he was kicking the shit out of that guy at the Street Scene, which made him seem only passably human at the time. An old chestnut came to mind with particular resonance—*you reap what you sow*—and my heart felt cold.

And by dawn the family had assembled in the Emergency waiting room, though only my mother and Uncle Giuseppe were allowed to see Joey in Intensive Care. My mother's calm and positivity came as a surprise—she was certain that Joey would pull through, that he'd wake up from the coma intact, fully himself, and the doctors corroborated her optimism. Though Joey was in a coma, his vital signs looked excellent; his hand was casted, the fingers would heal; his mouth would need extensive surgery, but his larynx was merely bruised, and the damage to his eye socket had not affected his vision; and Joey was clearly a *tough* kid—they said with knowing nods and reassuring smiles—so they had every reason to believe he would fully recover in time. How long that would take was another question.

Later that morning Vincenzo and I went down to the hospital cafeteria for a coffee. The serving staff wore hairnets and tight white clothes and almost all had asymmetrical faces. Medical personnel dominated the other tables, cheerful, eating heartily, telling stories.

My cousin wanted to know who I thought was responsible. When he saw I wasn't going to answer, he spoke.

"Better think this one through, cuz. Don't do nothing crazy. I know how hot you can get."

"I'm not hot, Vince. I'm okay."

He frowned, as if this calm of mine concerned him more than if I'd been raging.

"Think it has anything to do with that money?" he asked. "Or with Peters?"

"Eugene seems smarter than that," I said. "I mean, the heat's up with Fanelli's murder. Why would he risk more heat? I mean, for two grand? For Peters? Because if it points to Peters, it points to Eugene. He does nothing without Eugene's blessing."

"What about the Clubbers?"

"Yeah, this looks like their handiwork, except for the jackets. Charlie, the kid who got beat up with Joey, said nothing about these red jackets they wear when they're swarming. It's a thing with them. If they were sending a message or doing it to get back at me they would have made it clear, otherwise what would be the point?"

A happy nurse in a starched white uniform sat at the table beside us with a bowl of vegetable soup and a thick sandwich. A bearded doctor with a large variety salad joined her. The two exchanged words and chuckled as they plunged into their lunches.

"I dunno, man. Sounds like something for the cops to handle. People are getting killed. You don't want to be rushing in with your head down. Not if these animals are willing to kill you."

"Nobody's going to kill me," I said.

Vincenzo leaned forward. "What, you're bulletproof, Bobby?"

The couple beside us glanced over. I stared them down. They resumed eating, darting looks at us. Animals. I repeated the word in my head. It brought to mind green pastures and barns. No, not animals. Something else.

Vincenzo and I finished our coffees and went back up. Uncle Giuseppe stood in the hallway outside the waiting room with his hands behind his back, fatigued, unshaven. He was wearing pressed blue jeans. I'd never seen him in blue jeans. I offered my hand and he squeezed it tightly. He held it for a beat then let it go.

"Why don't you go home and get some rest, Bobby, grab a munch. You could use a shower, too, and a change of clothes. Let Vincenzo come with you. Your mother's okay right now. If there's any news we'll call right away."

I stood there as he walked into the waiting room, still feeling the warm pressure of his handshake. Vincenzo nudged me and we went out. Humid and overcast. Still wearing the green scrub top, I started sweating profusely, staining it in dark splotches. I had moved the Camaro to the visitors' lot but hadn't cleaned up any of the blood, and it reeked in there. I took out towels from the trunk and a bottle of Armor All I kept in the glove compartment, and my cousin and I wiped down the seats, the dash, and the floor mats as best we could.

"Lucky he didn't bleed to death, Bobby."

"Yeah, lucky."

I didn't feel very lucky. Hard to say what, exactly what, I was feeling. We boarded the Camaro and headed off to my house. Serious self-doubts started niggling me, questions about my own behaviour, and how it may have contributed to the chain of events that led to all this. Maybe I should have been more forceful earlier in the game. I had taken my eye off the ball for too long. I had shot off my mouth to sociopaths without thinking about the possible consequences. I wasn't dealing with rational human beings. Nor was I dealing with a rational situation.

Vincenzo, for his part, tried keeping the conversation light. Okay, something horrible has happened, but life goes on. We can't let sorrow and rage overwhelm us. Bones heal. Wounds scar over. Life goes on. Vincenzo's chatter distracted and, in the end, annoyed me. I needed to be alone to think. But he kept yapping away. About all kinds of shit that had nothing to do with anything. He loved me, this cousin. He knew exactly what he was doing.

When we got to my place, Mr. Warden sat on his porch wearing his bucket hat and looking pleased with himself.

"What's up with him?" Vincenzo asked. "Looks like he just won a lottery."

"Beats me."

Even had he won a lottery, I suspect the old bugger would have said nothing. But given that I thought his wife was back on the funny farm, if not pushing up daisies, his ebullient demeanour truly puzzled me. But then out of the house she tottered, Mrs. Warden, smiling as broadly as Mr. Warden, and wearing her bucket hat. She sat in the chair beside him and together they gazed at the green park and sipped tall glasses of lemonade.

Life is full of surprises.

Vincenzo and I went in the house and I took out some almondines and made a pot of espresso. The telephone rang. It was Demarco.

"Bobby, I heard. Is he okay?"

"He's in a coma, but his vitals are good. He and Charlie Tesser got jumped by a couple of guys with bats at Gage Park."

"Jesus. Who were these guys?"

"That's what I'm trying to figure out. They were wearing ski masks. I'd pin it on the Clubbers but these guys weren't wearing the red. They always wear those red jackets. But I've had this thing going on with Eugene and Terry Peters, I don't know—if they were going to nail anyone, why not me? Joey's nothing. If I wasn't in the picture, whatever. But I'm in the picture."

"Think they'll come at you, too?"

"Nah, Demarco. I don't see it. The heat's going to be really turned up now."

"Anyway, want me to come over?"

"My cousin Vin is here with me. We're heading back to the hospital after we grab a bite."

"Call me if you need anything. And don't do anything stupid. You don't really know who you're dealing with. Might be someone you don't suspect."

Something clicked when he said that. I would come back to it in time.

"Yeah," I said. "I even considered Albert the disco cop. Do you believe that? Thought he was going to shoot me the other day after I let it slip that I was still nipping over to Felicia's. But I doubt he even knows I have a brother. By the way, have you seen Nipsy around?"

"Yeah, he's back in the gym. Had his pec operated, but he's been working his legs. Why?"

"Just wondering."

Vincenzo and I drank espresso in the kitchen. He wanted to know who Albert the disco cop was. I told him it was a long story and that I'd save it for another time. I fried us eggs, cut up cherry tomatoes for a salad, and got a hunk of provolone from the fridge. I found a half-loaf of Sicilian cornbread in the breadbox and sliced it up. We went out back and ate under the pergola, covered over now with grapevines and leaves. My mother's rose of Sharon had flowered, its petals pinking the grass. Tomatoes red and green blotted the garden; baby eggplants shone. A basketful of basil on the table perfumed the air. I ripped off a few leaves and mixed them into the salad. We ate in near silence. Then some grackles started fussing in the Warden's maple tree.

We ate until we were busting. Then I went in and made another pot of espresso and brought it out with lemon cake and strawberries dressed in sugar and brandy. As I ate, I studied the makeshift scarecrow my mother had whipped together to scare the grackles and squirrels invading her garden, a monstrosity of aluminum foil, human hair, and a goalie mask that had once belonged to Joey. He never went far with hockey, his confidence too brittle, too easily chipped and cracked. And I thought of my father, the old-school Sicilian, who considered sports a hazardous waste of time. How much do they pay you to break your head? he'd ask me, believing football was the stupidest of sports. He never once came to see me play.

But one time he did come to watch Joey play hockey, a pee-wee-league game across the street in the arena that used to be there before someone torched the change rooms and the city shut it down. Joey's team, the Cardinals, wore red and white jerseys reminiscent of the Soviets. Beaten down from shiftwork, and showing the first serious signs of lung cancer, my father was a hard sell. But after a lot of pleading he agreed to watch Joey play this one time.

My mother teared up as we left the house—I think she knew by now that my father's days were numbered. He'd been losing weight for a year, not sleeping, complaining of chest and back pains, and that cough, that rattling, gut-wrenching cough, started seeming normal after hearing it for months. But the blood was a new thing. Bright red; his handkerchief bright red.

Joey played well that day, stopping a few sure goals with his blocker, and making a glove save that brought a vague smile to my father's face. Even if he was impressed he would have never shown it. Anyway, despite playing well, Joey let in four goals and his team lost 4-3. After the game my father asked him why he played goalie when all people did was take shots at him and then blame him for losing. He didn't meant it in a cruel way—and it didn't seem that terrible to me at the time—but I remember Joey being crushed by what he said, and after giving up double-digit goals in the next two games, he hung up his skates and goalie mask forever.

The one thing that always struck me was the essence of my father's question. Why let people take shots at you? In his Sicilian way of seeing the world, it was stupid and weak. Sitting back and letting people blast away at you.

"What's going on in that head of yours, Bobby?"

"Just thinking, Vin. Just thinking."

"We should get back to the hospital soon."

I put my hand on his shoulder. "Let me ask you something, Vin. If it was your brother and you knew who did this to him, what would you do?"

He thought about it. He didn't want to say anything careless, but I think he wanted to be honest with me. "It's a difficult question to answer, Bobby. I'm not saying it depends on the outcome, but we don't know what's gonna happen here. Joey could come out of it in one piece."

"You didn't see his face. His teeth were caved in."

"Ignore that for a second. What if he can get the teeth fixed and he comes out of it okay—and that can take time. But what if he does?"

The grackles flew off the maple in a small back cloud. Mr. Warden started up his Volkswagen. It sounded like an unwell lawnmower.

"What if he doesn't? What if he never comes out of the coma?"

Vincenzo craned his head and spoke in a loud voice. "That's all speculation. But if he dies... I mean, the police. The law."

"You think those idiots will find out who did it? I mean, come on. Two guys wearing ski masks with baseball bats. That's all they have to go on. Say it's your brother, Vince. In fact, say it's your mother—because if Joey were to die, it would kill my mother. Say it's your mother and unlike the police you know exactly who fucking did it?"

The Volkswagen sputtered off down the alley.

"Bobby, are you trying to tell me you know who did it? Because if you are..."

The telephone rang inside. I got up.

"Bobby—"

I went inside and answered the telephone. Uncle Giuseppe.

"Roberto, you better come. Joey's condition...They have to do a procedure for the pressure in his skull. He's bleeding."

"Be there in a few minutes, Uncle G."

Vincenzo recoiled at the news. He looked like he was going to be sick.

"I'm gonna grab a quick shower," I said. I still had blood on me. "I'll wait out front."

I showered and dressed in blue jeans and a T-shirt. We drove to the hospital in silence.

A feeling of dread that beset me quietly when we left my house overwhelmed me by the time we parked in the hospital lot. It took me a minute to get out of the car.

Vincenzo touched my shoulder. "Are you okay, Bobby?"

It seemed really bright at that moment, blindingly bright.

THIRTEEN

If I've learned anything since that summer, it's that prayers aren't often answered. The idea that a remote, supernatural entity, unknown and unknowable, upon hearing your murmured or impassioned pleas for intervention, will disrupt the laws of biology, chemistry, and physics to do your bidding is a recipe for a letdown, if not lunacy. I didn't pray on that day, but I know my mother prayed, and my aunts and uncles prayed. I watched them praying, as we waited. Vincenzo prayed. It reminded me of St. Lawrence Elementary, when Robert Kennedy got shot and Sister Michael Anthony had the whole school get on their knees and pray for him. I remember praying hard for Robert Kennedy, really hard.

The neurosurgeon came out of the operating room, mask at his chin, shaking his head. Uncle Giuseppe conferred with him briefly, then turned to the others with tears in his eyes. Screams followed.

I had never heard screams like that, and hope to never hear them again in this life. They seared through my brain like hot knives; they pierced my soul. I didn't want to be there; I didn't want to be Bobby Sferazza at that moment.

As I rushed out of the ward and out of the hospital, the screaming followed me. It followed me all the way home.

And I couldn't enter the dark house, afraid to go in and see it unchanged from a few days ago. I sat on my front porch and gazed at the twilit park. I couldn't see anything, not really—just a dark green mass, silver-edged—but it felt cool sitting there, quiet.

I tried to still the violent thoughts swirling in my head. I was circling the truth. Going round and round, circling it as if from the sky. And as the last pale dust of twilight lifted, black prevailed; the park yawned like a black gulf, streaked with black, peaked with black, and my thoughts continued circling, circling, closing in on a silver prick in the pitch black, a sliver, a pinpoint of light.

Then, giving me a start, Mrs. Warden appeared on my front lawn, in a gauzy nightgown, long white hair in braids, eyes glazed. Barefoot, she dragged her yellow heels through the grass like one of the undead. When I called her name, she stopped and raised her hands as though touching something before her, then she started walking again.

"Mrs. Warden," I said again. "What are you doing?"

When she was almost at my porch steps she stopped and smiled. A hard smile, her teeth clicked. Her head trembled. She kept smiling, fists clenched. Then she lifted her hands and started wildly thrashing at the air, as if bats or June bugs were accosting her. I stood up. I had no idea what she was doing. Sometimes your tolerance for fruitcake isn't happening. As I opened the door to head inside, Mr. Warden came out in a night robe, waving a flashlight.

"*Martha, are you there!*" he whispered.

She turned around giggling, and started toward the park, her nightgown fluttering like a giant moth in the yellow beam of the flashlight. Mr. Warden followed his wife across the street, but he lost a slipper on the curb, and by the time he recovered it she was gliding toward the soccer field like a ghost striker.

You'd think after twenty years of indifference you wouldn't give a shit about a person one way or the other. You could return the indifference without feeling the least bit inhuman or uncivilized. But in a reflex that surprised me with its suddenness and vigour, I found myself sprinting across the park toward the soccer field and Mrs. Warden, who had somehow reached it in seconds. I gently called her name as I approached, afraid to startle her, but she turned around smiling. The sky to the east, lit orange by the foundries, gave an impression of dawn. Mrs. Warden's smile, in that light, gave an impression of understanding.

"I know where the boat is," she said in a monotone. "It was right here, right here, right here. Right bloody here. We're going. Ernie said we're going. Are you the man? Why are we going that way? Ernie said the boat is here somewhere, over here..."

Mr. Warden waited by his porch. He looked worn out, his eyes bagged, hair in tufts. I thought he was going to be his usual reticent self and merely take the old bird off my hands and head back to their cage, but he offered me his hand.

"I want to thank you," he said. "She's been getting away from me lately."

His fingers were warm and thick. "That's okay, Mr. Warden. Ernie?"

"Oh, my name isn't Ernie. No, that's one of her *friends*. She has dementia."

"Sorry to hear that."

He took his wife by the arm and ushered her back inside.

The encounter was so odd I'd forgotten about Joey. But when I looked back out on the park where we had grown up, almost hearing my mother crying out his name—*Joey! Veni ca! Joey!*—I broke down. I sat on a chair in the porch and let it out. And I don't know how long I sat there weeping, maybe an hour or so, when Vincenzo pulled up in his Malibu.

"Come on," he said, and he took me to his house, where the aunts and uncles and my mother were mourning again, for the second time that summer; and while they were able to resign themselves to Uncle Sal's death, I couldn't imagine how they would deal with the loss of a son and a nephew of sixteen—it terrified me to think of it. As much as I didn't want to be there, finding it all so unbearable and unreal, I had, as my cousin reminded me, no choice. "It's times like this you have to step up." And as I dried my eyes in the station wagon and he pulled away from his house, he continued talking, and it was a good distraction. I loved my cousin; he was trying his best. Talking and talking to keep me from hearing the pandemonium in my own head.

The next few days unfolded like a weird fucking dream. The weather, sunny and perfectly dry with chalky blue skies and a fresh breeze gusting from the lake, sharpened the edges of everything, clarified, intensified—and yet the events themselves surged by in a seamless, stony blur. My mother, so calm and optimistic when she first arrived at the hospital, was now drugged and semicomatose; my aunts and uncles feared for her sanity. Uncle Frank also needed medication when his sobs became violent hiccups.

The thing I remember most about the funeral itself was black black black. Everyone in black, the casket black, my brother in black, the robes of the priest black, black clouds in the sky—after days of spotless skies it rained on that morning, it had to rain—and black my thoughts, blacker than black, receiving nothing, emitting nothing, not a flicker. Just black.

The grieving became repetitive, interminable, hammering away at everything I knew, insuring that I carried the weight of that grief in my bones. But the nuts and bolts of reality intruded even on this unfathomable grief: life had to move on, it would do so with or without us. Within a matter of days, perhaps mercifully, I was forced to defer my grief.

The police had questions. This time I answered them carefully, covering everything, leaving nothing out. I told them about Eugene's lost package and the two grand I was going to pay him. This puzzled them. Why didn't I go to the police immediately? I told them I feared for my brother's safety. So much for his safety, they said. But what about this two grand, why did Eugene not want it after all? I told them I didn't know. What was in the package? I told them what I was told, but how could one be sure?

"We already know Mr. Ciccone has been moving a lot of amphetamines. We also think he's moving cocaine. Your brother never mentioned cocaine, did he?"

"He never mentioned cocaine."

"Do you think Joey knew something he shouldn't have...or could he have stolen the package?"

"Joey didn't steal the package."

"Why are you so sure of this?"

"He wouldn't know what to do with it if he did. He was a fol lower, very low in the pecking order, just happy to belong. And I don't think he ever saw what was being moved. Eugene used guys like my brother to amuse himself. I don't think he would have entrusted Joey or other kids like him with serious quantities of anything."

"Fair enough. Did your brother ever mention Luigi Fanelli?"

"He didn't have much to do with Luigi. He dealt mainly with Terry Peters."

"We'll be talking to both Mr. Ciccone and Mr. Peters later today. If we have any more questions for you we'll be in touch. Thank you, you've been helpful."

On the way out of the police station—a short walk from the Press Club, where I hadn't been since the night of Joey's beating—I ran into Connie Fanelli, dressed in black, who burst into tears when she saw me. I expressed condolences for Luigi's death. She hugged me and said she was sorry about my brother.

"He was a kid, he didn't deserve that."

"No one deserves that," I said automatically.

Connie frowned. "That's not true, Bobby. Some people do deserve it. Some people deserve it big time. If I knew who shot my brother I'd kill him, swear to God. I wouldn't give a shit. For all of his bad, Luigi never killed nobody. They didn't have to shoot him like that right in front of the house. Fucking animals. They deserve better? But Joey, I don't know. I don't know why anyone would do that to a kid. He was just a kid."

"Are the cops still asking questions?"

"Yeah. But I think they've got a lead. Bet you a hundred bucks Eugene was behind it. Him and that piece of shit Peters. I hear you almost took that prick's head off at the Press Club."

This stopped me. I asked her where she had heard that and she said she couldn't remember. I told her to think hard. It was important.

"Oh, a girlfriend of mine—Gina—she was there the night those football players got into that fight. She said she saw Terry Peters beating up Eugene's ex Sue Allen, and how Bobby the doorman kicked him in the head and almost killed him. I would have kissed you if I was there. What's wrong, Bobby?"

"Besides the obvious?" If I smiled, it was not a happy smile. Word got around fast in this town. I hadn't mentioned the incident to the police. It didn't seem pertinent.

Connie read me. "You think Eugene and Peters had something to do with Joey's death?"

"Hard to say."

"I know what I said—about what I'd do—but don't do anything you'll regret."

"No."

We hugged again and she pulled a small notepad out of her purse, wrote down a number, and ripped off the sheet.

"Call me, if you want. If you need to talk or whatever."

"Okay." I took the note, folded it, and put it in my wallet.

As I walked away from the police station, a million things rushed through my head. But one thing became clearer to me: Eugene and Peters had nothing to do with Joey's death. It made no sense, even if they knew I'd dummied Peters. They would have been more direct. But then, what if they had a beef with Joey, after all? What if this thing with the package wasn't resolved? But what about the two grand? Why didn't Eugene take the two fucking grand? My thoughts swirled and sped in a monstrous merry-go-round. I couldn't still them. Eugene, Peters, Clubbers, Albert the cop, Lenny Hutton—not him—the Slompka brothers—not them—John the Greek and Dino Flex, no, no. Which left Ricky Tartaglia, Mad Dog, and Oscar.

Oscar. I hadn't thought of him. He hadn't even entered my mind.

Or he had and I let it go. But now I went back: I had seen him at the Press Club the night of Joey's beating. He was with Mad Dog; they were wasted. Oscar scrapped with Lenny Hutton; Hutton was punching him out until Mad Dog stepped in. Then we tossed them.

They didn't put up a fight. But did Oscar say anything? Did he make his intentions known in some way—a gesture, a look? And what about Mad Dog?

But how would they have tracked Joey to Gage Park that night? And what was he doing there at two in the morning? I hadn't asked Charlie Tesser about that, I don't know why. Two teenagers fucking around in a park at all hours. Nothing radical. What's to ask? Then they get jumped and one of them croaks. Story changes. I wanted to ask Charlie what they were doing there; I needed to ask him.

Before I went home I dropped by the Press Club to give Luciano notice. He often spent afternoons there going over the books and recovering from hangovers or the cocaine shivers. When I arrived he stood at the bar talking to a small hairy guy with a Roman nose. The club looked strange to me, like I'd never been there before.

"Oh, Bobby," Luciano said, rushing over with a stogie in one hand and hugging me. "I'm so sorry. My heart grieves for you and your *family*. It's a terrible tragedy. I hope you got the flowers, did you get the flowers? We sent a *huge* arrangement to Friscolanti's. I'm sorry I didn't make the funeral. But did you *get* the flowers?"

"We did, Luciano, thank you. My mother thanks you. They were beautiful."

"How are you holding up? I don't even *know* what to say to you."

"You don't have to say anything, Luciano. I came by to tell you I'm done. I'm outa here. I'm going to need a few days, and training camp starts in a couple of weeks. I'll be heading back to T.O. for good then. But thanks for the work."

"Bobby, did you ever meet Mimmo?"

The small hairy guy bobbed his head at me and waved. The deejay. His big hooped earrings made him look like a gypsy.

"He worked out *good* this summer, Mimmo, didn't he? Played the tunes nice. People danced when they weren't *braining* each other, ha. Tommy, not so much. Fifty-fifty isn't bad though. Anyway, I'm *sorry* to see you go. Your buddy Demarco gave notice yesterday. I'll have to hire a whole new crew. But business has been *slow*. That cocksucker across the street hasn't missed a beat, but that's the way the *cookie* crumbles. Win some, lose *some*."

"Take care of yourself, Luciano."

"Don't be a stranger. Bring your football pals for a night *out*."

The straitlaced, white-bread guys I played football with at the University of Toronto came to mind and I smiled. No, not their scene. Swearing made them skittish, for Christ sake. New York, New York was more their speed. I smiled all the way out of the Press Club and into the street. New York, New York was quiet, resting like a giant cyclops, its green canopy fluttering like a giant eyelid, with white-coated cleaners passing hoses through its yawning doors like dental floss. How it had escaped getting trashed was mystifying. I went to my car, uncertain of what to do next. My mother was staying with Uncle Giuseppe and Aunt Teresa for a while, pacified by Valium alone. I found it gut-wrenching to be around her, unable to contain my own tears, and felt guilty about that, but I also sensed an anger brewing inside of me, scalding, volcanic, bubbling up under the mantle of my sorrow, anger that wouldn't easily be cooled.

That evening Demarco and I chatted on his porch, accompanied by the tinkling fountain cherub, which lightened the mood as much as was possible at that moment. Warm and pleasant out, birds thrashed in the deepening shadows, and the sun expired in a flush of red dust. Mrs. Demarco brought us a tray with wedges of cold watermelon and cups of very sweet chilled espresso that made my teeth ache when I drank it.

Joey's death shook him to the core, Demarco admitted. It came as a wake-up call, a sign that it was time for him to get serious about his life, to quit fucking around. Time to leave childish things behind. And he and Pamela were getting along very well. She was at Mohawk College studying kinesiology, and upon graduation planned to open her own sports clinic.

"It's stuff like that I love about her. She knows what she wants and she's going for it."

"What do you want, Demarco?"

He fingered watermelon juice off his chin. "You know, man. I want peace. I want a peaceful life."

We both laughed, but when he clapped me on the back the tears started up again.

"I know, Bobby. I know. I wish I could do something for you."

He let me have a moment.

"I saw Charlie Tesser the other day," he said. "He was looking pretty down. His head still bandaged. Can't imagine what he's going through."

"He didn't come to the funeral. Where did you see him?"

"At the A&P with his mother. She didn't look so chipper either."

Wheels turned in my head. I needed to talk to Charlie. I needed to ask him questions I didn't know to ask him before. I needed to talk to him, but I knew it wouldn't be easy. His mother might not let him, and then if she did let him talk, no telling what he would say. He might clam up, afraid or too sad to say anything. Too traumatized. Or he might have a cop parked outside his door, just waiting for someone like me to come along. But I needed to talk to him, I needed answers, and calling him on the telephone wouldn't cut it. I needed to talk to him face to face.

"What is it?" Demarco said.

"Nothing. Think I'm going to shove off."

"Have the police said anything?"

"They've just asked a lot of questions. I think they've been giving Eugene and Peters the third degree, but mainly about Fanelli. Joey's an afterthought. They have no leads, no one with any real motive, no evidence, nothing. Just two guys in ski masks with baseball bats. How many people in this town own ski masks and baseball bats? Know what I'm saying?"

"I know what you're saying, Bobby. It's fucked up."

"A wasted life. And for what? Was it about that game?"

"What game, Bobby?"

Had Oscar made it about the game—about that one play? No fucking way; it was about more than the fucking game. The interception. The maybes. It had to be.

"Never mind, Demarco, I'm babbling."

"Okay, nothing new. But don't do it around strangers. Be objective. They won't be so understanding. See you tomorrow. Call if you need anything, or if you start getting ideas."

"I already have ideas, Demarco."

"I know you do." He squared up to me and put his hands on my shoulders. "Look, don't waste a second life. I know what you're thinking, Bobby. I know you're not gonna let this go. It's not in your nature. You're a dog. Once you get hold of a bone, forget about it."

"It could have been me," I said. "I could have gone the other way, especially after my father died. I was good at it, Demarco."

"Do you mean Joey? I don't understand."

But I didn't mean Joey. I meant that growing up where I did, fatherless, pissed off at the world, surrounded by sadness, and all but unguided, I could have easily gone the other way.

"I got lucky, Demarco."

"You're making no sense, Bobby. Go home, get some rest. Come for a workout tomorrow. Ned's been asking after you, and Nipsy can't wait to show you how much he can squat."

"I'll call you tomorrow."

Was it just luck? A couple of wrong turns, even this summer, and the dream would have come to an end. I wasn't totally self-deluded. I lived on my own edge. But no, it wasn't just luck. You had choices to make. You could choose among friends, girlfriends, lifestyles, careers. You could choose to live in this city or that one, read this book or that book, hang out with this person or another. And you could choose to stomp a stranger unconscious. And choose to hurl him down a flight of stairs. And you could choose to take a baseball bat to sixteen-year-old's face.

It made me sick in my soul to think about it. The act itself, its senseless outcome. What was achieved? Nothing. And the larger question: should a death like this go unavenged? Should it be accepted with a shrug as a meaningless event, with no real context, and no real consequences? How do you avenge an ostensibly random act of violence? Oh, but life is brutish and short. Sometimes you catch a bat to the face. But someone swung that bat. The perpetrators existed in the world, and walked around freely in that world. And no matter what, they had to pay. And I wasn't waiting around for the Law, or Fate, to take care of it, or Karma, whatever the fuck that was. It was up to me—my most human obligation—to right this wrong. No excuses. Someone had made the choice, and had thus married the consequences.

But I wasn't sure. I wasn't sure.

My cousin Vincenzo was waiting for me on my porch. The Wardens were inside. No need to see them at that moment. My cousin wanted to know where I had been. He was worried about me. They were all worried about me.

"Spent time with Demarco at his place shooting the shit."

"Your mother's been asking about you."

"I need a day or two, Vince. I haven't been right."

"You don't look that good. Have you been sleeping?"

"Not much. A wink here and there. That's not important right now."

"What's important then?"

Ah, Vinnie the mind reader. He knew me too well. They all knew me too well. And that was the problem then. Except that I didn't know myself as well as they did. Had I known myself I may have walked away, I may have jumped in the Camaro and bee-lined it to Hogtown, leaving all this shit behind me. But I didn't.

"Brought you some grub," he said. "My mother made manicotti. There's sausage, too."

"I'm not hungry right now. Come on in."

We went inside the dark house and I switched on some lights. An aroused fly began buzzing around a living room lamp, bumping into it, regrouping, and repeating the action. I tried to kill it with a rolled-up *St. Lawrence Church Bulletin* I found on the coffee table, swatting the lampshade with a thud, but it escaped death and buzzed into the darkness. The house smelled stale. Nothing had been touched for days. I asked Vincenzo if he wanted coffee but he said it would keep him up all night. He was back at work in the morning. I told him I didn't envy him but his eyes said he didn't envy me.

"I know, I have to find a new job," he said. "Don't wanna wind up like Uncle Sal doing thirty years in a factory. Might as well be in jail. Less taxes."

"Open a pizzeria. People in this town eat pizza like it's going out of style."

"Uh, I don't know if that's for me."

"What, making dough?"

"Always said you should take your act to Vegas, Bobby."

Neither of us laughed. Vincenzo was depressing me. He tried making small talk—When are you leaving for school? It's your birthday next week? Selling the Camaro? Coming back next summer?—but he could tell I wasn't in the mood, and after a while announced his departure.

"Ah, Bobby. This house used to be party central when we were growing up. Remember those birthday bashes? They'd stuff a hundred people into this place. Your old man would get the poker game going with my old man and the uncles, and the kids would bomb around the house and the backyard until a fight broke out or one of them peed themselves. Incredible. And your mother would make a hundred pizzas, it seemed like. And we would drink ten cases of Diamond Beverages, you always sucking on an orange pop. Those were good times."

"They're long gone."

Vincenzo cracked his knuckles.

"I don't know how my mother's going to come back from this."

"She'll be okay. We're still here. We'll always be here."

Vincenzo gave me a hug and a kiss on the cheek before he left and said he'd be back tomorrow. He told me to go visit my mother if I could and I said I would try.

FOURTEEN

A few days passed. I managed to see my mother, so heavily sedated she scarcely kept her eyes open, and visited with the aunts and uncles, who seemed awkward and apprehensive in my presence. I avoided Vincenzo and Demarco, not consciously, though I wanted to listen to myself for a change, to what my heart told me, and not to their well-intentioned but unhelpful and confusing counsel. I saw Nancy during this time. She had come to the funeral and we spent a few afternoons at her apartment listening to jazz records—she had purchased among others my favourite *Kind of Blue*, and Chick Corea's curious album *The Leprechaun*—and talking about books. I had read almost nothing over the summer, while Nancy had devoured every book I'd suggested and others she had discovered on her own. I felt self-conscious about it. More importantly, I had other things on my mind.

"You know, I don't get Hemingway," Nancy said, "that whole masculine code thing. It's such a bore. And sometimes he can be so childish, especially when women show up."

"Yeah, a bit awkward with the gals. But some of his short stories jump off the page, don't you think?"

"Why didn't he write in normal English? He felt of his knee. He felt of his knee. I must've read that out loud ten times and it never sounded right. Who says, He felt of his knee?"

"Where's that from?"

"English major, huh? It's from 'The Battler.' Otherwise it's pretty good. I like when they fry up the ham and eggs. Best part of the story."

And I thought, what would Hemingway have done in my position? A man who had written so powerfully about death and honour and grace under pressure, a man who'd handled guns all his life, who had been wounded in war, and who had shot himself to death, would probably not have hesitated. Then again, I wasn't taking any cues from a dead writer.

"Hemingway stories should be consumed like cigars, you know. Never back to back, and only infrequently. But now and then they're quite enjoyable, even soothing."

Nancy laughed. "I don't like cigars, but I know what you mean."

As she topped up her wineglass I thought about what I had said, how fatuous it sounded, how removed I was from such discourse, and I changed the subject.

"Let me ask you something, Nancy."

She sipped her wine and raised her eyebrows, waiting for the question.

"Do you love your mother?"

She opened and closed her eyes. "Of course I love my mother. We don't always get along. My dad says we're too much alike, but sure I love her."

"Don't get offended by this. I want to know, to understand, for myself I mean. Call it a thought experiment. But, let's say, that someone killed your mother—bear with me—and you knew who the murderer was and also knew that the person would never come to justice for the crime. What would you do?"

"That's a pretty creepy question, Bobby." Still, she took a moment to think about it. "I would, well, I'd call the police. I'd call them and I'd tell them what I knew."

"Forget the police, Nancy. Let's say there is no physical evidence, nothing whatsoever to link this person to the murder. But, somehow, you know. You know this person killed your mother and that they're going to get away with it."

She bit her lip. "I don't like this, Bobby. If you want me to say I'd go out and hunt this person down and kill them for killing my mother, I won't."

She held her wineglass with both hands and stared into it. Her eyes teared up.

"What's the matter, Nancy?"

"I know where you're going with this, Bobby."

"I don't know who killed Joey. I have my suspicions, but I don't know for sure."

"But when you know for sure, you're going to do what?"

"I'm still wrestling with that question."

And I wrestled with it for the rest of that day. Unable to eat or sleep, I bounced between bouts of crippling sadness and rages so overpowering I almost blacked out. I went through the options in my head, tried to piece together a picture of the future, but it looked vague to me, a bluish haze in the distance.

Next day after lunch I drove over to Charlie Tesser's house on Wood Street, a few doors down from the Picton Tavern, a favourite north-end watering hole. It was overcast but warm and clammy. I parked in the Picton lot and sat there staring at Charlie's place, its pink aluminum siding setting it off from its gun-grey and in-sulbrick neighbours. I had no plan, and hesitated going up and knocking on the door. Maybe I was hoping Charlie would pop out on his porch, spot me and come over. So I waited in my car.

A quarter of an hour later, three afternoon tipplers spilled out of the Picton Tavern and piled into a jacked-up black pickup with monster tires on the far end of the lot. They drove away hooting and hollering. The pickup backfired like a gunshot, giving me a start. I sat up and happened to see Fernando Coletto walking a red bicycle toward his house down the street. He had gone to elementary school with Joey and Charlie, and had come to the funeral with his mother and his kid brother Ralph.

"Fernie," I called from the car window.

He stopped the bicycle and turned. "Hey, Bobby."

"Can I have a word with you?"

"Yeah. Sure thing."

A gangly kid with pitted skin and braces, Fernando's bowl-cut black hair fit his head like a bad wig. Joey had always found him grating but simpatico. He slowly wheeled his bike over. I told him I had to talk to Charlie but didn't want to freak out his mother. I asked him to knock on Charlie's door and let him know I was here. I reached into my pocket for a twenty.

"Look, Fernie, I'll pay you for your trouble."

"You don't have to pay me, Bobby," he said in his whiny voice.

"Joey was my friend."

"Take it, get a bell for your bicycle. Will you do this?"

He reluctantly took the money and walked his bike over to Charlie's house and stood it on its kickstand. He opened the screen door and knocked. After a moment someone answered—I couldn't see who it was. Fernando looked back at me and held up his open hand. Unclear what the gesture signified; but after a few seconds Charlie exited the house, had a brief word with Fernando, then clapped him on the back and walked over to me.

He gave me an unexpected hug that filled me with emotion. For a brief moment I felt like I had my brother in my arms. Charlie's head wound had healed but dark circles under his eyes made him look haunted, unwell. I asked him how he was doing and he said the counselling helped, and he was trying his best to cope, but admitted to ups and downs.

"Some days I don't want to get out of bed. I just lie there staring at the ceiling. My mother says I sleep too much, but I don't sleep when lie I there. They gave me pills that make me feel like a frigging zombie. But if I don't take them... I keep seeing it again and again."

Sensing he was about to cry on me, I touched his shoulder and smiled.

"Sorry, Bobby. I can't shake it. It was unreal. Like a horror movie. And I keep asking myself why—why Joey, why me? But I don't know the answer to that."

"Listen, Charlie. I'm trying to find out why this happened, and find out who did this. I have to ask you something. What were you and Joey doing in Gage Park at two in the morning?"

"Like I told the cops, Joey and me were at Eddie's Billiards. This was around ten."

"Just you and Joey?"

"Yeah, we ordered a couple of those greasy little pizzas they make there before ten when they close the kitchen, and after that we played pinball. Around ten-thirty Manny the Toque from Mary Street came in and said there was a poker game at Frank DiTomasso's house over on Connaught in the east end, his parents were up north. Joey and I had played poker with Frank before. Manny drove us there in his van, and we played cards with Frank, Chuck, and Bryan Smith, who I knew from hockey, this guy called George from the east end that your brother knew, bit of a meathead, and Randy Walton, who used to live on Ferry Street, remember him? Joey and Randy never got along but Joey didn't mind taking his money—he won big that night."

"What did this George guy look like?"

"Hmm, he had a shaved head, sort of built, stocky, you know. Ugly mug on him. Your brother didn't like him, said he was a scumbag. Took all of his money, too. Joey was on fire."

"So Joey could play poker, eh?" It surprised me. All the men in my family played poker, but he'd never shown an interest—or at least I'd never observed it. He didn't seem cold-blooded or sly enough to be any good. Things I didn't know about Joey. Things I would never know.

"You kidding? He was a sharp. Said he learned to play from watching your old man. My old man says back in the day he was a sharp, so I guess it runs in the family." Charlie stopped himself with a shake of his head, perhaps clueing in that he was talking about dead people.

"It's okay," I said.

He smiled weakly and continued. "So we were there at Frank DiTomasso's till about one in the morning. And like I said, your brother cleaned house. He must have won at least a hundred bucks. The game broke up and we left and were cutting across the back lot at Gage Park—and it's dark there, all the lights busted—when all of a sudden this guy in a ski mask comes out from the trees behind us running at Joey and wham!—hits him across the face with a baseball bat. I couldn't believe what I was seeing. It felt like a bad dream. Joey went right down and then someone came at me from the side swinging a bat and cracked me in the head. I saw stars and almost went down but I shook it off and then he hit me again in the shoulder but dropped the bat. He started punching me in the face and then grabbed me around the head and tried pulling me down, but I got away and started running. He only chased me for a few feet, he was kinda fat, and then he stopped. I kept running right to the park entrance, but it was dark and I tripped hard over a concrete barrier. That's when I hurt my knee."

A man in his mid-forties wearing a fedora came out of the Picton Tavern with a big smile on his face. He saw us and nodded. I nodded back. He weaved his way to a lime-green Gremlin parked across from the Camaro, its fatuous Kamm tail facing us, and climbed in. He sat there for a minute or so, rolled down his window and stuck out his elbow, but didn't start the engine. Then I saw his head tip back on the headrest and figured he was taking a nap before he hit the road.

"So I'm lying there and my knee is banged up and it hurts so much I want to cry and then I look up and see the guy who hit Joey running at me, really fast. And I don't know how but I get up and start running, even though my leg is gimpy and I can't move very fast, and I keep running without looking back. I was afraid, Bobby. I thought they were going to kill me."

"You thought right, Charlie." I didn't want him to feel any guilt. "They would have killed you if they could have, or at the very least fucked you up. Go on."

"I was trying to run and I hear this yell and then all kinds of swearing and I turn around and realize that the guy chasing me didn't see the concrete barrier either and must have hit it as hard as I did, if not harder, because he was really moving. And so I kept running across the park and then I hid behind the fountains. I hid there and waited."

"Did they come looking for you?"

"I didn't see them again, didn't see anybody. The park was real quiet. My head was bleeding. My leg was bad but I managed to get back to the parking lot, and Joey. When I went up to him and looked at his face, I didn't know what to do. I stood there for I don't know how long, like, paralyzed. Then I snapped out of it and saw that he was still breathing and trying to talk but his mouth was all bloody and his teeth were broken. Then I remembered there was a phone booth near the front gates. I went there and called you."

The guy in the Gremlin, arm dangling from his window now, began snoring so loudly Charlie stopped talking. It might have been a solution for my insomnia, a few beers and a rich nap in a green Gremlin. Charlie asked if anything he told me rang a bell. And I said it sounded like a random beating. Except that one thing struck me.

"The guy who ran after you was fast, eh?"

"Yeah, that guy could move. I was scared shitless. No way I was going to outrun him even if my leg wasn't messed up."

"And you didn't see this guy up close at all?"

"No, Bobby. I was a few feet away when he whacked Joey, but with the ski mask on... I don't know what more to tell you."

"One more thing, Charlie, and then I'll leave you alone."

I went into the Camaro, opened the glove compartment, and took out a yellow envelope, with the photograph Oscar's mother had given to me. I showed the photograph to Charlie.

"That's you and Oscar Flores, back in the Cathedral days. Joey and I used to go to all the games. I'll never forget that touchdown you scored, Bobby."

"Okay, yeah. Listen, Charlie, I want you to look at Oscar in this photograph. Really look at him. What do you notice?"

As he studied the photograph he seemed uncertain, like he wanted to say the right thing, to appease me, or to comfort me, and not something stupid.

"What do you notice that's different about Oscar?" I said, pressing him a bit. "Different from me, for example."

He continued studying the photograph, biting his lips, tilting it this way and that. Finally, his eyes lit up and he pointed. "Oscar's teeth I mean, his tooth. It's silver or something. My grandmother used to have one like that."

But it didn't click with Charlie. He shook his head and shrugged. He failed to see the connection I was trying to finesse—Oh yeah, the tooth!—and if it didn't strike him naturally, if I had to force it, then it couldn't be valid. But that didn't exonerate Oscar. It was dark, too dark for Charlie to notice such a small detail. And he was running for his life. It proved nothing. I hugged Charlie, thanked him, and told him that if anything else occurred to him to call me.

"I miss him," Charlie said. "I miss Joey."

"Yeah," I said. "He'll be missed."

The guy in the Gremlin abruptly pulled in his arm, opened the door, and with one hand holding firm his fedora, plunged his head out to vomit. A neat yellow splash on the asphalt and everything was better. He pulled back his head, closed the door, and returned to his siesta.

I waved at Charlie as he limped back to his house. It made my heart heavy to watch him and I hoped he'd be okay.

On my way home I replayed Charlie's account in my head again and again. I wanted to make something out of what I'd been told, but after going over it a dozen times, I found nothing there. It sounded like a random attack. Wrong place, wrong time. And that would have been fine, except that I'd never heard of anyone getting attacked with baseball bats in Gage Park. I wasn't even sure they had taken the money he won that night at poker. In all the confusion, it didn't occur to me to check his pockets. It didn't add up. What was the likelihood of two dudes in ski masks prowling around Gage Park at one-thirty in the morning, waiting for a random victim to happen by—to roll or beat into a coma? How many people walked through Gage Park at one-thirty in the morning?

Not exactly an entertainment district, this neighbourhood: not a bar or restaurant for blocks, and the park itself all but deserted even in the daytime, when you might see a handful of oldsters walking their pooches, a few kids on bikes, but that was it.

A random attack made no sense. I wished I had checked Joey's pockets. That would have told me something. But whether or not they rolled him, a key piece of the puzzle was missing. Something putting the thugs in Gage Park at precisely that time of night. A solid and logical component that would cleanly click into the other pieces.

At my house I fried two eggs and ate them with tomatoes picked that morning from the garden. Not knowing when my mother might return from Uncle Giuseppe's, I did my best to maintain the garden, hosing it in the morning and at night, cleaning up weeds, and picking anything ripe. The scarecrow spooked the grackles, if not the squirrels. But despite the frequent raids, I'd already collected baskets of tomatoes, zucchini, and eggplants.

Though I hadn't been to the gym in more than a week I was still taking Dianabol, doing vigorous calisthenics in my bedroom, and going for runs around Eastwood Park. I figured I could get through training camp without being in my best shape, but training camp was the furthest thing from my mind. I wasn't certain there would be a training camp for me. Demarco and Vincenzo called me daily and we spoke, albeit briefly. They were both caught up in their own lives, and good for them.

Then one morning a Constable Steve Morse called; he wanted to see me as soon as possible down at the station. Believing there had been a break in Joey's case I felt, perhaps unreasonably, euphoric. I drove to the police station and presented myself at the front desk.

Constable Steve Morse was a big blond man with eyes like Jeff Bridges but a body like George Kennedy. He shook my hand and walked me to an interview room next to the reception area where he instructed me to sit in one of the wooden chairs by a table. He sat across from me and opened up a white folder. I anxiously waited for him to tell me what I hoped to hear, but he began our conversation by declaring that no new leads had surfaced in the case of my brother and Charlie Tesser, and in his estimation none would unless a witness or one of the perpetrators came forward out of the blue.

"I'm sorry about that, Mr. Sferazza. I know how disheartening it must be. But the reason I called you here is because we're conducting an investigation and you might be able to help us."

"Help you?"

"Caesar Booth was jumped in the back alley of the Press Club last night—down the street, yes—and beaten very badly with... brass knuckles. I know, bizarre. He's in St. Joseph's right now with severe facial lacerations, a broken jaw, and a cracked clavicle. The owner, Mr. Mercanti, reported seeing two tall men get into a dark Lincoln Continental in the alleyway shortly after the beating. He didn't get the plate numbers. But do you know of anyone who would want to hurt Mr. Booth? Or of anyone in possession of brass knuckles?"

"Did you say two *tall* guys got into the Lincoln?" Not Eugene and Peters, obviously. And what was it with the brass knuckles? Only in Hamilton.

"Yes, *very* tall is Mr. Mercanti's precise description. Anything else you can think of? We know he boxed at a local gym, but he seemed to have no problems there."

"Hmm. He did get into a beef a few weeks ago with a guy who might have been Johnny Papalia's nephew."

Constable Steve Morse raised an eyebrow at this and wrote down the name on a legal pad. "Papalia still has a lot of influence in this town," he observed. "Wouldn't put it past him to send out his dogs for family pride or whatever."

"Then again, if Papalia sent someone, Caesar might not be in hospital right now, if you know what I mean. When you work in one of these joints you never know who has a hate on for you. After two weeks away I still look over my shoulder. It's been a crazy summer."

He nodded. I wasn't telling him anything he didn't already know. He thanked me for coming and apologized again for having nothing new on my brother, but he found my information interesting and promised to pursue the lead. I left the interview room disenchanted by the officer's use of the words *information* and *lead*, as if he didn't get it from ten other sources already, but in the end I didn't care.

When I stepped through the reception area I saw a stocky skinhead in ragged denims being ushered into the station by an undercover cop, or so I assumed given that he looked like a hippie but had a badge dangling from his handwoven hemp belt. The skinhead wasn't cuffed but the hippie held him firmly by the elbow with one hand and with the other pushed him along. Reluctant to the point of impertinence, the skinhead cried, "I didn't set anything on fire! I didn't set anything on fucking fire!"

I did a double take. The voice sounded familiar, but the shaved head threw me off. Then I got a better look at the guy, now wrestling with two uniformed officers as well as the hippie, and realized it was Gorgeous George, the Slompka brother who'd sported the long blond hair that inspired his moniker.

The officers restrained Gorgeous George, and with a lot of thumping and grunting hauled him off to the back. George fought like a baby tiger but the officers proved too powerful, especially after one of them sprayed him with something from a metal canister that made him scream like Minnie Ripperton. I exited the police station smiling. I had enjoyed watching that wrangle, and it made me forget my own troubles briefly. Then I got in the Camaro and sat there for a few minutes before I started the engine, sat there and pieced things together in my mind like a jigsaw puzzle, with every piece clearly defined. Still missing a piece or two, but the overall picture emerged. Now it was a matter of finding the missing pieces. Biding my time and doing things in a calm and straightforward manner. I wasn't going to get excited, or get hot, or go on a rampage. I didn't feel that way at all. I felt okay.

Clear-headed. Like I had been called on a blitz and I knew exactly where I was going, exactly how to get where I needed to be.

Next day I went to the gym and Ned expressed his condolences and told me I still looked great. I explained I wasn't in for a workout but looking for Nipsy. I needed to talk to him. Ned said he wasn't around but he'd likely be there that afternoon. I told him it was urgent, if he could flip through the rolodex and give me his telephone number I'd be obliged. At first he balked, but reconsidered, and within seconds had the number written on a business card.

"Once again," he said, "I'm truly sorry for your loss, Bobby. You're a good guy."

"Thanks, Ned. I'll be seeing you."

"Will you be back for a workout sometime?"

"You bet. You know I love this place."

My heart was racing. I was short of breath. I tried to calm down. Not easy once I got excited. The roids rocketed me into high gear fast. I sped home.

At home I paced around, staring at Nipsy's telephone number. I went out and sat under the pergola but my restlessness drove me back inside the house. I gathered myself and dialled the number; when I got a busy signal I almost fainted. I had to calm down. I took a long cool shower and tried not to think about anything beyond calling Nipsy, and being done with it.

After I dried off and put on fresh clothes, I went down and dialled the number again. This time I got through.

"Hercules. Pleasant surprise. What can I do for you, my man?"

"I need to see you."

"Uh-huh. That can be arranged. Meet me at the Tim Hortons on Highway 20 at, say, one o'clock. I'm heading up for a workout right after. Did Demarco tell you I'm squatting over five hundred pounds these days?"

"Amazing, Nipsy. I'm impressed. Watch yourself with those big weights. But yeah, one o'clock is fine. See you there."

Too agitated to sit around the house, I went to Uncle Giuseppe's to visit my mother. When I got there Aunt Teresa told me she was sleeping but to come in for an espresso.

"Are you hungry? I have ravioli left over from yesterday. I can heat it up for you."

"No, I'm good. How is she?"

Aunt Teresa shrugged. "I don't know, Roberto. She sleeps and sleeps from the pills. But when she doesn't take the pills she cries. I don't know what we're going to do. She can't go home like this. She can't go home now. She can't take care of herself."

"Maybe she needs to see a doctor."

"She already saw the doctor. He said it will take time. And he gave her the Valium."

"I mean a psychiatrist. She might need to see one. If she gets any worse—"

Aunt Teresa covered her face with her hands and shook her head. It was too much. The sorrow, the strain, the responsibility. I put my hand on her shoulder. "Zia, don't cry." What the hell was I doing? I couldn't meet with Nipsy. Crazy to even think about it. I wasn't a gangster. I wasn't cold-blooded. How would I live with myself? And if my mother managed to recover from Joey's death, did I want to finish her off with an act that would in effect destroy my life?

Except that I wasn't insane, and destruction is relative. Joey's life was destroyed. No getting around that. But I didn't plan to die; and when everything was said and done, I planned to be able to look at myself in the mirror, and sleep well at night, even if in a prison cell. I'd live and sleep with my choice; it would be mine. And concluding, in that instant, that only my death would truly break my mother—if she wasn't already broken—I calmed down and refocussed.

There was no turning back.

The Tim Hortons on Highway 20 was a busy place. Wearing headphones, Nipsy sat in a booth bobbing his head with his eyes closed, and sipping a pink drink through a striped straw. I tapped him on the shoulder and he popped his yellowy eyes open. He was wearing white shorts, his absurd quadriceps muscles massed under him like black alloy manifolds. He pulled his headphones back and flashed a toothy smile.

"Hercules. Well, well." He stood up and gripped my hand in a jive shake, then he squeezed my shoulder. "Sorry to hear about your baby brother. Demarco told me. My heart goes out to you. That's a bad bad thing, man, young kid like that. I'm telling you."

"Thanks. It is a bad thing. But you have to move on."

He sat back down. "Yeah, you got no choice but to move on. We cannot question the ways of the Lord. 'The wind blows and we are gone,' as my momma used to say." He sighed and turned to the matter at hand. "So, you taking the step?"

"Well, sort of." He was talking Winstrol; I wasn't. "How's the pec, Nips?"

"Healing. I won't be benching anything in the near future, but I'll be squatting Stelco and Dofasco, brother. Lemme tell you. Ha ha. So, what up?"

"Let me grab a coffee."

"Okay, boss."

And as I waited in that lineup—the glassy-eyed patrons as oblivious to me as I was to them—I knew I was making a choice, *that* choice. With a clear mind and a clear conscience. And I knew that I could live with myself if I did; but if I didn't, I knew my life would be insufferable.

At some point you do the unimaginable, because doing nothing is more unimaginable.

Behind the counter the servers zipped around with jaw-grinding focus and efficiency, their doll eyes unblinking. I wondered if Tim Hortons laced its java with Benzedrine, that would have explained a lot. I purchased my coffee and returned to a perspiring but serene Nipsy.

"We should get in on one of these Tim Hortons franchises," he said with a nod at the never-ending lineup. "They're a gold mine."

"We should," I said, not really paying attention.

"You okay, Hercules? You look..."

"I was wondering, Nipsy. Know where I can get some brass knuckles?"

He frowned, then realized my request wasn't serious.

"Brass knuckles," he said, snapping his fingers. "You had me going there for a sec."

FIFTEEN

Charlie Tesser called me a few days after we talked. He had remembered something.

"That guy George," he said. "After your brother busted him out at the game, he hung around the house for a while, but he left before we did. That was around midnight, something like that. Didn't think nothing of it at first—the guys in the ski masks were a lot bigger than him. But then I thought what if—"

There it was. The connection I'd been looking for between the poker game and the beating: Gorgeous George. "It makes sense now," I said, interrupting Charlie.

"It does? You think George had something to do with it? Like, he got somebody to roll us? But I had no beef with him. Joey beat him for his money fair and square, that's poker. And those guys, Bobby, they weren't trying to roll us."

So what the fuck were they doing? One way or another I was going to find that out.

"Charlie, don't worry about it anymore. What's done is done. Nothing we can do will bring Joey back. It's just one of those fucked-up things. It could've happened to anybody."

Charlie dropped his head. "I got lucky."

"Luck, whatever, you're walking and talking. Get out there and live your life." There was one more thing. "Charlie, how do I get a hold of Frank DiTomasso?"

"Manny has his number. I'll call him and get it for you."

Charlie got me the number later that morning and I called

Frank DiTomasso. I caught him heading off to the cottage with his family. He was surprised to hear from me and expressed sadness for Joey's death. "Some poker player, your brother." When I asked him about George Slompka he told me he just got out of jail, and was likely staying at his mother's place on Beechwood near Ivor Wynne. He hung out during the day with thug buddies and dime-dealers across the street at Scott Park, near the baseball diamonds. Frank offered me his phone number.

Calling George on the telephone wasn't an option. That afternoon I cruised around his neighbourhood, hoping to spot him. I even parked near his house for an hour but no one came or left. A few skinheads drifted by, but not George. Then I parked the Camaro in the Scott Park lot and walked over to the baseball diamond, where some kids were playing softball. Behind the backstop, near the grandstand, Gorgeous George stood with three malnourished delinquents, all teeth and eyes. He didn't see me coming; I was on him before he could react. The juniors took off; George didn't even try to run. I told him we needed to talk. He said he didn't want to talk.

"You've got no choice, George. We're going to have a talk."

His dirty blue eyes darted about.

"What do you think the alternative is?"

He took a quick look at me. Not eager to find out.

"Let's walk," I said, touching his arm.

He hesitated, but after a nudge his feet started moving. We crossed the street to Ivor Wynne Stadium and went around to one of the less conspicuous side gates. The air was thick and humid; I felt swollen. George stopped there, panting. His faded blue T-shirt stuck to his skin; I could see his puckered nipples through it. His wrists looked raw and red as if they'd been in ropes.

"Tell me about the night of the poker game," I said.

He frowned. "What poker game?"

"At Frank DiTomasso's place over on Connaught."

"Frank who? I don't know no Frank Tomatoes. Never been to Connaught."

"Come on, George. You played there a few weeks back. You must remember."

"Nah," he said, closing and opening his eyes. "Never been there."

"I know you were there," I said. "My brother was there, too. Joey, remember Joey?"

He shrugged and looked at the ground. "Yeah. I remember him. He was winning all the money that night." He froze. "You don't think... You don't think because of the money that I... Fuck, man. No way that I..." His voice trailed off.

"George. Listen. I don't think you hurt my brother. That's not where I'm going with this."

He put his hands on his fuzzed-over head.

"Why'd you cut your beautiful hair, George?"

"Fucking scabies," he said, holding up his scarred wrists as evidence of his suffering. "Ever had scabies?"

"Can't say I have, George. Sounds unpleasant."

"Unpleasant?" He bared his brown stubs of teeth. "That's funny. That's a funny word."

"I need to know who you talked to after the card game."

He said he couldn't remember. How could he remember that far back? He smoked so much weed and dropped so much acid his memory was shot. I asked him if he had talked to Oscar or Mad Dog that night. After a hesitation he said he might have. Maybe that night. But he wasn't sure. He crossed his arms on his chest. No, he wasn't sure.

I punched him in the nose, not too hard.

His head snapped back. His eyes teared up and he grabbed at his nose. Blood gushed through his fingers.

"You didn't have to hit me!"

"It'll help you remember." I handed him a paper tissue I had in my pocket.

"You're nuts," he said, pressing the tissue to his bleeding nose. "I don't know what I'm s'posed to remember. Maybe I did go there. Maybe I did go to Mad Dog's. So what? What does that mean?" His eyes filled with tears. "I didn't fucking do nothing." He shook and wept.

"Listen to me. Did you talk to Mad Dog that night? Think hard. Did you mention the poker game? George?"

When he didn't respond I raised my fist.

Turning his face, he blurted, "Well, I would've told Mad Dog I busted out of the game."

"Did you mention Joey to him?"

George wiped the blood and tears away from his face and took a deep breath. "My mom kicked me out for smoking joints in the bathroom. I'd been crashing at Mad Dog's place till things cooled off. Went there that night. Told him I'd been playing cards at Frank's place, and busted out. He wanted to know if they were still playing and how much money was on the table. I said they'd play till one or two, you know, and there was a couple of hundred bucks, tops. So he gets this idea to drive over to Frank's place in the van, throw on some ski masks, and rob those guys. I said no way, that's not cool. You don't do that. But Oscar was there. Oscar wanted to know who was at the game." George stopped and bowed his head.

"Go on," I said. "Oscar wanted to know who was at the game. What did you tell him?"

"He was all coked up and drinking Jack Daniels straight from a bottle. When I mentioned Joey's name he got this weird look on his face but he didn't say anything else. They didn't mention the card game again. We hung out for a while, smoked a few doobs, then Oscar said he needed more coke and the two of them went out in the van. Didn't think they were going to jack the game. Mad Dog told me to stay and watch the house."

I needed nothing else from Gorgeous George.

"What are you gonna do?" he said.

"I'm going home for a nice cool shower."

"Fucking psycho," he said, blood bubbling from his nose.

"You could use a shower yourself, sunshine. You smell like boiled tripe."

When I got home I took that shower and felt better. I put on fresh jeans and a black T-shirt, ate a bite of bread and cheese, took my pills. At around three that afternoon Demarco called.

"What's going on, Bobby? How are things? I was thinking about you."

"Good or bad thoughts?"

"You came up in our conversation last night."

"I'm the subject of conversations now?"

"Pam and I were talking and I said, I wonder what Bobby Sferazza is doing right this second. And she said, Whatever he's doing I hope he's safe. Wasn't that a sweet thing for her to say? Wasn't it? What's going on with you?"

"Nothing new to report. My mom's still staying with my aunt and uncle. I'm getting my shit together for school."

"When are you taking off?"

"Couple of days. Training camp starts in a week."

"Ready for the season?"

I didn't answer the question; I was having trouble concentrating. Training camp, the season, Toronto—how remote they felt, despite their proximity.

"You okay, Bobby? You sound, I don't know, distant."

"Distant, yeah. I guess it's going to take time to come back."

"I can only imagine." He paused. "By the way, did you hear about the Press Club?"

"No, I didn't."

"Saturday night about twenty Clubbers charged the doors and trashed it. Sent everybody scattering. Beat the shit out of the door staff. Jerome and a few of the new guys wound up in hospital. Even poor Diego caught a beating. Anyway, the Press Club is closed until further notice. I hear Luciano skipped town."

"All good things come to an end."

"Good things and bad things."

And that was true. A great equalizer, annihilation.

The muggy day inched toward a conclusion. It would come, that was certain, and it calmed me to think of this certainty. Despite the nebulous skies, sulfurous air, and querulous grackles warring with themselves, I ate a dinner of bread, salami, and tomatoes outside, under the dense green pergola. Not a leaf moved, the air was so still. Like trying to breathe soup. I ate slowly with swollen fingers and sweat pouring off my brow. Two tart black plums completed the meal and I felt sated, if not peaceful.

Vincenzo dropped by after dinner. He had come from Uncle Giuseppe's and said my mother was sleeping.

"That's all she does these days."

"Maybe it's better she does."

I didn't want to talk about my mother.

He glanced around the house with his hands on his wide hips, unconsciously sniffing. It smelled stale in there. I'd have to open a few windows. What else was he going to say? He looked me in the eyes. What could he say? Nothing that would change anything. I offered him espresso and he accepted; we drank it out back under the pergola.

"The garden looks good," he said, surveying the bounty. "You must be taking good care of it. Nice. It'll make your mother happy. At least the garden is good, you know." He knew what he had just said meant nothing, so he switched gears. "Any word from the police?"

"About what?' I said, tracking a squirrel rampaging through the zucchini. "Just a sec." I picked up a rotten tomato and hurled it at the rodent, missing by inches.

"About Joey, Bobby. Any word about Joey? You should get a slingshot for those squirrels. My old man swears by them. He picked off three or four last year."

"Vince, I'm heading up north for a couple of days with a lady friend. We're going to stay at her cottage. In case your folks decide to call or come by. I already told Uncle G."

"Sounds good, Bobby. A little rest before school. Clear the head."

"I'll be gone two or three days. When I get back I'll have to talk to Uncle G about my ma."

"That's a tough one, Bobby."

The squirrel reappeared. This time a small green tomato left my hand truly and pinged it off the head. It went scrambling under the fence into Mr. Warden's backyard and then shot up into the maple tree, where it chittered and shook its tail with outrage.

"Nice shot," Vincenzo said.

I looked at him. He asked me what was wrong in a serious voice. I smiled; it made him uncomfortable. What could be wrong? What the fuck could be wrong? The smile said it all, no?

We finished our espressos in silence. I had nothing more to say to Vincenzo and he shoved off a few minutes later.

Exhausted by heat and stress I went to bed and fell asleep instantly. I dreamed I was chopping down a tree in Eastwood Park with a hatchet. Chunks of wood fell away with each stroke. Then I realized the tree was a man and I had chopped off slabs of his chest and abdomen, exposing his writhing organs and ribcage.

I opened my eyes to darkness and crickets chirring, went to the bathroom and splashed cold water on my face; then I looked at the face, puffy, florid, bemused—and all but unrecognizable. The whites of the eyes had a yellow cast; acne reddened the forehead. I touched the hair and it felt greasy. I sniffed the sour armpits. I showered again. I washed my hair twice and scrubbed my face with an exfoliating cleanser that left it raw and sensitive to the air. Beads of blood formed at my scalp line and I dabbed them with tissue paper. My teeth looked yellow; I touched them and they felt loose, sending twinges into my bleeding gums. I rinsed out my mouth, splashing red clots into the sink, the sight of which sickened me. I flipped up the toilet lid and with my hands on my knees bent over and vomited. I emptied myself. Then, empty, hollow, I rinsed my mouth again and went to my bedroom to get dressed.

Before heading out I stood before Joey's bedroom door; no one had been in there since the night of the beating. I turned the doorknob, pushed open the door. It was dark, except for the Mott the Hoople poster glinting on the wall behind the bed. I didn't switch on the light, didn't want to see things any clearer. I shut my eyes for a moment, and breathed.

When I stepped out, Eastwood Park was black and soundless, save for sighing trees. Mr. Warden sat on his porch in a black night robe clutching a glass, illuminated by a green camping lamp; ice cubes tinkled. I continued down the stairs. Then I heard him cry out and looked back. He sat there, drink in one hand, the other hand covering his eyes. His shoulders shook.

I walked over, went up the stairs, and stood behind Mr. Warden as he wept, glass in hand. I touched his shoulder to comfort him, but he jerked away and stared at me, horrified.

"It's me," I said, "your next-door neighbour."

"Oh." He waved and drank from the glass. "Well, she's gone. Martha's gone."

Gone? I thought. I surveyed the park.

"No, I mean *gone*." He pointed with his finger to the ground.

"I'm sorry to hear that," I said, wondering if he knew about Joey.

Other neighbours had paid their respects—Mr. and Mrs. Sullivan, the Fingernagel family, the Crea clan, the LeBlancs, Yummy and Margie, to name a few—but we didn't even get a card from the Wardens. Unless they didn't know, and I'm not completely certain they even knew Joey existed. Still, I felt for the old guy, not deeply, but as one suffering human to another, though tender words eluded me. But I commiserated with him in my mind, if that means anything. Life is pain. I wanted to say that to him, that life is pain, but it seemed inappropriate under the circumstances. And yet what could I have said instead?

I left Mr. Warden on his porch, to his sorrow, his solitude, his gin. He didn't say goodbye, he didn't say anything; he simply picked up where he left off, sniffling and drinking himself numb. That was one way to go.

Without delay I drove the Camaro down to Holton Avenue and passed Oscar's house. The lights were out, his mother likely working till morning. But he'd come home eventually. I parked half a block down the street and checked my Omega: ten o'clock. I figured I'd wait. He would show up. I switched the radio to the jazz station and lowered the volume to a whisper. The air was thick and humid. Even with the windows down I found myself gasping. I sat there sweating for an hour. Not a single moving car or human appeared on the street during that time.

Then, in the side mirror, I saw a man in a clear plastic raincoat approach with a sleek Doberman pinscher. As they passed the Camaro I thought I'd be observed, but the Doberman pulled the leash taut, and charged a black cat fixed on a lawn a few doors down. The man's shoes clapped behind the lean bounding dog as he fumbled to rein him in. Meanwhile the cat sat there calmly, licking a paw, as if this were old hat, with a predictable outcome: a sharp yank brought Fido to a yelping halt, and the satisfied feline disappeared into an ink-black alley.

Thunder rumbled in the distance; the air smelled ionized and radically green. I rubbed my throbbing temples, glanced at the silver Madonna trembling on my dash and stilled it with a finger. More thunder. More trembling. Then single slack raindrops splashed the windshield and thudded the fabric roof. I gripped the .38: cool and dense in my hand; it felt heavier than when I first handled it. I repeated Nipsy's instructions: aim at his chest and squeeze the trigger, then go up close and put two in the temple or the back of the head. Two for sure. Two taps would do it. A blue bolt of lightning ripped through the sky; more thunder, then rain started pouring.

The gun felt like an anvil in my hand. I carefully let rest it beside me on the console and switched off the crackling radio. Wind gusts rocked the Camaro, water streamed over the windshield. Another flash of lightning lit up the interior and made my eyes wince. Raindrops rattled the car hood and pummelled the roof with such force I thought it would give.

So much for my plan. I considered driving away, and rethinking everything, when in the rear-view I saw a hooded figure limping down the street. He stopped at the Flores house. I sat up in my seat and turned around to watch through the rear window. The figure stiffly climbed the porch steps one by one. He stood there for a moment, shaking water off his shoulders and arms. He flipped back his hood and I caught a brief glimpse of his grey face before he turned to the door and let himself in.

It must have been Oscar.

The .38 gleamed on the console. I gripped it and lifted it to my chest.

It had to be Oscar.

This was it, then. I cleared my head. I knew how to focus. I could shut everything else out, all the chattering, the doubts, the dispiriting projections. All I had to do was think of my brother's face on that night in Gage Park and a marvellous, exhilarated calm came over me. This was the right thing. This was the only thing. As I reached to open the door I heard a vehicle coming. My hand froze. Behind me headlights blazed and jewelled the falling rain. A horn honked twice. I slumped down and peeked in the drizzled side mirror. A dark red van had stopped in front of the Flores house; I couldn't tell who was driving. Seconds later Oscar came limping down the stairs, moved around to the passenger's side, and climbed in. He slammed the door shut and the van pulled away from the curb.

As it passed me I caught a glimpse of the black-bearded driver: Mad Dog.

The Camaro wouldn't start on the first go. Took exception to the rain. I waited a few seconds, steadying my breath. The engine caught and I revved it up. Then I put the car in gear and eased away from the curb.

The rain fell in straight grey sheets that blurred the street lights and traffic lights into luminous smudges. The roads streamed with rainwater and heavy trees shook off their excess, splotching the Camaro with greasy leaves and gobs of sap. The windshield wipers swiped and thumped with effort. The windows fogged up.

The Camaro whooshed and splashed up semi-flooded Holton Avenue until I was almost at Main Street, where the van had stopped at a red light, left-turn signal throbbing. I slowed down beside a parked pickup truck. When the light turned green and the van made a left onto Main Street I drove to the intersection and caught the light as it turned amber. I straightened out the Camaro and checked my rear-view mirror. My heart jumped.

A police car was tailing me.

I glanced at the .38, then again at the rear-view. The police car slowly closed the distance between us. With as little motion as possible I reached out my hand, popped open the glove compartment. Then I grasped the .38 and eased it forward.

We were coming to a red light at Ottawa Street. The rain continued pelting down. The van slowed to a stop and I saw in the rear-view the police car inch up to mine, and in that moment, as my hand eased the gun from the console to the glove compartment, red lights started flashing and a siren yowled to life. My arm jerked and the gun barrel clanked against the glove compartment door, knocking it out of my hand to the floor mat.

I sat back and tried to think quick but my brain wouldn't budge. There seemed no recourse out of that fix. I was fucked. Flooring it crossed my mind, racing right out of town and out of that life, but the rain—maybe the rain—snuffed that idea.

Now in full wail, red lights flaring in the downpour, the police car swerved to my driver's side. I waited for the signal from the cop to pull over. But instead of pulling me over, he continued ahead, toward Mad Dog's van. The traffic light was still red. As the police car slowed down, the van lurched forward and fishtailed through the intersection.

A crossing sedan swerved away from the van at the last second. A canvas-covered transport truck roaring along the wet black road about fifty metres behind the sedan did not. Veering late, the truck slammed the front of the van with a metallic concussion that I felt on my skin, bevelling the passenger's side like tinfoil, and spun it violently toward the far corner of the intersection, and a concrete light post. The skidding van hit the light post broadside in a burst of glass and concrete shards, and wrapped itself into a steel U at the base. Steam billowed from the shattered engine compartment, rising into the torrent.

Two hundred metres down the road, the screaming transport truck rocked to a halt.

Moments passed. My hands were frozen on the steering wheel. I couldn't move, couldn't breathe. All I could hear was the rain drumming the car roof.

First thing I saw was the cop climb out of his car, putting on a plastic-covered cap, eyes popping as he took in the smoking crash site. He turned and looked in my direction, then ducked back into the car and fumbled with his radio. I shut my eyes and asked myself if this was really fucking happening. Did I just see that? An impulse to laugh at the absurdity of the situation quickly died in my throat.

Next thing I saw was Mad Dog emerge from the wreckage, face covered in blood, blood streaming from his beard, his fingertips. His right arm was bent the wrong way. He staggered a dozen paces, his black mouth opening and closing. He collapsed there in the street, in the rain.

The cop jumped out of his car. Holding his cap and holster he hurried over to Mad Dog, his shoes splashing up water. He bent down and touched Mad Dog's neck; then he stood up and jogged to the van. Distant sirens wailed.

And perhaps I should have been satisfied or even relieved that it went down this way, that some divine force had intervened, or that blind chance had prevailed. Any way you cut it, justice was served, and I had no blood on my hands. I could get on with my life. But the truth is that far from finding satisfaction or relief with this conclusion, what I felt was thwarted, denied, empty. It's difficult to accept ourselves as puppets of chance.

However way it all went down, I wasn't off the hook. Not by a long shot. Chance had not absolved me; I was staring into an abyss.

The cop moved to the crumpled passenger's side of the steaming, hissing van. When he got there he turned away abruptly, as if dodging something. Then he started back to his car through the ceaseless, straight-falling rain.

Salvatore Difalco was born and raised in Hamilton, Ontario, where he attended Cathedral High. He graduated with an MA in English from U Of T after winning an SSHRC Fellowship. He has worked many jobs including counsellor at the maximum security Peninsula Youth Centre. He was an editor and regular contributor at *Toro Magazine*. He is the author of one book of poetry and two collections of short fiction. *Mean Season* is his first novel. He currently resides in Toronto and works as an Italian translator.

Other Books From Mansfield Press

Poetry

Leanne Averbach, *Fever*
Tara Azzopardi, *Last Stop, Lonesome Town*
Nelson Ball, *In This Thin Rain*
Nelson Ball, *Some Mornings*
Gary Barwin, *Moon Baboon Canoe*
George Bowering, *Teeth: Poems 2006–2011*
Stephen Brockwell, *Complete Surprising Fragments of Improbable Books*
Stephen Brockwell & Stuart Ross, eds., *Rogue Stimulus: The Stephen Harper Holiday Anthology for a Prorogued Parliament*
Diana Fitzgerald Bryden, *Learning Russian*
Alice Burdick, *Flutter*
Alice Burdick, *Holler*
Jason Camlot, *What The World Said*
Margaret Christakos, *wipe.under.a.love*
Pino Coluccio, *First Comes Love*
Marie-Ève Comtois, *My Planet of Kites*
Dani Couture, *YAW*
Gary Michael Dault, *The Milk of Birds*
Frank Davey, *Poems Suitable for Current Material Conditions*
Pier Giorgio Di Cicco, *The Dark Time of Angels*
Pier Giorgio Di Cicco, *Dead Men of the Fifties*
Pier Giorgio Di Cicco, *The Honeymoon Wilderness*
Pier Giorgio Di Cicco, *Living in Paradise*
Pier Giorgio Di Cicco, *Early Works*
Pier Giorgio Di Cicco, *The Visible World*
Salvatore Difalco, *Mean Season*
Salvatore Difalco, *What Happens at Canals*
Christopher Doda, *Aesthetics Lesson*
Christopher Doda, *Among Ruins*
Glenn Downie, *Monkey Soap*
Rishma Dunlop, *The Body of My Garden*
Rishma Dunlop, *Lover Through Departure: New and Selected Poems*
Rishma Dunlop, *Metropolis*
Rishma Dunlop & Priscila Uppal, eds., *Red Silk: An Anthology of South Asian Women Poets*
Ollivier Dyens, *The Profane Earth*
Laura Farina, *Some Talk of Being Human*
Jaime Forsythe, *Sympathy Loophole*
Carole Glasser Langille, *Late in a Slow Time*
Suzanne Hancock, *Another Name for Bridge*
Eva H.D., *Rotten Perfect Mouth*
Jason Heroux, *Emergency Hallelujah*
Jason Heroux, *Memoirs of an Alias*
Jason Heroux, *Natural Capital*
John B. Lee, *In the Terrible Weather of Guns*
Jeanette Lynes, *The Aging Cheerleader's Alphabet*
David W. McFadden, *Be Calm, Honey*
David W. McFadden, *Shouting Your Name Down the Well: Tankas and Haiku*
David W. McFadden, *Abnormal Brain Sonnets*

David W. McFadden, *What's the Score?*
Kathryn Mockler, *The Purpose Pitch*
Leigh Nash, *Goodbye, Ukulele*
Lillian Necakov, *The Bone Broker*
Lillian Necakov, *Hooligans*
Peter Norman, *At the Gates of the Theme Park*
Peter Norman, *Water Damage*
Natasha Nuhanovic, *Stray Dog Embassy*
Catherine Owen & Joe Rosenblatt, with Karen Moe, *Dog*
Corrado Paina, *The Alphabet of the Traveler*
Corrado Paina, *The Dowry of Education*
Corrado Paina, *Hoarse Legend*
Corrado Paina, *Souls in Plain Clothes*
Corrado Paina, *Cinematic Taxi*
Nick Papaxanthos, *Love Me Tender*
Stuart Ross et al., *Our Days in Vaudeville*
Matt Santateresa, *A Beggar's Loom*
Matt Santateresa, *Icarus Redux*
Ann Shin, *The Last Thing Standing*
Jim Smith, *Back Off, Assassin! New and Selected Poems*
Jim Smith, *Happy Birthday, Nicanor Parra*
Robert Earl Stewart, *Campfire Radio Rhapsody*
Robert Earl Stewart, *Something Burned on the Southern Border*
Carey Toane, *The Crystal Palace*
Aaron Tucker, *punchlines*
Priscila Uppal, *Summer Sport: Poems*
Priscila Uppal, *Winter Sport: Poems*
Priscila Uppal, *Sabotage*
Steve Venright, *Floors of Enduring Beauty*
Brian Wickers, *Stations of the Lost*

Fiction

Marianne Apostolides, *The Lucky Child*
Sarah Dearing, *The Art of Sufficient Conclusions*
Denis De Klerck, ed., *Particle & Wave: A Mansfield Omnibus of Electro-Magnetic Fiction*
Paula Eisenstein, *Flip Turn*
Sara Heinonen, *Dear Leaves, I Miss You All*
Christine Miscione, *Carafola*
Marko Sijan, *Mongrel*
Tom Walmsley, *Dog Eat Rat*

Non-Fiction

George Bowering, *How I Wrote Certain of My Books*
Rosanna Caira & Tony Aspler, *Buon Appetito Toronto*
Pier Giorgio Di Cicco, *Municipal Mind: Manifestos for the Creative City*
Amy Lavender Harris, *Imagining Toronto*
David W. McFadden, *Mother Died Last Summer*

To order these books, visit www.mansfieldpress.net